Praise for Jayne Rylon's *Healing Touch*

"One of my favorites by Jayne."

~ *Guilty Pleasures Book Reviews*

"A great turnout by Jayne Rylon. Fans, new and old, will not be disappointed."

~ *Fallen Angel Reviews*

Look for these titles by *Jayne Rylon*

Now Available:

Nice and Naughty
Where There's Smoke

Men In Blue
Night is Darkest
Razor's Edge
Mistress's Master
Spread Your Wings

Powertools
Kate's Crew
Morgan's Surprise
Kayla's Gifts
Devon's Pair
Nailed to the Wall
Hammer It Home

Hot Rods
King Cobra
Mustang Sally
Super Nova

Compass Brothers
(Written with Mari Carr)
Northern Exposure
Southern Comfort
Eastern Ambitions
Western Ties

Play Doctor
Dream Machine
Healing Touch

Compass Girls
(Written with Mari Carr)
Winter's Thaw
Hope Springs

Print Anthologies
Three's Company
Love's Compass
Powertools
Two to Tango
Love Under Construction

Healing Touch

Jayne Rylon

Samhain Publishing, Ltd.
11821 Mason Montgomery Road, 4B
Cincinnati, OH 45249
www.samhainpublishing.com

Healing Touch

Print ISBN: 978-1-61921-513-9
Digital ISBN: 978-1-60928-861-7

Editing by Christa Desir
Cover by Kanaxa

First Samhain Publishing, Ltd. electronic publication: December 2012
First Samhain Publishing, Ltd. print publication: November 2013

Dedication

As always, to the readers first. A huge thank-you to every person who has made it possible for me to keep reaching for my goals.

And also to myself. For all the hard work of the last six years. From the first word I ever wrote, the opening of *Dream Machine*, to this sequel...how far *my* dream has come.

The sacrifices were worth it.

Author's Note

This work is an erotic fantasy and not meant to portray realistic therapeutic relationships between doctors and patients. The author has great respect for the ethical guidelines set by the psychology profession, but they make for a boring story.

Chapter One

Luke Malone couldn't believe he'd lost his erection. He poked his half-hard cock with the tip of his index finger as if the annoyed jab would suddenly make his tool spring to attention. Instead, his junk swayed, coming to rest against his thigh. His balls hung low and loose, not tucked tight to the trunk of his body where they usually clung while he played voyeur.

On the bed in front of him, his two best friends made love as though they were the only people in the universe, never mind the sole inhabitants of their plush master suite. Becca's sighs had escalated. Full moans escaped her succulent, parted lips as Kurt focused the full intensity of his prowess on the woman who'd brought all his dreams to life. And then some.

Kurt glided up her torso from where he'd spent the past ten minutes lavishing attention on her admittedly killer rack. Instead of devoting the majority of his brain cells to his fascination with Becca's tits, Luke found himself wondering what it might be like to love a woman enough to infuse every gesture with ultimate affection. He'd never have imagined the man who had been his scientific college roommate capable of delivering such tenderness.

Not once did Kurt put his needs ahead of his lovely wife's. Despite the must-be-painful state of his boner, which hung heavy and dark between his thighs, Kurt hadn't attempted to penetrate the moist paradise Becca offered up with the arching of her body. And Luke knew from experience just how amazing she felt when passion turned her wet and needy.

The velvety heat of her pussy hugging him... Fucking amazing.

Enticing. His cock made a half-hearted attempt at bulking

up.

Curious about all aspects of human sexuality—appropriate, considering his profession—Luke experimented on himself as he watched the show his best friends put on. Idle strokes along the spongy length of his shaft plumped the flesh. Still, the resulting chubbiness didn't warrant the label *hard-on.*

He didn't freak.

He didn't blame his poor performance on high blood pressure or some other physical dysfunction.

He didn't pretend to misunderstand the directive from his uncooperative libido.

Nope. As a therapist who often dealt with sexual issues, he diagnosed himself as having a clear case of disinterest peppered with a healthy sprinkle of self-pity and a dash of envy. Okay, more like a supersized helping of jealousy. He'd never coveted another man's lover, until now.

And still Kurt toyed with her. He dragged his fingers up and down her arms, making her gasp. What could make a man like Kurt—a man who reveled in sexual exploits of epic proportions as the outlet for his inner control freak—repress his own desires? Had his wife forged his needs into something stronger?

Could loving a woman be that much…*more*…than physical?

Deflation stole the trace of rigidity Luke had mustered. For the first time in his life, he felt as though he'd missed out on something spectacular, despite the wild bedroom adventures he'd indulged in as a pillar of the local kink scene. He rubbed at the ache that had taken up residence in his chest lately.

Kurt trailed one finger along the perimeter of Becca's smile and shivered.

Luke sighed. He took himself in hand and stroked, picturing a sweet, caring cutie who'd give it all up to him—plenty of sex and even more soul. Some measure of firmness began to add heft against his roving palm.

His best friends whispered to each other in the stillness of the magical place they'd transported themselves to. Luke leaned back in the chair, spread his legs farther apart and cupped his balls in his free hand. He teased the underside of the wrinkled skin, trying desperately to impose his face on the receiving end of Becca's amorousness.

Why the hell couldn't he visualize it?

Maybe because he'd never earned a woman's full trust and devotion, despite a lifetime of preaching to his best friend about opening up. Sure, he'd thought he'd had his heart broken plenty of times, and had returned the favor a few more. But those almost soul mates paled in comparison to the real deal.

Hell, maybe he should have brought his sunglasses inside with him. Or a welding mask. Sparks flying between the two sexy, sweaty bodies that ground together in front of him would not have come as a surprise. Kurt had insinuated his thigh between Becca's and they writhed against each other as they kissed.

And kissed.

And kissed some more.

Kurt captured Becca's wrists in an unshakable grip, not that she would try to evade her husband's touch. He pinned them above her head and sank deeper into their exchange. Nips, licks and sucks made their claims on each other audible.

Their bodies danced in a rhythm only the couple could hear. No matter how hard Luke strained, he couldn't get in tune with their unique song. They would gladly have allowed him to join in—adding a harmony to their melody, as he often had this past year—but today he couldn't bring himself to do more than observe. He studied their bond, hoping to discover a clue. He had to find a way to erase some of the shadows that had been dimming the light Kurt had always accused him of living in, carefree and lucky.

Why couldn't he regenerate the brilliance he'd taken for granted? Maybe he'd always mistaken a glow for this shining beacon until he'd had something to compare his fond liaisons to.

Damn it.

He abandoned his self-relief attempts entirely, interlacing his fingers and resting his joined hands on his abdomen. At least all this recent frustration had helped tone his body. Contours of the muscular ridges and valleys along his belly did a little to restore his pride. Still, hours of sweating out his dissatisfaction in the gym hadn't gotten rid of the despair that had chased him to his best friends' open arms, and their bedroom, on a random Sunday afternoon.

Thirty-four was too damn young for a midlife crisis. As the head of Elembreth University's psychology board, it was his business to know so. He refused to wallow.

Hell, maybe he should have let Kurt fuck this all up. Then Luke could have made a play for Becca when he'd had the chance. He shook his head, clearing the traitorous thoughts. As if she would have settled for him. Besides, it wasn't her alone that was so special. Not even the sexual gymnastics they'd engaged in for the past twelve months could account for the drastic changes in the pair—Becca more bold, Kurt more caring.

No, it was the bond the two lovers shared that worked miracles.

As if to prove his theory, they didn't seem keen to indulge their naughtier tastes today. Instead, their mating was pure vanilla. All breathy promises. Luke found himself drooling.

Were they trying to tell him something? Could they sense his recent ennui with fetish play? The weakening of the thrill meant even his more extreme public scenes at Dark Side had satisfied him less as his longing for something deeper festered inside. He felt like a pirate with a fake map. *X* no longer marked the spot.

Becca had gone as far as broaching the subject of his escalation after he'd violated his usual limits by imparting intense sensual pain on the woman who'd begged him to cane her at the club last weekend. That'd never been his thing before. Truthfully, it never would be. He'd hated her yelps, despite the obvious ecstasy toning them. Afterward, he'd declined her offer of relief, and had gone home alone instead.

Luke wished he hadn't brushed off Becca's concern in reflexive denial.

Sure, he enjoyed the shit out of a good spanking, or the gadgets the couple seemed to revel in using, not to mention their proclivity for bondage or exhibitionism, to name just a few varieties of their libertine pursuits. But *this*...goddamn.

Maybe his friends planned to show him what he hadn't allowed them to say?

Kurt nuzzled Becca's cheek. They seemed to melt, fusing together tighter. Saccharine smiles reached all the way to their eyes, sweet enough to give Luke a toothache. Then, *finally*, Kurt reached between them, aligning his cock with Becca's drenched opening. Her body held him there, poised on the brink of penetration.

When Kurt shifted ever so slightly, he flexed his hips until her soft flesh yielded to the steel of his erection. Luke groaned, living vicariously. He completed one final double check and measured the difference between Kurt's solid shaft and his own quasi-stiffy.

Thank God his friends were way too preoccupied to notice his disgrace.

Becca moaned. She tried to utter something, maybe encouragement. Garbled cries of pleasure and desire filled the space. Kurt's heart heard and translated her wishes into action. She relaxed when he began to pick up the pace, shuttling in and out of her body with escalating fervor.

The thick carved-wood headboard—complete with embedded carabiners for no-muss, no-fuss trussing—began to tap against the wall. Percussion kept time to the seduction taking place three feet away from Luke's perch.

Becca opened her legs wider, accommodating Kurt as he drilled deeper, harder and faster. Neither one of them was an easy lover. They thrived on intensity in both their professional and personal lives.

Heels drummed on Kurt's ass in time to his rocking. Each

thrust seemed to drive his wife higher, and not just on the satin sheets they preferred. She mewled—a vulnerable, needy sound she hadn't been capable of surrendering not long ago. Before their love had given them both permission to grow and change.

Luke admired Becca's tenacity. She'd fought for this. Had refused to take Kurt's bullshit and had steered them both to a happily-ever-after that seemed more like an ecstatically-ever-after. Continuing her relentless demands, she squeezed every last drop of pleasure from her husband. Her legs wrapped around his hips and her pussy clenched so hard Luke could see the flex of her abdominal muscles from his outpost.

Dropping low, Kurt used a few of the tricks up his sleeve to get even. He rotated his hips as he plowed into Becca's waiting grasp, making sure to stroke her clit with his pelvis. A fine sheen of sweat broke out over his tan skin. Luke would have bet it came from holding back, not from exertion. After all, the sick bastard ran more than five miles to kick-start most mornings.

Or at least he had, before wake-up sex replaced the jog as his favorite form of exercise.

Sprinting now, Kurt plunged into his wife. She met him halfway on every stab of his hips. Digging her heels in, she balanced herself perfectly to accept the force of her husband's fucking. Lovemaking, really.

Luke didn't think either one of them had blinked yet.

They stared into each other's eyes.

Kurt stroked so far in and out, the head of his cock was visible before he drove home again. The pair groaned in unison when he bottomed out, then evacuated to start the cycle over in earnest. Just when Luke expected screaming and frantic sex to make an appearance, a measure of serenity overtook both Kurt and Becca.

Their faces smoothed out, sublime in their ecstasy. Kurt's lunges turned liquid. He glided back and forth for several circuits. Advance and retreat.

Their chests pressed together as they breathed in sync.

Luke leaned forward in his chair. A knot stuck in his windpipe.

This was the moment he'd been waiting for.

"I love you," Kurt murmured to his wife.

"I love you too. So much." A tear formed in the corner of her eye. He captured the dampness as it trickled down her check, lapping it away with his tongue.

"I have you," he promised. "It's okay to let go."

"Only if you're with me." Becca puffed.

"Always."

Luke closed his eyes while they splintered. For the first time, he felt like an intruder.

Becca sighed. She snuggled deep into the warmth and protection of her husband's embrace before her eyelids fluttered open. Her rosy cheeks blossomed when she spied Luke and smiled. Her brows knit a tiny bit as she scanned down his chest to the limp penis dangling between his thighs.

"You already came?" She chuckled. "I guess we got a teensy bit carried away. Sorry, I didn't notice. I know how turned on you get when we watch you too."

Luke ignored the laser-beam stare Kurt shot in his direction from behind the softly rounded shoulder of his wife.

"Actually, you didn't miss anything." Luke shrugged as if it was no big deal. "I, uh, guess I'm having an off-day."

"What?" Kurt blinked a few times.

Luke couldn't fault the man for needing some extra recovery time to kick start his brain. But he'd better get the hell out before Kurt's notorious logic reengaged, or they'd never let him escape without an impromptu session. Luke didn't think he was ready to examine his issues in depth, whether Kurt and Becca were the best therapists in the nation or not. How could they understand when they had everything he lacked?

"Sorry. We were kind of boring today, I guess." Becca grinned. "I promise we'll be more exciting next time."

Luke rose from the leather wingback chair they'd furnished

in the corner of their bedroom exclusively for him. His place of honor would be empty for a while. Possibly forever. Because he wasn't sure his heart could handle the blackness swamping him lately. Temporary relief always gave way to long-term loneliness.

As he neared the bed, Becca mistook his intentions. She wrapped her dainty fingers around his lifeless dick.

Wincing, he pried her loose. He gathered his jeans and tugged them on. "Not today, Becca. Thanks, though."

"What's wrong?" She tried to sit up.

Kurt's wasted, limp body lay over her, pinning her with his dead weight. She didn't seem to mind, except his bulk didn't permit her to reach Luke.

"Nothing for you to worry about, sweetheart." He leaned down and placed a light kiss on her forehead while one of his hands squeezed Kurt's shoulder. "Thanks for inviting me today, but I'd better get going."

"Do you have plans?" She tilted her head.

Does watching reruns in my empty house count? He didn't answer her as he turned his back and faced the door.

"Luke. You're not going to join us anymore, are you?" Her whisper froze him midstep.

"I don't think so." He couldn't meet their concerned gazes. Wouldn't risk them glimpsing the agony shredding his heart. Losing this intimacy...it would hurt. He couldn't deny sharing their exhilaration, even tangentially, had satisfied some unusual bent in his sexuality. But he'd been using it as a crutch.

Enough was enough. Time to man-up and go for what he wanted. All the way. Not just as a third wheel in their relationship.

It couldn't be healthy to rely on them for his happiness.

"We're here for you, Luke." Becca voiced what Kurt demonstrated with a clap on the thigh. Luke took another step away, breaking the connection with the guy who'd been his best friend for over two decades. "Go, if you need space, but know we'll be here waiting. With open arms. And ears. Don't shut us out. Let us help you like you did for us."

"I hear you, Becca." He hated the raspy way his confirmation sounded. "I just need some time to think. Thank you."

"We love you," she murmured.

"I love you too." He stumbled across the threshold, picking up steam. "But I have to go."

"Drive safe on that thing!" Becca called after him as he crashed down the hallway toward their front door and the fresh air outside. Suddenly, the tightness in his chest wouldn't allow him to drag in a full breath.

"Your office. First thing tomorrow," Kurt bellowed just before the ornate wood and glass shut behind Luke. "Don't make me kick your ass!"

Luke chuckled despite his pain. The dirt bag could try it. Wouldn't be their first fight, but he could hold his own and then some.

He straddled his custom bobber, strapped on his helmet and revved the engine. A long, hard ride would clear his mind. He hoped.

Chapter Two

Luke grumbled as he tried to read his scribbles off the crumpled list in his hand. He paused to decipher his doctor's writing. It really had gotten illegible lately.

"Excuse me." A soft voice distracted him from his squint.

He glanced up in time to see a woman hesitate as she approached from the opposite direction, a half-full basket dangling from her arm. Sure, he hadn't left a big gap, but the pretty, slender lady could have easily slid by.

"Sorry," he apologized, parking his grocery cart at the very edge of the aisle.

"You're fine," she murmured with a shy smile.

He stared as she took a deep breath then darted through the opening. Her long hair swished against the curve of her waist, which he'd bet he could nearly wrap his hands around.

Too bad she wasn't on his menu for this evening.

Now you're going to cooperate? He rolled his eyes at his hardening cock, which had an instant appetite for the demure brunette who disappeared around the corner. He resisted the urge to follow her.

Barely.

Nothing much piqued his interest these days.

Maybe deciding to try his hand at cooking would be another flop. He'd test-driven enough hobbies intended to shake him out of his funk—golf, woodworking, voyeurism and landscaping—to recognize another lemon looming on the horizon.

After all, what he really craved had nothing to do with the dozen or so items his housekeeper had dictated he purchase for his culinary experimentation. If only there was a store he could patronize to browse for a life partner...

Lately his house echoed, reminding him of his loneliness as he paced during sleepless nights. He'd thought those would vanish once he'd reached some of his goals. But now that he'd hit both career and financial milestones, the nest egg he'd amassed rotted in his bank account with no hope of being used for something worthwhile like a vacation house for two or retirement plans or a fancy wedding or a kid's college education fund. Without someone to share his successes with, they seemed sort of...pointless.

Shaking himself from the gloomy thoughts, he focused on the scrap he'd torn from his notepad. What could he possibly need for his stir-fry that would start with a *z*?

Zucchini!

He nabbed a decent bottle of St-Emilion Bordeaux from the wine section on his way to the produce display at the front of the store. Didn't it figure? A heart-shaped ass was presented to him as the woman he'd inadvertently trapped bent over to rummage through a crate of onions on the cracked linoleum.

If he hadn't loved this place on entering, he did now.

Luke couldn't say he'd ever shopped here before. The emphasis was certainly more on the product than the displays, something he found refreshing after the overly bright fluorescents of his usual megamart.

He might have to start frequenting the place, which touted *the freshest vegetables at lowest prices.* After passing it a million times before—since it was on the street between Kurt's office and his house—he'd decided to alter his routine, hoping to change his broader course. Something had to give. Soon.

The damned adorable clientele here had lifted his spirits already. He didn't claim to be a perfect man. Or even a decent one. No, he slowed down to relish the view as long as possible as he approached.

As if she sensed his gaze, she made her selection then peeked over her shoulder. Maybe she always checked her back.

Something about the momentary flicker of fear in her wide,

brown eyes tugged at him. He considered saying hello, starting a conversation, yet he guessed she'd bolt the instant a stranger approached. Especially a man who looked as hungry as he must.

Who'd hurt her? he wondered.

She nibbled on her glossy lower lip—a natural, pale pink.

Luke offered her a gentle smile. She ducked her head and zigzagged around a low-hanging, cheesy cardboard arch that had seen better days. The path took her the long way to the lettuce. He shook his head and resisted the urge to give chase.

At least four different types of zucchinis were nestled at the very end of the row of pallets. The store had clearly run out of space and stuck them in the narrow lane. The awkward configuration left him surrounded by vegetables on three sides while he dug through the offering as if he could tell by osmosis which he should add to his selections. It was such tight quarters he'd had to abandon his cart at the opening, winding through the admittedly colorful and fragrant vegetables to reach the bins.

"How the hell do you tell which one to pick?" he muttered to himself.

Or so he thought.

"The freshest ones still have a moist end on the stem. The skin should be a little prickly but shiny." The woman he'd refused to stalk, despite the directive from his crotch, offered assistance in a melodious voice that made him think of candlelight and fancy silverware, instead of the basic white plates he'd eat off tonight.

She didn't enter the narrow section, waiting on the wide swath of linoleum outside its boundaries while he floundered. Probably she just wanted him to get the hell out of her way again.

"Ah, thanks." He smiled at her, using her criteria to select what he thought was a prime specimen. "What about this one?"

She shook her head. "Almost, but no. It's too big. The ones that are about six inches long or less have better flavor. Don't take one that's too fat either."

Luke almost swallowed his tongue. At least choking kept his crass remarks from rushing out before his better sense could filter them.

How old are you? Ten?

"Better?" He exchanged the vegetable for one that conformed to all of her rules.

This time she beamed at him, and the expression transformed her from appealing to exquisite. "Perfect. Would you mind handing me one too?"

He focused on discovering the ideal zucchini for her, shifting several layers until an exemplary summer squash appeared. Something about her encouraged him to apply himself for the first time in a while.

Who would have thought?

"Here. This one." He held the best out to her. Not a single mark marred its skin, flawless like hers.

She blanched and froze.

"What? It's not good?" He tipped his head.

"It's great. Sorry, I just—can't go in there." She waved her hand between the enormous boxes of produce.

"Ah, no worries." He didn't pry. He'd never met someone who was lachanophobic but he knew rare and unusual things existed in this fucked-up world. Maybe she was afraid of one of the other vegetables or the creepy crawly things that could easily be hiding in the cracks after stowing away on the organic haul. More likely, of being too close to a man, especially one as tall as he was. He tried to slouch, making himself as unimposing as possible.

"Here you go." He slipped the zucchini into a plastic bag and handed it to her at arm's length.

"Thank you." She shot him a sad smile laced with something that looked like regret then bolted while he wrapped up his find the same way.

"You're welcome," he murmured to her retreating back. If

she'd stuck around a moment or two longer, he might have asked her to share the meal he was about to prepare. Then maybe he'd have had a reason to really try to get the recipe right.

Crossing the last thing off his list, he wandered toward the checkout lines. Only two were open. Of course, he slid behind the skittish woman, who had her eyes glued to the green numbers flashing prices as the cashier rang her up.

Her slender shoulders tensed when he encroached on her territory. So he pretended to read trashy stories from tabloids housed at the back of the queue space. Not that he gave a shit about Tom Cruise's supposed two-headed alien baby.

She relaxed visibly when he shuffled far enough away to guarantee her unhindered exit route. Out of the corner of his eye, he watched her take a few bills from her wallet, along with an impressive bunch of coupons and a loyalty savings card.

"Would you like to add five dollars for the Elembreth Women's Shelter?" the cashier asked by rote.

"What will the total be with the donation?" The woman riffled through her purse for another single and some change.

"Twenty-six dollars and forty-three cents."

She paused, eyeing her purchases. A small sigh passed her lips as she plucked a bag of mini candy bars from the assortment, leaving only essentials behind. "Would you mind restocking these for me?"

"No problem. Not many people say yes. But I've heard that place is good. The owner here...she says she owes them everything."

"I believe it." The woman glanced over at Luke as if afraid he might be annoyed by her brief delay. "How about now?"

His heart melted when she handed over all her cash to cover the bill, getting only a few coins in return.

Wanting to say something, he couldn't find the words.

A part of him roared for him to reach out. To stop her from leaving. Ask her on a date, though he could tell she wasn't really available, regardless of whatever her relationship status might be.

She packed and collected her reusable canvas totes then left the store, with him still staring after her. When she stopped on the corner outside, waiting for the light to change, the cashier cleared her throat.

"Plastic bags okay for you, sir?"

"Yeah, that's fine." He acted before he could think better of it, snatching the candy off the shelf and passing it over the scanner, which beeped brightly as it registered the bar code on the treat. "Go ahead and ring up the rest of this stuff. I'll be right back."

Luke dashed out the door.

The zucchini expert, on constant alert, must have sensed him nearing. She flinched at his hasty approach.

He stopped short, closing the gap one step at a time, the bag of chocolate replacing boring zucchini in his outstretched hand.

"For your help." He willed her to take it.

She bit her lip, hesitated, then shrugged a loop of material off her shoulder, opening one of her bags.

After tucking the candy inside, Luke backpedaled slowly. He didn't take his warm gaze from hers. "Thanks."

That dazzling smile made a reappearance a moment before the light changed and she trotted across the street as if her burdens weighed nothing. Three or four times, she whipped her stare over her shoulder as if verifying he didn't intend to tail her.

He wondered if she shopped at VegVana often as he resumed his place in line, ignoring the dirty look from the guy behind him. He could learn to love this food group if necessary.

"That was really sweet." The cashier fluttered her lashes at him. All he saw was the memory of soft brown eyes and a riot of long, wavy hair.

"Yes, she was," he sighed.

"Damn. Two nice people in a row. That's gotta be a record." The woman pouted when he didn't respond to her flirtations. "Have a nice day."

"You too. And I think I just did."

He slotted his purchases into the saddlebags of his motorcycle, whistling.

It'd been a long damn time since he'd felt like this. A bag of candy was a small price to pay for hope.

Maybe cooking would become his new favorite pastime after all.

Chapter Three

Brielle Norris hated the trembles zipping along her legs from hips to toes. Pretty soon her knees would knock together beneath the airy bohemian skirt she'd opted for this afternoon. Ridiculous. It was as if she strolled through the Arctic instead of the blazing summer heat she'd endured on the bus ride across town. Three parkas wouldn't have kept her from shivering.

Just thinking about spilling her guts to a stranger had her doing an about-face, spinning on her heel in the marble foyer of the high-rise building she'd been referred to by the operator of the university's anonymous health services hotline. She couldn't believe she'd actually found the guts to call the toll-free number. Or for that matter, that she'd tucked the business card with the info into the pocket of her clean, secondhand black slacks a day earlier. She'd found it in a Plexiglas holder beside the sink in the bathroom of her new office.

Hell, it'd taken her almost seven weeks of working in Elembreth University's Science Department—and more than a dozen failed attempts—to find the nerve to shut herself in the tiny, no-stall deathtrap at all. But she'd done it. And the literature boasting free mental health support had seemed like a sign.

She couldn't live impaired forever. At least, she didn't want to.

Coworkers were starting to wonder. She slipped out to the fast-food joint across the street multiple times a day. They couldn't know she didn't have a real addiction to trans fats so much as she had to use their large, bright facilities. Returning with something off the dollar menu justified her trip, and eased her guilt for using the restrooms, without denting her tight budget.

Brielle couldn't afford to lose her job as a student services coordinator, even if the title was a fancy way to describe something that felt like a glorified gofer.

She was fairly sure she'd only gotten the position because they were desperate. Two women had gone on maternity leave. At the same time, a guy had quit to run away with his boyfriend to some remote South Pacific island, where they intended to live the good life as pool boys at a glamorous resort. She wished she were that bold.

With no experience and no qualifications to recommend her, it seemed like she'd fallen into the right place at the right time. Maybe Fate had decided to give her a break. Brielle worked hard and learned fast, no matter how trivial the tasks they assigned her, but she knew only too well that sometimes her quirks were more than normal people could comprehend or tolerate.

Sometimes putting up with her weirdness was too much to ask.

Like it had been for Brad.

Squeezing her eyes shut, she gripped the handrail on the inside of a tiny wedge of the revolving door. It spun around on the boundary of the building she had intended to flee from. Quitting was not an option. Not if she hoped to change her future. She committed herself to going all the way around instead of taking the easy way out by collapsing on the sidewalk, no closer to ending the horrible ride filled with fear her life had become. She clung to the shiny bar until she escaped...right back inside the lobby of the tower of terror.

Why the hell couldn't they have a regular, old-fashioned door?

Enough running. Enough sacrifice.

She needed help to stop the cycle of pain she'd allowed to dominate her universe for far too long. Playing the victim had never suited her.

When she popped into the pristine, air-conditioned heaven—or hell—for the second time in less than a minute, the receptionist, who might have worked here since the building opened in 1952, gave her a wan smile. "Back again so soon? How can I help you, dear?"

"I have an appointment with Dr. Malone and Associates." She tried not to wince when the lady nodded as if to say, *No kidding, you could really use a shrink or twelve.*

"No need to be nervous. Luke's offices are on the top floor. Just wait until you see the view from up there. *He's*— Er, I mean, *it's* gorgeous." She tossed Brielle a conspiratorial wink that made her guilty for thinking such harsh thoughts about the other woman. Maybe she needed to add paranoia to the list of ailments she sought treatment for.

But didn't it freaking figure? Top floor.

"The elevators are right over there, around the corner." The receptionist waved a manicured nail, decked out in sensible taupe polish, in the direction most of the foot traffic seemed to flow toward.

"Where are the stairs?" Brielle had her limits. And the tight enclosure of the door had nearly done her in. No way could she handle being stuck in a brass box for the eternity it would take to reach the summit of this ivory tower just to see the honorable, and apparently sexy, Dr. Luke Malone.

It didn't matter how damn good he was.

"Honey, that's twenty-six floors up." The receptionist stopped chuckling when she realized Brielle didn't join in. "You know, they're real long flights of steps. These ceilings are high."

Brielle simply waited, tapping her foot.

"All right, have it your way. I'll call and let them know you'll be a few minutes. Go down the hall then turn left after the Ficus tree."

Brielle nodded. She hurried off before she could change her mind again.

The heavy metal door clanged shut as she began her trek.

Somewhere around the fourteenth floor she began to wonder if the elevator would have been so terrible. The thought alone had her breathing double time. She slowed to avoid turning into a sweaty mess by the time she reached the summit. Good thing she had experience sneaking down the fire escape when her father had gotten drunk enough not to notice. The skill had likely saved her life as a teenager. Plus, her apartment complex's super hadn't taken the *Out of Order* sign off the hazard they called an elevator since she'd moved in to her modest third-floor flat six months ago.

Probably for years before that.

Grocery shopping had become a strategic test as she picked up a bag or two of supplies on the way home each day to avoid the logistical nightmare posed by a boatload of packages. If she ditched the bus a stop early, she passed right by VegVana and the general grocery store next door to it. From there, the walk and climb weren't so bad. Plus, she saved the money others might have paid in gym fees.

Without purchases to lug today, the giant blue numbers painted on the cement walls ticked off the floors she passed at a steady pace. Exertion distracted her from the tumult of emotions bouncing around in her core.

Could she really do this?

Brielle huffed out a sigh when the enormous *26* on the door in front of her came into view. She took a few deep breaths on the landing, then exited the stairwell. A stroll to peek at the office wouldn't hurt anything. No one said she had to go inside.

A squeak escaped her when she nearly barreled into a tall man who occupied a lot of space in the hallway. He rested his shoulder on the wall, arms folded over his broad chest and feet crossed at the ankles. His suit fit like a glove, highlighting his trim waist and the long lines of his torso. A quick twist allowed him to check the shiny silver watch gracing his wrist.

"Under ten minutes. Not too shabby," he admitted. "Sometimes my friend Kurt and I race. But not after lunch out. Especially not after gyros from the street meat truck that comes on Wednesdays. We've learned that lesson the hard way."

At his rambling, a laugh bubbled up from beneath the layers of worry, doubt and tension stratified endlessly inside her. Maybe she wasn't the only nervous one in Dr. Malone's lair. "Yeah, that doesn't sound like a great idea."

Grateful, she lifted her gaze, then stumbled back when she recognized the candy man from VegVana. "You! What are you doing here?"

Had he followed her? Panic clawed at her throat for a moment. Until he clarified.

"Ah, sorry. I should have officially introduced myself. I'm Dr. Luke Malone." He slowly extended one of his big hands. Not in a grab for hers, but in invitation. It stayed steady, allowing her to decide if she should accept it or not.

Everything about him gleamed in the sunlight streaming through the skylights. His almost too-long, blond hair, his dazzling white teeth and cuff links she'd swear were studded with diamonds. The only thing ruining the effect was an out-of-place goatee, drastically darker than the rest of his gilded perfection.

Brielle swallowed hard and stared. Part of her jumped for joy at seeing him again, especially now. Another sliver screamed at her to run. Something about him mesmerized her, and that couldn't be good. She'd trained herself to keep her wits handy when it came to men.

"You must be Ms. Norris?"

"Brielle Kelly Norris," she answered on autopilot. She gulped when her palm disappeared inside his. Had she chosen to meet him halfway or had he enchanted her with his golden demeanor?

All smiles and light, he erased some of her uneasiness. Somehow his size didn't frighten her, though she knew she'd be wise to retreat a few more steps. Out of his grasp. Away from his heat. This was the man she'd have to embarrass herself in front of. Repeatedly. At least for the duration of the five free sessions the university covered. No use getting attached.

Then again, it helped to know he wasn't flawless. His clueless expression in VegVana went a long way toward helping her feel on footing slightly more even.

"Pretty name. You okay?" He tilted his head as he examined her respiration. "Is it all right if I take your pulse?"

"I think so, Dr. Malone," she whispered.

"Please, call me Luke." His light hold lingered, thumb brushing over her wrist. The gentle touch certainly didn't make her heart hammer any less. "Tell me if it becomes un-okay at any time and I'll let go. Agreed?"

She nodded.

"Good. Mrs. Allerton, from downstairs, said you looked like you might be a runner." He shook his head at the receptionist's term. "I thought it'd be best to meet you out front. Wouldn't want you tumbling down the stairs if you changed your mind. Twenty-six flights is a lot. A return trip, with fifty-two, is insanity."

She opened her mouth to deny her urge to flee. But closed it, preferring not to lie.

"It's okay." He didn't release her hand, not that he could have since she didn't ease up her grip on his. Instead, he turned toward the office she spotted over his shoulder. "Many of our patients are frightened at first. You don't have anything to worry about here."

A snort escaped before she could prevent it.

"Well, yeah, maybe a few things. But I'll let you fill me in on those when you're comfortable. Let's go inside and talk. Maybe I could interest you in a glass of iced tea." He lulled her with his easy manner. "Everything is up to you. You're the boss. Nothing you can't handle."

"Thanks." She bit the inside of her cheek, hoping she didn't prove him wrong. Her dry throat begged for the drink he offered.

"No problem." He drifted closer, still in lock step with her, when she didn't flinch. "Really, Brielle. You'll see. You're safe here. I promise."

How could he tell exactly how to comfort her? He must have earned his reputation as the best in his field. The hotline worker had assured her she'd gotten lucky. Dr. Malone had only recently started seeing patients again, in addition to his duties as department chair, even though that'd meant he'd sacrificed his Saturdays. His selflessness swayed her, just like his kindness had the day she'd run into him a few weeks ago.

Reading people seemed like second nature to her escort. In ten seconds, he'd given her more reassurance than Brad had in seven years. How could she have been so blind? Maybe because she hadn't believed men like this existed.

She stumbled.

Luke wrapped his arm around her waist, supporting her as they crossed into his space. Glass and chrome sparkled everywhere. It was so open to the outside she could forget there were walls at all. Sky hung above them. City stretched out below. She'd never visited a spot that made her feel less closed in. Less caged.

Part of her relaxed. A fragment deep down that hadn't taken a breath...maybe ever.

He smiled at her as he led her to an angular black sofa.

"Would you like that drink first? Or are you ready to talk?" He only released her hand when she'd settled into the surprisingly comfortable leather. "Sorry, I don't have any chocolate to offer you. I should put a bowl out."

"I'm tempted to take the coward's option and delay our discussion." She scrubbed a hand over her face. "But we'd better get down to business. There's only so much we'll be able to fit in my five sessions, and I'm afraid that'll hardly be enough time to scratch the surface."

"Why do you say that?" Luke turned his back, not pressuring her to respond but inquiring idly as he poured them both a tall glass of tea from the pitcher on the lacquered side bar. Ice clinked against the gorgeous crystal, adding to the luminosity of the space.

"Because I'm pretty screwed up." No sense in beating

around the bush.

"We all have our moments, Brielle." Something about his huff made her curious.

"You?"

"Of course. Sometimes more than others." He handed her the tea, then rubbed the nape of his neck. Part of her nearly volunteered to do it for him. How could he affect her like this? No one ever had. And after Brad, she thought no one ever would. Just being around him was a relief.

"Thank God." She grinned when his eyebrows raised. "Everything about you, this place, seems so unblemished. I wasn't sure you could understand."

"Try me." He surprised her by sitting beside her instead of in one of the chairs across the coffee table. "Do you mind?"

"No." Brielle was pleased to find it was true. "You don't have to ask. If you freak me out, I'll let you know. It helps to feel less...alone."

"I agree." He nodded. "It's easy to let life overwhelm you when you shoulder all your burdens single-handedly. I'm fortunate to have good friends, ones I've known for years, but lately it seems I can't share with them without risking their feelings. Being gagged like that... It's miserable."

Knowing he could relate helped her divulge her secrets. "Exactly. It was such a relief to have the hotline operator to talk to the other night. Things get particularly bad in the dark. When I can't sleep. And I lie there and think. Too much. It was easy to whisper my fears into the phone, and reassuring to know someone was listening, even if she couldn't do much to help."

"I know what you're saying. Still, I think the operator did a pretty damn good job of assisting. After all, you're here. Doing something different about your problems. Finding a new solution. Something better than getting by. I assume you've suffered for some time?"

"Yes. Years." She swallowed hard, unable to say more.

"Then at least this is a step in the right direction. What you've been doing hasn't resolved your issues. I hope we can work toward that goal together." Genuine concern tinged his wish. At least she assumed it did. If not, he was a world-class actor in addition to a renowned psychologist.

"I have a phobia," Brielle blurted.

"You're not afraid of heights." He smiled as she stared out the window, scanning from soaring birds to pavement in order to avoid looking into his eyes.

"Nope." She laughed. "Small favors."

"I wondered when you didn't take the elevator. Some patients are scared of falling." He sipped from his glass.

Brielle couldn't help but stare as condensation gathered then dropped from the tumbler onto his chin. His Adam's apple flexed when he wiped the beads from his stubbly chin. He paused to scratch at it.

"Your goatee is dark." Speaking aloud hadn't been her intention. The anomaly caught her off-guard.

"Weird, right?" He laughed. "I've never grown the thing out before. But lately, I don't know, I guess I've felt like making a few changes myself."

"Keep it." Her smile reflected his. "No one can be perfect, you know. At least, not without annoying everyone around them."

"Is that so?" He grinned.

"Yes. You need some idiosyncrasies. As long as you don't go too far and frustrate people by being a freak." She sighed.

"Has someone accused you of that?" A cloud floated above them, shading his face.

"Yes." She glanced away again.

"Because you're afraid of—"

"Being closed in small spaces." A shudder raced up her spine. She took a big gulp of tea to wet her dry mouth.

"Plenty of people are claustrophobic, Brielle." He set his glass down, leaving wet rings on the clear table. "It's a very common affliction."

"You're talking about people buried alive in a coffin, submariners freaking out miles under the ocean or...I don't know...something actually scary." She shook her head. "This is different."

"How?"

"I like that your doors are open." The glass panels pinned against the wall left no doubt she could escape.

"No one else is working this weekend." He shrugged. "There's no one to overhear us."

"Right. But I could leave if I wanted to."

"At any time." He held his hands out, palms toward her. Another shadow crossed his face. "Though I hope you'll give me a chance to help."

"I think you already are. After my boyfriend—well, my ex-boyfriend, Brad—made it clear I was no longer welcome..." She couldn't divulge the whole truth yet, maybe not ever. "I didn't think I could share again. You make it easy."

"Thank you, Brielle." He smiled sadly. "Though I'm not quite sure what we're talking about yet. For the record, it sounds as if your boyfriend didn't support you as you needed. Moron."

He muttered the last under his breath. She caught it anyway.

"Is that your professional opinion?" Her giggle cut off. Would he construe her innocent amusement as flirtation? Awkwardness wasn't anywhere on her agenda for the day. Not that she'd have a chance with a man like him. He was...above and beyond.

"Hell, yes. My personal one too." He scrubbed his face with knuckles. "You make it hard for me to separate Luke and Dr. Malone. That's not a problem I usually have, Brielle. I've known you less than ten minutes and I can already tell you're extraordinary. I could tell the day we met in VegVana. There's something different about you."

"Yeah, like the way I can't brave the produce aisle? Or get in a freaking elevator? Or how I sweat myself to sleep in a panic most nights. Or don't drink coffee in the mornings so I won't have to endure a visit to the tiny bathroom in my office." *Or always have to be on top when I have sex so I don't feel stifled. Or how I ended up driving my boyfriend away with all my rules and regulations for living day in, day out in a state slightly less than full-blown hysteria.*

"No, like different *special*. I told you, phobias are common."

"Is *special* code for a pain in the ass?" She grinned.

He choked on the next swallow of his tea. "No. I reserve the term *complex* for those types."

"Good to know."

"Do you want to tell me how you developed an aversion to tight spots?" He left another door open.

And she felt safe enough to walk through it without hesitation.

"My mother died when I was six. My father wasn't interested in raising a kid or in the settled life without her. After my mom... He abandoned our house. Just moved one day. I found out later he didn't even try to sell it. Left it to rot—empty, overgrown. I don't remember a ton about my mom, but I know she would have hated that.

"He stopped at a gas station that afternoon. He tried to leave me too. I should have let him. I screamed and cried until he realized he couldn't get away with dumping me so easily. It was less effort for him to tote me along and make it look like things were fine to the outside world.

"So he moved us to some tiny place in the city. Somewhere near Fifth and Livingston. Where fewer people noticed any particular kid."

Luke squeezed her hand lightly. "That's no neighborhood for a child. Hell, I would lock my doors when I pass through if I didn't ride a motorcycle."

"After that, I remember my dad always being there,

drinking or doing drugs. I'm pretty sure he worked for criminals. Sketchy guys would come in at all hours. They'd wake me up with their yelling, and fighting. I don't know how he had cash all the time. It sure as shit didn't look like he was loaded in our pigsty. But he gambled a lot. Partied a lot. Had sex with random women who latched on to his sometime-wins. There was no way for me to avoid it in that place."

Brielle took a deep, shaky breath. "I tried to stay out of the way. Keep from being noticed. I put some pillows and blankets in a sloped closet under the stairs to the roof. At first, it made a great hideout. I didn't mind, except that it didn't even have a light, so when my dad closed the door..."

She shivered.

Luke allowed her to gather her composure before continuing. He wrapped her fingers around her tea, which she chugged.

"It's okay if it's too much." Kindness radiated from his eyes, the same gorgeous blue as the sky behind him.

"I can do it. This isn't the hard part." Brielle took a deep breath. "I liked when my place would get spider webs because I hoped their owners would eat the other bugs.

"After a while, it became a routine. As soon as I came home from school, he would lock me in there to keep me out of the way while he did whatever he did. I stole a flashlight from school and I would search for batteries in the garbage. Sometimes I could score ones that weren't totally dead. Or those Glow Stick things at Halloween. Those were the best.

"Until later when he wouldn't let me stay out, even if I asked to sleep in my bed for a night. Then it wasn't my place to hide anymore. It was my dad's way of getting rid of me. My refuge turned into a cell."

"Jesus," Luke muttered so low she figured she wasn't supposed to hear. But he seemed to be sitting closer now. "I'm so sorry you had to endure that, Brielle. Can I ask something? It's not a judgment. I just want to understand."

"Go ahead." Glad not to have to carry the conversation, she

waited as he phrased his question.

"Did your dad threaten you? Hurt you? To keep you from telling people at school what he was doing?"

"No. I mean, there were times when he drank that he'd take a swipe at me. Not very often." She slumped in the seat. "I know, it's stupid. Even Brad accused me of bringing it on myself. But...it felt wrong to leave my father."

"Because he was your only bond to your mother?" Luke asked.

"Maybe, in some way." Brielle shrugged. "But also because he was my dad. I didn't want to abandon him, like he tried to do to me that time. He needed me there. Even if it was too hard for him to bear being around me. Too painful to remember."

"How do you know that, Brielle?" Luke narrowed his eyes.

"One time I ran away." Her eyelids fluttered closed as she remembered. "I was nine. We went to the university's topiary park on a class trip. The designs and the glass conservatory were so beautiful. I just...didn't want to go. I hid in the bathroom until my class left without me. I made it a little over a week before I was starving and cold. So cold. It was winter, and the guy living between the dinosaur and the train, who said I could share his fire, tried...things. I kicked him in the nuts and ran straight home."

"It's okay," Luke murmured. "You survived. You did whatever you had to in order to make it to the next day. That's okay, Brielle. That's what you're supposed to do. It's human nature. Instinct."

"I couldn't cut it. I had to go back." A curse threatened to escape. Either that or tears. But it had been a hell of a long time since she'd allowed herself to cry. Neither her dad nor Brad had put up with weeping. Luke wouldn't appreciate waterworks either.

"What I'm hearing is a sense that you failed." Luke shocked her with his insight. He cut through all the bullshit on top and dove to the heart of the matter.

"Maybe if I had tried something else..."

"Maybe you wouldn't have endured." His tone grew slightly stern. "You may not have lived to fight again. You made the best decisions you could at the time. As a nine-year-old girl, I'd say you did pretty damn well for yourself."

"Thank you." She wished she could hug him. Sure that wasn't appropriate, she wedged her fingers beneath her legs on the sofa. Maybe someday in her life she'd find someone who allowed her to express herself. Brad hadn't welcomed unsolicited contact either.

"Do you want to tell me what happened when you went back?" he prodded quietly.

Brielle paused.

"You don't have to. We've already shared a lot for our first session. Whatever you're comfortable with is fine."

"Is our time up soon?" She couldn't believe the reading on the clock above his desk.

"I was going to break for lunch. You could join me if you'd like to continue another hour." He smiled, encouraging her.

"How about the abridged version? I'd like you to know." She bit the inside of her cheek.

Luke nodded. "I'm listening."

"I climbed up to our apartment that night, using the fire escape for the first time. I wanted to see what was going on. Had he even noticed I was gone? It was late. I should have already been in my closet. When I got to the top, there was only one light on. No people. No chaos. My dad sat in the room with empty bottles, broken, everywhere. He had a gun in his mouth and his finger was on the trigger."

"Brielle," Luke whispered.

This time she reached for his hand and he linked their fingers.

Why couldn't it have been so simple with her father? "I shoved open the window. The locks had never worked right, nothing to steal anyway. I ran inside and yanked the gun from his hand. It was so heavy. He looked at me and passed out as if he'd seen a ghost. He didn't wake up for almost a full day after that. I was afraid he would die."

Neither of them said what she was thinking... She would have been better off if he had.

"From then on he was careful to lock me in the closet right away. Every night. Usually before I'd eaten dinner. And even when I used the bathroom or took a shower, he would make one of his friends watch me. Always." She shuddered.

"You're so strong, Brielle," Luke murmured to her. "To have gotten through it all, mostly intact. Trust me, you're doing great. Amazing. I see patients all the time who have been challenged by far less than you, yet haven't coped as effectively. I'm impressed with your resilience. Your bravery. Do you understand how tough you are?"

Seldom in her life had someone praised her. The compliments went to her head, making her bold and confident. Enough to spit out the rest of her story. The important parts anyway.

"When I was seventeen, he pissed someone off. Bad. I was locked in my closet for the night. I heard arguing start. This time was way worse than others. There were guns in our apartment a lot of the time. They didn't really frighten me. I never realized how loud it would be..."

"Your dad killed someone while you were in the closet?" Luke's blend of empathy and quiet anger—not *at* her, but *for* her—helped her divulge the truth.

"No." She swallowed hard. "Someone murdered him. Blood and...other gross gray stuff floating in it...ran under the door to my closet. I stayed quiet so they wouldn't do the same to me. But I was stuck. In there. With the smell. And the bugs. No food, or water, or bathroom. Or light. For days. I think it was the stench that eventually drew enough complaints, even in that hellhole, to bring the landlord's son to investigate. Brad. He found me. Let me out of my closet. I'm not sure which of us was more surprised. Or scared."

"This was your boyfriend?" Luke tilted his head.

"Yes." She winced. "For seven years. He took me in. I owed him everything. I tried not to bother him with my drama."

"Is that what he called your phobia?" Luke practically growled.

Brielle scooted an inch or so away. Seeing, for the first time, some danger in the dazzling man she'd come to trust in an instant. Just like Brad. Damn her. When would she learn?

"I'm sorry." He calmed immediately. "I'm not angry with you. But I'm standing behind what I said before. That guy did not deserve you. Not at all."

"He kept me."

"Like you were some stray animal? A dog? His pet?" A glint of something icy froze his blue eyes.

"It didn't seem that way to me at first." She hung her head.

"Nothing in your life was normal. You couldn't understand how twisted his treatment was, Brielle." Luke lifted her chin. "Don't confuse opportunistic with altruistic, please. He used you."

"Until the sex and my cooking and cleaning weren't enough to offset the *drama* anymore." She gritted her teeth. No way could she spill the rest. Not yet. Not even to Luke, no matter how he called to her on a basic level.

"Is that what he told you?" A flush crept up Luke's cheeks. Did he get this upset by his other clients' revelations?

"Yes." She sighed before skirting the truth. "And he didn't even wait for me to finish moving out before bringing some new woman into the place I thought was our home. I left everything. Walked away. At first I took odd jobs to pay for food. And I found a shelter. They helped me get on my feet. But I wasn't ready to talk. So I started over."

"That sounds like a smart thing to do," Luke reassured her. "Everything you've built now is fresh. Completely yours. A great foundation for your future. I'm sure it's been harder than I can imagine—"

She choked back a sob.

"But you're doing it. You're still surviving. You have work, a place of your own and...you're here."

"Begging for help," she whispered. "I want to be normal."

"Remember, that means messed up in some way." Luke sighed. He scrubbed his hands through his hair. "I think that's a good place to stop for today."

Disappointment rushed through Brielle.

"At least with this formal session." He stood, rubbing his flat abdomen. "Would you like to join me for that lunch now?"

Suddenly she craved nothing more than that. Her stomach growled. "Yes."

Luke Malone held out his hand.

And she grasped it like the lifeline it was.

Chapter Four

Luke knew down to his marrow that if Brielle got even a glimpse of the pure destruction in his thoughts, he'd lose her. She'd run and never look back. He wouldn't blame her either after all she'd told him. Schooling his features, he offered her his hand and silently pleaded for her to accept his support.

When her long, slender fingers landed on top of his palm, he did a mental jig. He closed his hand around hers for a brief squeeze. Not enough to trap her. "Come on, I know a great place around the corner. It's one of my favorites. Do you like sandwiches?"

"Um, yes." A long pause put him on alert.

"What is it?" He slowed down, trying not to rush her into anything. "You can change your mind at any time."

"Is it expensive?"

Luke knew better than to offer to pay. She had to have her independence. God knew, she'd earned some. He considered the menu, a little ashamed that he didn't even weigh things like that in his choices these days. "You tell me. You can get a half sandwich and a bowl of soup or a salad for under five dollars. The portions are big enough that my best friend's wife usually takes some home with her for a second meal too."

"I can swing that." Brielle beamed.

"Great." They meandered toward the front door of his office. "If you have to use the restroom, the one on this floor has five stalls, a big sitting room attached and a sky light. The sandwich shop's is far less spacious."

"Thank you." The full blast of a smile from Brielle nearly knocked him over. She was naturally beautiful. Not because of caked-on makeup or manmade touch-ups. Some of the women he'd attributed the title to in the past had relied on gimmicks to perfect their presentation. None of that was necessary for Brielle.

In the weeks after their run-in at VegVana, he'd wondered if he'd imagined her stunning loveliness. He hadn't. Her chestnut hair fell in waves to her waist. The fullness of her lips had had him longing to kiss their plump softness from the moment she'd burst from the stairwell. Out of nowhere, his absent sex drive had roared to life. At the most inopportune time possible.

It'd been a month or so since he'd slunk out of Kurt and Becca's bedroom. The longest period of abstinence he'd imposed since he was sixteen. No wonder he was having trouble controlling himself when faced with a gorgeous woman. One he desperately hoped he could assist. Even if it meant stifling his own reactions to her.

As he waited for her in the hallway, he recited all the reasons why instant attraction didn't matter in this case. Chemistry couldn't justify violating the patient-doctor relationship, no matter how badly he wished it could. She seemed to trust him and she honestly needed help. He wouldn't risk damaging her chances for recovery.

Luke had treated plenty of vulnerable, gorgeous women in his career. None of them had affected him like Brielle did. The connection burning between them didn't come along every day. Maybe he could use it to facilitate her healing.

When she emerged, she hovered by the door to the stairs.

"Brielle, do you know how phobias can be treated?" He didn't join her just yet.

"Isn't that your job?"

He barked out a laugh. "Yeah, I suppose it is."

"No, really, I don't." She flushed.

"Why would you? You're not a psychologist." He hoped she didn't balk now. "One way to treat phobias is through systematic desensitization, which means encouraging a patient to live through their fears. They have to realize the terror is irrational and overcome it a little at a time in a very controlled environment. The trigger stops being frightening when you face your phobia and grind it into dust."

"You mean I have to get locked up." She paled. Her eyes grew wide and her breathing turned erratic. One hand steadied her against the wall, but she wobbled anyway.

Holy shit. She was going to pass out.

Luke lunged for her, wrapping her in his arms and guiding her to the floor. Dazed, she blinked up at him, questions dancing in her rich brown eyes. "Put your head between your knees. Breathe slow and deep. With me."

They dragged in a lungful of air together. Then released it. Again and again.

"Better now?" Luke drew circles on her back, surprised by how much of her he could span with one hand. She hadn't seemed so little when she'd held under the pressure of relating her childhood to him. Part of that could be attributed to her boxy, ill-fitting clothes.

"Yes. Sorry."

"Don't apologize. It's my fault. I shouldn't have sprung the treatment plan on you like that." He tucked a wisp of her hair behind her ear so he could monitor her expression. "We'll go slow. Really slow. Only taking another step when you're ready."

"How is that going to work in five—no, four—more sessions?" She dropped her forehead onto her knee and wound her arms around her shins.

"It's not."

She wilted beneath his gaze.

"We're going to have to work longer than that on something so ingrained in your psyche." He wanted to rub away her frown with the pad of his thumb, but he held himself in check. Barely. "I hope you weren't expecting a silver bullet. This is going to be hard. But we'll get there together and the effort will be worth it in the end."

"I can't afford therapy." She shrugged. "You'll have to teach me as much as possible, then leave the rest to me."

He didn't doubt she would bust her ass to vanquish her demons. But some things couldn't be done solo. She needed assistance. Support. Or she risked lapsing into a state worse than her current coping permitted.

"Forget about the insurance thing. I'm committed to helping you." He patted her bare knee, positive she had no idea how much of those magnificent legs she flashed at him with her skirt sliding up her thighs. "Whatever it takes. We'll get through this together."

"I can't let you do that," she answered without lifting her head.

"Why not?" He blinked.

"Because you shouldn't have to work for nothing," she objected.

"Our practice provides sliding-scale therapy for those in need. We're committed to preventing costs inhibiting people from getting the help they need." That was the truth, though he didn't intend to seek payment for her case. Helping her would be gratifying enough. Something about her meager subsistence had him feeling guilty for his success anyway. It was a small thing. But he could do this. Wanted to do it.

"Really?"

He nodded.

"Okay, then." She perked up. "I would be grateful for your help."

"So you tell me. Are you ready to ride the elevator?" He rose, but she didn't follow his lead.

"I—" She hesitated.

"Okay, that's answer enough. If you can't say yes right off, then you're not prepared. That's all right. Remember, you're in control. You decide what's comfortable, or within your limits to try."

"It's just that we're so high up. The thought of having to stop and wait a bunch of times on the way down, the door closing me in after each person we pick up...” She began to hyperventilate again.

“Shh. Deep breaths, remember?” He smiled when she caught herself before blacking out. “I understand your concerns. They’re valid. I don’t mind walking. If we get to a point where you think you’d like to try the elevator instead, all you have to do is say so. I’ll be with you the whole way, no matter what you decide. Okay?”

“Sure.” She unfolded the human pretzel she’d morphed into, accepting his assistance to climb to her feet.

“So, what do you do for a living?” When she didn’t respond after they’d gone down two flights, he figured she didn’t intend to answer.

“I’m sorry. I’m a little confused.” She turned at the end of the landing and started down another set of stairs.

“About what?”

“Is this typical?” She tipped her head up to look at him. In the dim stairwell, her eyes looked huge and innocent. So much of her life had been unusual, she had no point of reference for normalcy.

“What?” He had to make sure he understood her question.

“Going to lunch with a client?” Brielle called him out. “The things we’re talking about now... Are they for the case or because you want to know?”

“Ah, that.” He shook his head. “Nothing about today has been standard for me. No, I very rarely, if ever, interact with my patients outside of my clinic. It’s important for my clients to know that we are not friends.”

“Oh.” She bit her lip, quiet for a few more flights before nodding. “I understand. It makes sense.”

“To be honest, Brielle, I like you. I admire your strength. Maybe someday, when you no longer need my services, we could reevaluate that boundary.”

“I think I would enjoy that.” She skipped down the next step and three more, picking up speed until he had trouble keeping up with her spritely bouncing. Ahead of him, she ducked through the door to the second floor.

"Brielle, we still have another flight," he called after her.

"I know. I'd like to take the elevator." She smiled over her shoulder before pausing. "Unless that's dumb. It's only one floor."

"No, that's not in any way silly." He smiled wide at her as they rounded the corner toward the elevator. "It's fantastic. I'm proud of you."

"I haven't actually done it yet." Her finger shook when she poked the button.

Luke cupped her shoulders in his hands and turned her to face him. "Listen to what I'm saying. You're safe. There is nothing that can hurt you in there. The doors will open as soon as we're down one floor. I'll be with you. Keep breathing. Focus on your heartbeat and making it steady. Then I want you to say this to yourself: I'm okay. This is temporary. I'm not trapped in here. I'm okay..."

She joined him in practicing the mantra. They'd repeated it about twenty times before the bell signaled the car's arrival.

Brielle stiffened instantly beneath his palms. "You don't have to do this. Only what you're comfortable with. There's always next time."

The doors began to slide closed with them still on the outside.

"No!" She jabbed the arrow again. When the opening was at its widest, she latched on to his arm, dragged him inside with her and closed her eyes. A deep breath expanded her slender ribs, enhancing the swell of her breasts. As she exhaled, she began to chant aloud. "I'm fine. This is just temporary. We are not locked in here. I am safe. You are with me."

Luke didn't mind her revisions. Whatever kept her calm and began to coach her consciousness into accepting the truth was fine with him.

Brielle did such a great job, she didn't seem to notice when the car slowed and the doors slid apart, welcoming them to the lobby.

"We're here." He tapped her on the shoulder.

"What? Already?" She looked up at him and grinned, then did the cutest little conga he'd ever seen in his life out of the elevator.

And in that instant he knew they had some major problems. Because despite every oath he'd ever sworn, he wanted one of his patients.

Brielle launched herself at him, giving him no time to do more than react. He caught her in his arms and used their momentum to swing her around, instead of crashing to the floor in an undignified pile of limbs. "I did it!"

"Yes, you did." He hugged her tight before setting her onto her tiptoes. Did she have to smell so delicious? "Congratulations."

"Same to you." They grinned as they passed a bewildered Mrs. Allerton. "You're amazing, Luke."

The way his name flew off her tongue, familiar and reverent, stirred something deep inside him. So did the confidence in her bearing when she marched to the revolving door, tucked into one of the cubbies and shoved right through her fears.

Brielle floated alongside Luke as he led her to one of his favorite cafes. She couldn't believe how much hope he'd bestowed in a single session. Sure, she was messed up. Majorly. It would take time and an enormous amount of energy to make real progress. Still, she actually believed it could work.

If only she'd tried this years ago.

Regret had no place at the table with them. She shoved it away. The reality was she hadn't been ready. Hiding in Brad's house had been a convenient excuse. She could see that now. And if she had reached out for help, she likely would not have found Luke or a counselor as well suited to her.

His light, gentle style mixed with some smart-assery met all her needs perfectly. Without him, she had no doubt today could have been a disaster. So she decided to give him what he'd asked for. "I'm a student services coordinator for the Science Department of the university."

"In the Franklin Building?" He whipped his head toward her. "On State Street?"

"Yep, that's the one."

"I know it well." His lips pinched tight as though he wanted to add something, but stopped himself.

"What is it?" Brielle touched his arm lightly, startling them both.

"Uh. My two best friends have a practice on the second floor. I'm there all the time. How haven't I met you before?" He shook his head.

"I haven't worked there very long, less than two months." She winced when she recalled the temporary jobs she'd struggled with before that.

"Ah, yeah. I've been sort of avoiding Kurt and Becca most of that time." A frown marred his features.

"Becca..." She tapped a finger on her lips. "Does she have red hair? Green eyes? Always smiling? Goes everywhere with the tall, dark-haired doctor? The really serious one?"

"Yes, that's her." Luke laughed. "She hasn't quit with that grin since she and Kurt finally hooked up last year. Kurt's been my friend since middle school."

"You're so different." Afraid of offending, Brielle didn't mention that the man had frightened her at first, until she saw how much he adored his wife and the respect he treated her with.

"No kidding." Luke shrugged. "Well, I guess in some things. We have a lot in common. How we get there tends to be by opposite directions. It makes for a great match-up. Same as Becca and Kurt. Becca is terrific. She draws Kurt out of his brainiac ways and makes him smell the roses, you know?"

"I could see that. I like her." She recalled how the woman always stopped to chat, not pretending Brielle was invisible like so many others did.

"That's good. Really good." A smile spread across Luke's face, warming it even more and bringing life to his super blue eyes. "I think—"

"What can I get for you today, Dr. Malone?" The girl behind the counter batted her lashes at Luke so hard Brielle thought she could feel the breeze.

"The usual, please."

"And you?" The server stared down her nose at Brielle as if she didn't already know she wasn't a suitable companion for the gleaming man beside her. She tarnished his polish.

So busy talking, she hadn't bothered to read the menu boards. A glance up revealed too many choices to run through quickly. "What's the usual?"

Luke laughed. "Grilled ham and cheese with a bowl of chicken noodle soup and a side of fries. I admit it, I have the stomach of an eight-year-old."

"That sounds terrific. I'll have the same." She could have done another happy dance when the cashier glared in her direction.

"I'll bring those right out."

Luke led her to a booth in the corner. He helped her slide in before taking a spot on the opposite side. When she peeked up, his face was somber.

"Brielle." He paused.

What had changed in a matter of seconds? Her stomach sank through the floor.

"I can't be your doctor."

"What?" All her euphoria fled, deflating her like a sad balloon. It had been too good to be true. Him. His support. The hope of a life unburdened by fear. "Why? It's too much, isn't it? There's no chance I can be normal."

"Like hell." He leaned forward, planting his elbows on the table and capturing her hands between his. "You did so well today. I'd say your prognosis is very good. With the right help."

"Then why?" She hated the disappointment choking her, making her questions ragged.

"Because of this." He lifted his index finger and wiggled it between them. "I can't be professional with you. I won't be unbiased or objective. There's been something here since the zucchini and it's going to interfere. I won't take that chance with your well-being."

"Oh." She blinked. He felt it too. "I understand."

But she hated the thought of starting over with someone new, someone who wouldn't be Luke.

"Dr. Williams—I mean, Dr. Foster. The new Dr. Foster. Becca," Luke corrected. "She can be exactly what you need. You said you like her. Trust me. She's amazing at her job. I wouldn't hand you off to just anyone. In fact, I hope you'll let me stay involved. If you want, I'll go with you. We can work on this together. They often deal with couples' counseling. I'd team up with you if you wanted."

"But Becca would be in charge of my case?" She toyed with the edge of her napkin, reveling in the warmth of his hands cocooning hers. Not once did she have the urge to break free of his tender restraint.

"Yes." He smiled. "She'd take the lead. I know you have a lot of sorting out to do in your life right now, but if you'll let me, I'd like to be part of it. Would you be okay with that?"

For the second time in one day, Brielle thought she might cry. Until the server dropped a steamy platter of fries and grilled ham and cheese between them with a resounding *clank*. Apparently she and Luke weren't the only ones who could detect this crazy bond.

"Thank you." Brielle reserved her sweetest tone for the jealous cow.

When the girl sashayed away, Luke chuckled. "Sheathe those claws, kitten. You don't need them. If it makes you feel better, Becca doesn't get along with Chastity either."

"That's her name?" Brielle nearly shot water out her nose.

"Pretty ironic, isn't it?" He appraised the server's too-high skirt hem and too-low neckline. Not in a way that hurt Brielle's feelings. In fact, it highlighted how differently he regarded her—with far more...interest. Or Becca, with more admiration.

Several bites of delicious gooey cheese and fresh bread later, she couldn't restrain her curiosity any longer. Something had her intuition on high alert. "You talk about Dr. Foster...Becca so fondly. Familiar. Is she—?"

"Go ahead. What would you like to know? I'll share anything you ask. How can I do any less after you trusted me with the skeletons in your closet?"

She couldn't suppress a shudder.

"Sorry, no pun intended. You know what I mean." He swiped a crumb from her lip. "Ask."

"Has she always been just a friend?"

"No." He didn't hesitate or qualify his response. No excuses followed either. "What? You didn't expect me to be honest?"

"I guess not." She stared as he spooned up some soup, slurped the broth then cleared the star-shaped noodles from the utensil. "You're so different."

"Good or bad?" He licked the last drops from the silver, making her toes curl.

"Not too shabby." She grinned when he tapped her shin below the table with the toe of his shoe.

"Now you're heading for complex, Ms. Norris."

She laughed until she realized he was staring at her, his silverware still suspended above his empty bowl.

"What? Do I have something stuck in my teeth?" She scrubbed at them with her tongue then smiled wide.

"No. Nothing like that." He attempted to disguise his smirk behind his napkin. "You're distracting me. Look, I don't plan to deceive you. Not now, or ever. Kurt and Becca went through a tough time when they were getting together. Kurt did some things I didn't understand. Made some bad choices. It almost cost him the woman of his dreams. I won't take a chance with people who matter to me. I will always be honest with you, I swear."

"Thanks. I can take it. I'm pretty sure." She smiled ruefully. "So your best friend married your ex-lover. Isn't that awkward?"

"Oh." He set his empty plate aside and leaned back. "I guess that's what most people would assume. It wasn't like that at all. Becca has always been Kurt's first."

"You two cheated on him?" Brielle couldn't imagine Luke would do something like that. Had she read him all wrong? People were capable of unthinkable things in the right, or wrong, circumstances. She knew all about that.

"Definitely not." A grimace twisted his lips. "I wouldn't normally disclose personal information about a doctor to their patient, but considering how intimate this could get and the relationship between us all, I think you have a right to know before you sign on. Kurt and Becca are unorthodox therapists anyway. In their personal life they like to experiment. Sexually. They've asked me to join them or watch on occasion. I've been the third in ménages with the couple on and off for the last year. Off for over a month now."

Ah, so *that's* why he'd been staying away from State Street.

Part of her gaped, wondering how two people in love could want...that. But then she questioned why having three people share positive affection would be any less gratifying than a couple exchanging respect and desire. In fact, the more the merrier she imagined.

"Why? I mean, why stop now?" She elaborated before he could explain the allure of a threesome. That part she'd have to think about some more. Later. When she was alone.

"My heart hasn't been in it. Physical pleasure wasn't enough anymore. Things degraded to the point where I couldn't...perform."

"Wow. You weren't kidding earlier about everyone having their moments." Brielle whistled.

"Rub it in, why don't you?" He faked a pout before a wicked gleam darkened his eyes. "Somehow I don't think that's a *moment* I'll be having again anytime soon."

Sort of the opposite of overcompensating with an enormous chromed Hummer in the middle of the city, Luke's easy admission made her sure sexual prowess wasn't something he worried about. What would it be like to sleep with a man like him? Someone unselfish, fun and caring?

The stuff fantasies were made of, she imagined.

"It would be great if you could say something right now." Luke's fingers twisted his straw wrapper into a knot.

"You think *I'd* judge *you* after all we've shared this afternoon? Hardly. Thank you for telling me that. I would have felt weird talking to Becca about, you know, everything, and wondering. Or finding out later. I would have felt foolish."

"Does that mean you'll do it? You'll meet with her and see if she's a good fit for your counseling?" Luke seemed to hold his breath.

"Yes." With him by her side, she thought just maybe she could do it.

"One more thing."

"Uh-oh, I don't like the sound of that." She finished her lunch, wiped her mouth and tossed her crumpled napkin on top of the wreckage of their plates, unable to remember the last time she'd devoured her food with such gusto.

"I mentioned Kurt and Becca's uniqueness earlier. I think you should also be aware that they are known for utilizing unusual, but highly effective, methodologies in their practice. They're not conventional in any sense of the word."

"I got that from the threesome discussion." She grinned. "If you haven't noticed, I'm not very by-the-book myself. What about my life has been ordinary?"

"Right. So now that you're not my patient anymore..." He smirked. "Can I pay for your lunch? We could call this our first date."

A *what*? A real-live-boy-and-girl-go-out-to-dinner-and-get-to-know-each-other thing. She'd gone on one and not even realized it. With him, everything seemed organic, completely natural.

"What the hell? Sure." She grinned like an idiot when he plucked her check off the scratched hardwood and pumped his fist.

"Since I'm on a roll, will you let me drive you home? Mrs. Allerton saw you get off the bus. It'll be packed, and can't be comfortable in this heat. On my motorcycle, you won't be closed in."

Why would she say no? She couldn't drum up a single reason. Except that her whole world had turned on its axis in one afternoon.

Still, the idea of clinging to him while they raced through the wide-open air—irresistible. "Okay, but on one condition."

His raised eyebrows had her amused again. "Bold, Ms. Norris. Let's hear it."

"Take the long way."

"You got it." He tugged her from the booth, leaving a few crisp bills in their wake without bothering to ask for change.

Luke winced when he rolled up in front of the shabby apartment building Brielle pointed to over his shoulder. The motion pressed her soft breasts into his back completely. He could all too easily imagine what it'd be like if she were riding him instead of his bike.

He'd driven them around the entire city, through some of his favorite scenic routes. The ten-minute commute had turned into almost an hour of sweet torture. Yet he didn't relish the thought of letting her go. Not when he'd finally found someone who held his attention for longer than the couple of minutes it took to attend to baser needs.

He braced them on the pavement, groaning softly when

Brielle peeled herself off him. He missed her light weight and the clutch of her arms around his waist. The plan he'd formulated on their journey came pouring out. "I'll call Becca when I get home and see what her schedule looks like this week. What time do you usually work until?"

"Six. And I have an hour lunch break." She glanced away. "But I'm not sure I can handle going back to my job after, you know?"

"Of course." He reached for her hand, brushing her knuckles with his thumb. "It'll be emotionally draining, I'm sure."

"I'm a little worried about people from work noticing me going to Becca's office too." A flush deepened the effect of the wind on her cheeks.

"It's none of their business what you do on your own time." He sighed. "I understand though. I can join you at their office in the evenings. Unless I'm already over there for meetings, it would be hard to find time during the day. I don't want to rush you either. Or possibly Becca would consider the weekends so she can lead some in-depth sessions."

"I'm already being difficult. You're calling in favors for me. Inconveniencing her isn't my goal."

"You don't understand. This is what we do. It'll give her a great deal of satisfaction to work with you. And, my guess is—if anything—you two will have trouble not breaking the no-friend rule too. I think you'll get along really well."

"If you're sure..."

"I am." He stared into her rich chocolate eyes.

"I guess I should go inside now." She extracted her hand from his gentle hold.

"Brielle..." Her name rolled off his tongue. Nothing else would come, despite the snarl of emotions making him feel alive for the first time in months.

Terrified too.

When he struggled to find the right thing, she let him off

the hook.

"Thank God. I don't know what to say either, Luke." Walking backward, she took a step and then another until the magnetic field bonding them seemed to lessen a bit.

"Wait a minute." He stood, digging in his back pocket for his wallet. Fishing around, he located a card then held it out to her. "My number. Call me if you need...anything, really."

"Thank you. For everything." The thick paper earned his envy when she clutched it to her chest. "Mmm. It's warm, like you."

"Screw this." He reached down and placed his hands on either side of her face. His fingerless gloves prevented him, somewhat, from touching her supple skin. Leather didn't seem to bother her in the least. Her lips parted and she held still as he descended. The featherlight brush of his lips across hers did nothing to ease the hunger gnawing at his guts.

He'd imagined this since the day their paths had crossed, regretting that he hadn't slipped his card to her along with the candy that afternoon.

Time to make up for that mistake.

Once, twice, he kissed her before sealing their mouths in a deeper exchange.

Music blared from someone's open window. Carly Rae Jepsen's "Call Me Maybe" instantly became Luke's favorite song. Brielle tasted so honeyed. Her lips moved in time to his, meeting him halfway on every motion, as if she could project where he'd venture next. No awkwardness stole the perfection of the moment. They met and matched as though they'd been made for each other.

A simple kiss from Brielle affected him more strongly than the raunchiest club sex he'd ever indulged in. With any partner. Even the ones he'd convinced himself he loved.

Infatuation, maybe.

He'd been there, done that enough times to know that this was something else entirely.

Lost in heat, he advanced their kiss from a chaste exchange to something resembling a claiming. When Brielle nipped his lip, he came to his senses and backed off. Breathing hard, he chastised himself for pressuring her. She didn't need him adding to the confusion today would certainly bring. It seemed impossible they'd only been introduced hours ago.

She touched the tip of her index finger to her lips, smiled and began her retreat once more. This time, he let her go with his contact info laid against her heart, where her hand pressed it to her chest.

"When I left this morning, I never expected this. It's...a lot. I have to go now."

"I know." He nodded. "Take some time to reflect. I can wait."

She seemed as torn as he was between needing distance to deliberate and craving more of the drugging, if simple, pleasures they'd shared. "Luke, you're turning out to be very...*complex*."

He gawked at her for a second then burst out laughing. "My friends are going to adore you. And for the record, so do I."

A wave and a smile later, she disappeared behind a bed of wildflowers.

Luke's smile still hadn't faded as he drove away, glancing in his mirror at least a dozen times before rounding a bend in the street.

Chapter Five

"Get in the closet, Brielle."

It was Brad, not her father, who ordered her this time.

"No!" She thrashed in his iron hold as he dragged her across the floor of their bedroom by one arm. Her shoulder burned as she writhed. The hardwood afforded her no purchase. "Don't put me in there. I swear. I'll clean the bathroom better."

"Damn straight you will." He swung her around like a rag doll.

Her ribs connected with the edge of the molding that surrounded the door, stealing her breath. He jammed her inside, kicking her when she tried to scramble out despite the lightning scorching her side.

"Don't act like you hate it. You chose this. Asked for more. You did this to yourself." He glared at her when he swung the door shut. "You're so fucked up. I can't believe you actually want this."

Her leg shot out, preventing the closet from closing. "I don't! Brad!"

"Bitch, if you crack the wood, you'll pay for that too." He became quiet and cold. She knew better than to challenge him when he got so dangerous. "You said it yourself, Brielle. You're curious about being held down. About why you liked shutting yourself in the closet in the first place. Now you're going to get your wish, you freak."

"I take it back. I didn't mean it. This isn't what I pictured. Brad! Don't leave me in here. Please, Brad. Please. I'll do anything." When her begging fell on deaf ears, she resorted to action.

Her survival instinct kicked in. She smashed into the door.

The sturdy construction of the old plaster and solid panel didn't budge. That fact didn't keep her from trying. She banged on every surface until her hands and feet were bruised and throbbing, maybe broken. Lying on the ground, she could see a shard of the outside world. Enough to calm her a bit.

That's when she realized Brad still lectured her. "You causing all this drama isn't making me want to stay, Brielle. Maybe it would do you good to have some time alone to think about how messed up you are and how lucky you are that I know what you really like."

"No! Brad! No!"

And when he plunged her into complete darkness, flipping off the living room light, deserting her in her own personal hell—probably to fuck his new girlfriend—her shouts turned to screams.

Brielle slumped with her shoulders leaning against the wall as she perched, wide-awake, in bed. Cold sweat saturated her cotton nightgown. The air mattress she slept on didn't exactly have a headboard. Or a frame at all, for that matter. But the pile of pillows she'd collected from garage sales did the trick. She could make mounds out of them to help steady herself without feeling trapped.

All the lights blazed in her apartment after the nightmare that had wrenched her from slumber. The closet. That fucking closet—her sanctuary turned hell on earth. Had her father even had to steal *that* from her? And Brad... What a disaster. After seven years together, she'd thought she might be ready to open up about the root of her issues. Had hoped maybe exploring her fantasies would help them grow together instead of drifting apart.

How wrong she'd been.

She couldn't afford any more bad decisions when it came to the men in her life. This time she might not survive.

Brielle stared at the business card propped against the lamp on the floor beside her bed. Blue and gold, it shone. The weakest part of her yearned to dial the number printed across the bottom.

Luke.

But the strongest fragment knew if she was truly to heal, the courage to change had to originate from within.

A quick flick of her fingers flipped the card over so she wouldn't be tempted to use the crutch he'd so graciously given her. Especially not at two in the morning. Or three. Or four, because she'd probably still be awake then too. Instead, she hugged one of her pillows to her chest and rocked while repeating the chant he'd taught her. "I'm okay. I'm not trapped. I'm safe. No one can hurt me here. I'm okay."

Maybe if she said it often enough, it might start to be real.

Tuesday afternoon, Brielle stared out the open segment of her cubicle. If she put her chair on its highest setting and strained, she could peek out the window across the aisle to the parking lot. Denying she craned her neck every time she heard the roar of a motor would be futile. But it didn't seem like Dr. Malone had any intention of ending his boycott of State Street in this century.

Hell, maybe he had twice as many reasons to avoid the area now.

So busy spying, she didn't register the logo on the delivery truck that had parked out front. Until her phone rang.

She jumped. No one called her. Email did the trick for the lazier employees in her office. Everyone else simply walked over or shouted for her to come to them.

"H-hello?"

"This is In Bloom. I have a delivery for a Ms. Brielle Kelly Norris."

"That's me." She resisted the urge to pull the phone away from her ear and gawk at it. No one had ever sent her anything. It wasn't even her birthday.

And only one man would use the middle name she'd practically stuttered when her nerves and his influence had overwhelmed her.

"The front door requires an access card for entry, ma'am. Would you mind meeting me there?" He grunted. "I can follow you in. This is a heavy one."

"Um, that's fine." She barely remembered to say thank you before hanging up.

Flying past the stairs in the hallway, she thought back to her descent from Luke's office. How could she miss a man she'd only known for a few hours?

Absorbed in her thoughts, she nearly collided with a woman who'd just turned the corner from the stairs, heading toward the Science Department instead of out into the sunshine.

"Oh crap!" They dodged and ended up grasping each other's forearms to stabilize themselves.

"Brielle?" Fiery red hair, which the woman calling her name possessed, could only belong to one woman in the building.

"Becca." What were the odds?

"Hey, sorry about that. I was actually coming to see if you wanted to go for a walk with me so we could discuss a few things away from prying ears. I'm not sure if you get breaks at all." Becca paused, tilting her head. "Were you in a hurry?"

"Actually, yes. I was letting someone in." She blushed.

From the shadows, where she hadn't noticed him, Kurt raised his chin in their direction. "I've got it, ladies. You chat."

Brielle sighed and relaxed a little.

"Does my husband make you nervous?" Becca smiled. "Please don't let him. He's all bark and no bite. A complete softy inside."

"I find that hard to believe. He's so...no-nonsense. Even the way he walks, without wasting any effort. Direct. Brusque. Efficient. Yeah, I guess you could say he intimidates me a tad."

"Here, this should help." Becca pointed in the direction he'd disappeared.

They faced the original Dr. Foster together. He held an enormous vase of flowers to the side of his chest, trying to peer around them. Becca was right. The mental image of Kurt completely buried in Gerbera daisies would go a long way toward taking the edge off his bearing.

The women chuckled together.

"Oh sure, keep laughing. Luke is going to love this story. He probably paid extra to set me up. Figures that asshole would send the biggest arrangement in the universe." Kurt shook his head. "How am I going to top this?"

"They're gorgeous, but I already have everything I want." Becca avoided most of the flowers to peck her husband's cheek.

"How do you know they're from Luke?" Brielle stammered. Not that anyone else would be sending her an enormous bouquet.

"Besides the fact that he's texted me about nine million times this morning asking if the delivery truck has been by yet?" Kurt rolled his eyes.

And the spell was broken. Brielle officially voided her initial hard-ass impression.

"Oh." She couldn't help the smile tipping up the corners of her mouth. At least Luke had been thinking about her maybe half as much as she'd obsessed over him.

"Yeah." Becca scooted over so her husband could pass them in the narrow hall. "Why don't you go put those on Brielle's desk so we can hash a few details out?"

"You got it." He sniffled, then turned his head as an enormous sneeze echoed through the stairwell. "Good luck with these, Brielle."

"Thank you." She hoped he understood the flower delivery service was the least of what she appreciated. Luke's friends were treating her like one of their gang. Not some broken, battered woman. It made all the difference in the world.

"So..." Becca plopped onto the stairs, patting the spot

beside her. “I hope you don’t mind. I love wearing high heels. Sometimes they aren’t ideal for a full day of standing and walking though.”

“I can see that.” The stiletto platforms were amazing and deadly. “I’d break my neck if I ever attempted those.”

“You get used to them.” She smiled kindly. “Plus Kurt appreciates them so it’s worth the sacrifice. It’s crazy the things you’ll do for the right person. Speaking of... Luke told me about your case.”

“Ah yeah. Hopeless, right?” The laugh she attempted sounded fake, even to herself.

“Not at all.” Becca put her hand on Brielle’s knee. “We can talk about that stuff later. How does Saturday around ten sound?”

“That’d be fine. Are you sure it’s not imposing? You don’t usually work weekends, do you?” Brielle measured Becca’s reaction.

“I don’t, no. But Kurt and I would do just about anything for Luke. He’s part of our family.” She winked. “And a friend of his is a friend of ours. He said he was pretty straightforward with you. How does that make you feel about me?”

“You really are a shrink, aren’t you?” Brielle winced.

“Sorry. I didn’t mean it that way.” Becca squirmed a little in her skirted suit. “I guess I’m asking if you’re sure you’re comfortable sharing intimate details of your life with me, knowing I’ve slept with Luke.”

“Based on the way he described it, yes.” She nodded. “I appreciate you both being candid with me. I guess I have the same to ask of you, though. Are you going to be able to separate your past with Luke from any future he and I might have together? Will anything come in the way? I’ve got to tell you, I asked for help for a reason. I need it. And I don’t want to waste time or get derailed because of some bizarre tangle of unrelated nonsense.”

“Believe me, I’d be thrilled if Luke could find a hint of the happiness Kurt and I have. If you bring that to his life, I’ll be grateful."

"Then it's settled." Brielle nodded.

"But aren't you even the teensiest bit jealous? I mean, I have had insanely good sex with him and my husband. At the same time." She might as well have buffed her bright red nails on her blouse along with the claim.

"Enough." Brielle stuck her fingers in her ears. "I'm trying to be polite, but I have my limits. I don't think your husband would appreciate a catfight at his practice. I will pull your hair and scratch your eyes out if I have to."

"Thank God. I was afraid maybe you didn't feel the same way about Luke as he does about you."

"You're testing me?" Brielle bristled.

"I told you, he's more than just a buddy of my husband."

"Don't worry. I can't think about much other than him. It's infuriating."

"Great. In that case, would you please call the man?" Becca lowered her face into her hands. "He's going bananas waiting to hear from you. I'm not sure what kind of spell you put on him. Good job, though. He's completely smitten. And afraid to chase you if you need room. Why haven't you reached out?"

"Do you think he's only interested because of some weird pity thing?" Brielle hated that she voiced her concerns. Still, if anyone would know, Becca would.

"Are you kidding?" The doctor looked more her age when she wrinkled her nose. "No way in hell. In our line of work, we see people every day that we empathize with. Never, and I mean *never*, has he sought more with a patient. You have no idea how irregular this is for him. Talk to him."

"I will." She nodded when the lump in her throat prevented her from admitting she'd been afraid to dream so big.

"Soon." Becca stood as Kurt's footsteps clicked toward them. "He wants to invite you to a function we have to attend tomorrow night. It'd be lovely to have you with us."

"What? Another date?" Brielle wasn't sure which of the

revelations to process first. “What kind of event is it?”

“Becca was awarded top honors for most influential researcher of the year. Across all disciplines at the university.” Pride oozed from Kurt’s every pore when he mounted the stairs and hugged his wife from behind.

“Don’t listen to him. We’re both receiving the accolade. It was his invention that made it possible. I was just along for the ride. His subject.” A blush stained her cheeks.

“And don’t you forget it.” He laughed when she turned to smack his stomach, which didn’t flex a bit. What was it with these doctors and their commitment to being ultrafit? Damn.

“So you’ll come?” Becca seemed eager for her answer. “With Luke?”

“Let the woman talk to him directly, matchmaker. Break time is over, Dr. Foster.” Kurt tickled his wife. When she squealed, he scooped her into his arms and toted her easily up the rest of the stairs. He called down from above, “Fair warning, Brielle, I took a picture of your desk phone, with the extension showing, and texted it to Luke. You might as well call him before he caves. Save him a little face, would you?”

“I left his number at home.” She couldn’t risk temptation that strong.

“I jotted it on your blotter. So you’ll always have it.” He chuckled when Becca reached up to lay a big sloppy kiss on his cheek.

“You sentimental fool,” she murmured, barely loud enough for Brielle to catch it. “I love you.”

“Love you too, baby.” He stared at her with pure adoration until Brielle felt like the proverbial fly on the wall.

“See you tomorrow.” Becca called over Kurt’s shoulder when he rushed them to their office and ducked inside.

Brielle raced through the hall and to her desk. Flowers blossomed everywhere. Spring and the scent of happiness filled the air, covering the slight musk of her space. Two women popped in within seconds. “Those are gorgeous. Who sent them? Do you have a boyfriend?"

They hadn't spoken to her beyond a polite hello in the seven and a half weeks she'd worked there, but the moment flowers showed up, every woman in the place turned to mush. How would she stand a chance of holding her own with Luke?

He was obviously an expert in a game she'd never played before.

It took five minutes to bring herself to snatch the card from between the jewel-toned petals. Inside were two brief lines.

I miss talking with you, and the sound of your voice.

Call me, please.

Doodling hearts around his phone number didn't help Brielle convince herself she could muster any sort of poise. She'd practically reverted to high school. Except back then she hadn't been able to experience the carefree crushes of a typical girl.

Sometime around the fourth attempt she made to muster some bravado, practicing what she intended to say, her phone rang. She closed her eyes and took a few deep breaths.

On the third buzz, she answered. No sound would pass her lips.

"Brielle?" Luke's voice mesmerized her. She hadn't imagined the smooth, rich texture of his tone. "Hello?"

Oh, right. She actually had to talk instead of sitting there wrestling the butterflies in her stomach. He completely scrambled her brain. "Hi."

"Three days and that's all I get?" His smile was evident even through the phone lines.

"Thank you for the flowers. They're stunning." She laughed softly. "You're making my coworkers jealous."

"As they should be," he teased. "You're by far the prettiest, sweetest and most irresistible of them all."

"How would you know?" A thought crossed her mind. "Have you gone out with someone in my department? Or *stayed in* with someone in my department?"

"You're the only woman on the first floor of the Franklin Building who's ever caught my eye."

She snorted, clapping a hand over the receiver so he wouldn't catch her indignity.

"Complex. For sure," she muttered.

"I missed you too." He didn't sound like he was joking. "In fact, I was wondering if I could see you again."

"For the award ceremony tomorrow?" She still couldn't believe it.

"Ah, you ran into Becca then?"

"Yep. Just a few minutes ago. We bumped into each other, literally, in the hall." She twirled her pen absently on the desk. "We also set up an appointment for Saturday at ten. I hope that works for you, if you're still interested..."

"That's great. I'm putting you in my calendar right now." He paused. "As long as you're sure."

"I'd appreciate you holding my hand, yes." Relief flooded her.

"Then it's settled. So, how about tomorrow? Will you keep me company through all the dull stuff up until Kurt and Becca's award presentation? Bland chicken, cheap wine, probably even some dry cake... Come on, you know it sounds fabulous." She could picture his eyes sparkling.

"Honestly, it does. Spending time with people who care enough to endure that to cheer each other on... Well, that's a big deal to me." She sighed. "I'm just not sure I have anything to wear. It sounds fancy schmancy."

Luke laughed. "If it wasn't such an enormous milestone in their careers, I'd bail and lure you somewhere fun instead. Somewhere dress code doesn't matter. Maybe to my house, where you don't have to wear anything at all if you prefer."

"Complex." She shook her head.

Then she seriously considered it for a nanosecond.

She'd never been somewhere proper. This event would surpass her experience, even if the dry chicken didn't meet his high standards. What fork should she use? What would she wear? Surely, her sundresses wouldn't be formal enough, especially not paired with the old lady sweater she used to camouflage the fact that she'd never owned a strapless bra either. Going without certainly didn't seem classy enough for his date. "Luke, I really appreciate the invitation. If I could, I'd love to. It's just not possible."

"Okay, Brielle, I understand. I guess I'll see you Saturday then." Disappointment reverberated in his voice.

She could relate. Suddenly, she felt like Cinderella longing to attend the ball. Except she already knew that's where her prince would be. In his world. A million miles from hers. And he deserved a princess on his arm.

"Right." A week had never seemed so long.

"Will you call me before then?" He seemed uncertain for the first time.

Damn, she was screwing this all up. "I didn't want to bother you with my drama."

"Brielle." The steel in his tone melted almost instantly with the hiss of air he exhaled. "I'm not your ex. Or your father. I'm interested in you. All of you. If you want to call and talk about nothing, that's great. If you need to talk about something, I'd be honored if you picked me to listen."

"You're going to be sorry you said that at two in the morning." She dropped her head to her forearm on her desk, cradling the phone between her neck and ear.

"Having trouble sleeping?" His concern caressed her through the phone.

"I can fall asleep. I just can't stay that way." She lowered her voice so no one would overhear her weakness. "Nightmares. But I've been using the technique you taught me to calm myself afterward. It works. Most times I can squeeze in a nap before my alarm goes off."

"Damn, Brielle." He muttered something she couldn't understand. "You shouldn't have to go through that alone. You have my number. Use it. Let me help."

"We'll see." She didn't plan to drag him through her muck.

"Holy crap, you're stubborn." He laughed softly. "What does it say about me that I like that?"

"Someone once told me that being normal means being messed up." She grinned.

"Very true. Wise man." He groaned. "Sorry, Brielle. I have to go. My admin is shooting me a death-ray glare for being late to this meeting."

"Of course. And it's not like you can pretend to be oblivious with all that glass." His crystal cavern probably bustled with activity today. She should have realized how busy he was. Taking up his time in the middle of the day... Well, he'd called her, hadn't he? "Have a good day. Thanks again for the flowers."

"My pleasure. Truly." He sighed. "Saturday is a long time from now, isn't it?"

"An eternity."

"Call me?" Papers shuffled in the background.

"Maybe." She couldn't help but smile at his exasperated growl.

"Complex woman," he moaned. "Later."

"Get back to work, Luke. You're late, remember?" She hung up to the sound of his laughter.

And every time she looked at his flowers, she smiled right back.

Chapter Six

Brielle wondered how long it would be before one of her neighbors complained about her screaming in the middle of the night. She clutched her chest, willing the pounding of her heart to steady some. "I'm okay. I'm safe here. I'm okay."

Her eyes fluttered closed as she repeated the mantra. It seemed that each night she recovered faster from the terrifying visions that haunted her dreams. A mental picture of Luke, holding her hand and promising to keep her safe, didn't hurt.

Talking to him earlier had only made her craving for him stronger. The taste hadn't staved off her hunger. Before she could second-guess herself, she jammed her hand beneath her pillow and retrieved his card—a bit worse for wear since she'd slept on it a few times.

After lunging for her phone, she typed in the digits she'd pretty much memorized anyway. He answered on the first ring, and barely into that, spurring her to assume maybe it was an automated message service instead of his personal line. *Damn.*

"Shit. Are you pissed? I didn't think you'd be able to see me."

"Luke?" She canted her head, trying to make sense of his rambling with the dregs of panic still settling around her.

"Yeah. It's me, sweetheart," he crooned. "Are you all right?"

"I think so. Just the usual after-midnight bullshit. I wanted to hear your voice again. To chase away the gloom." Haziness began to dissipate. "What were you talking about?"

"Look out your window." He sounded funny. A little nervous.

She crawled from bed and tugged on the edge of the purple botanical sheers she'd made from bargain-bin fabric. They'd come out pretty damn nice, if she said so herself.

After scanning the area below her third-story window, she said, "I don't see anything."

"By the oak tree." A small glimmer caught her attention.

"Is that you?" She gasped. "And is that a lighter?"

"Yep and no, I don't smoke. It's a simulation app on my smartphone. I downloaded it the time Kurt and I saw Carrie Underwood in concert."

"Are you joking?" It was probably best he couldn't see her expression.

"Nope." He chuckled. "What? She's hot and there were tons of pretty girls there. Besides, I like lots of different kinds of music."

"Me too." Brielle frowned. "But the only concert I've been to so far was the free show the university orchestra gave on the lawn of city hall for Memorial Day."

"Hey, I was there too. I enjoyed Brahms' "Symphony No. 1" the most."

"Me too again. Although the *Star Wars* theme was a close second." She giggled.

"I knew you had good taste." He grunted. "I wish I'd met you that night."

"I wasn't ready, Luke." A grimace reminded her that this hadn't begun as a social call. "Hell, I might not be now. I'm definitely not a good bet. So...why are you staked out?"

A long pause ensued, spawning some reservations on her part. If she'd only met him at VegVana she'd probably be freaking out to find him lingering this time of night. But now she worried she might have become the doctor's pity case. Worse, what if he had been thinking of a way to tell her they really lived in separate worlds after the whole award-ceremony rejection?

"I seem to be experiencing some insomnia of my own and thought I'd go for a ride. I guess I just sort of ended up here."

"I'm not sure if that's sweet or kind of stalkerish." She ran her fingers over the perfect seam of her curtains. Gooey insides proclaimed it adorable, despite her false protest. What if she could help his mind rest too?

"Maybe a little of both," he acknowledged.

"Probably so." She couldn't believe how quickly he'd distracted her from the gnawing terror she'd broken free from minutes ago. Usually it was an hour before she stopped shaking so hard her teeth clicked together.

"Are you going to invite me up? Give me a tour?" He sounded so hopeful she couldn't bear to disappoint him.

"That should take about two-point-three-seven seconds. This isn't exactly an Italian villa, you know?" She tore around the apartment, ensuring her underwear had all been stuffed completely in the hamper, tossing her half-full glass of water into the sink and fluffing her tangled sheets until they didn't look as though she'd been wrestling demons in her sleep.

"I'm not a snob, Brielle," he reminded her. "I don't give a shit how fancy your apartment is or isn't. As long as you're there, that's what counts."

"Good thing." She couldn't believe she was about to do this. "It's on the third floor, no elevator. Unit 317."

"Don't you have to buzz me in or something?" he wondered.

"Nope. None of that high tech stuff here." When she reached the door, she slid the chain off the rickety lock. "Not much reason anyway. Most of the residents do all right, but they're not dripping diamonds."

"I wish you had a dog, at least. A big one. With a mean bark." Air puffed between his phrases. He must have taken the stairs two at a time because he reached her far more quickly than she could have made the journey.

Smart on his part, since she'd already begun to reconsider.

Shaky in the aftermath of one of her episodes, she'd have no defenses against his charm. No way to prevent him from running rampant through her private retreat or tending the sprouts of her affection, which grew for him. Suddenly she wished she had a deadbolt for her heart.

"Brielle?" He rapped softly on the door, nudging it open. Broad shoulders encased in a trendy gray coat filled the frame. Her gaze wandered to his chest, where a faded T-shirt with *Elembreth University* printed in a navy arch hugged his pecs.

"Welcome." She spread her arms, gesturing to her home. "Make yourself comfortable."

"Don't mind if I do." The sneaky bastard took the opening to insinuate himself into her embrace. He bent down and enfolded her in his arms.

Their hug went on and on, each of them basking in the heat and comfort provided by the other. Luke's protective grasp squeezed more of the awfulness of her nightmares from her mind, replacing it with something that still ached, but in a much better way.

Roving hands massaged her back, dissolving the knots there.

"You're trembling, Brielle," he whispered in her ear, kissing her temple as he retreated. "Are you cold?"

"In here?" She shook her head. Ceiling fans and open windows made it almost bearable. Certainly not chilly.

"Adrenaline will do that." He appraised the dark circles beneath her eyes. "You sounded so scared when you called. I wish I had come up and knocked when I first got here. Or, hell, I should have asked you to dinner tonight. Maybe I could have stayed."

"Presumptuous much?" She raised an eyebrow.

"Uh, now that you mention it, that could have been fun too." He rubbed against her as if the pressure of not being touched was almost too much to bear. "What I meant is maybe I could have coached you on some methods for shaping the content of your dreams to avoid getting so frightened."

"Is that really possible?" If she could master a technique like that...*everything* could be different.

"For some people." He nodded. "Becca and Kurt uncovered

proof during their Dream Machine experiments. They need more data, more testing and more studies to pass academic muster. Still, it seems that certain dreams are expressions of subconscious desires. They stay pure and candid, almost like REM sleep acts as a truth serum. Kurt used Becca as his primary subject to support that body of work."

"I think I'm still with you." Brielle adored how animated he became when discussing his job. She wished she had something to be that passionate about.

"But the kind of dreams that happen to a person, as if they're watching themselves star in a movie, they're a little different. Kurt and Becca hypothesized that humans are hardwired to run a variety of plausible scenarios to determine possible outcomes in difficult situations. Sort of like the best simulator in the world. They also think that if an event is traumatic enough, the process can break and get stuck on one particular event. Maybe because the person can't find an acceptable solution. Or maybe something to do with the dreamer waking up before the scenario is finished, in the case of something horrifying."

"You're saying dreams are a way for someone to decide what to do in real life?" She scratched her chin, imagining the choose-your-own-adventure books she'd loved to check out of the school's library to distract her from the world beyond her closet.

"In complex situations, yes, I believe they could be. Or when the nightmare event is historic, I think dreams could be a person's mind trying to see a way to have done it differently. Some kind of visual regret." He stroked her hair. "So if you're having the sort of dreams where you're stuck in a rut, the same things happening night after night, we could concentrate on changing the outcome."

"Wow. I love it when you get all nerdy." She patted his cheek. It was that or burst into tears. There could be a way to end this madness?

Unsure of whether it was her relapse or his presence that

spurred her wash of frailty, she allowed herself to lean on him for a few rare seconds. When she stiffened her arms and shoved off his chest, breaking their bond, he didn't try to trap her close. Although he could have, with one hand tied behind his back.

"When you're ready, just ask," he whispered, allowing her to put some space between them.

"So. Yeah." Nibbling her lip seemed to draw his attention. "This is my combo kitchen and living room. Nothing special."

"Except that you live here. That's a huge bonus, as far as I'm concerned." He ambled toward her pile of sheet music—everything from the Beatles to old church songbooks—collected from flea markets she'd scoured this spring and summer. Maybe someday she could add a piano and teach herself to play it. Next he scanned the milk crates she'd stacked into an artful display. Odds and ends littered the shelves in between them.

The last sale she'd gone to, when the university students moved out for the semester off, had yielded a couple of self-help books she'd splurged on but hadn't worked up the guts to crack open yet. Luke's fingers traced the bindings, stopping on one in particular. It was called *Healing Touches*. "Not to brag, but Kurt and I conducted some studies that appear as documentation in this one."

"Seriously?"

"Yeah. I'm sure one of our less successful students couldn't wait to get rid of his required reading. Looks like it's in mint condition. Never used." He shook his head, chuckling. "Too bad for him. A bunch of our better students have used this thing to put the moves on their lab partners."

"I've been procrastinating in reading those books myself. I was afraid that if I tried and nothing worked..."

"Having a possible solution on the shelf in case of emergency is better than having a dusty book written by know-it-alls who can't fix your problem, right?" His wry grin lit her up inside. Someone who understood her, when had she ever found that before? More rare than an affordable instrument at a rummage sale, he was precious to her. Already.

"It's a little freakish and sort of nice being around you, Becca and Kurt." She smiled. "It's like I hardly have to talk at all."

"You don't have to if you don't want to." He braceleted her wrist with his fingers and tugged lightly, walking backward until they sank onto her couch. "We can snuggle in silence until you're settled enough to try hitting the hay again. You need to catch up. How long has your sleep been disturbed?"

"Since my dad... Worse since I left Brad's."

"I can't believe that asshole kicked you out." Luke's fingers curled into a fist.

She didn't bother to correct his assumption.

"Though I'm glad he did. Getting away was the best thing you could have done."

"I know. Believe me. I wasn't planning to stay after..." Despite his understanding, she couldn't bring herself to reveal the full circumstances of her exit yet.

"It's okay." He petted her hair, trailing his fingers on to her lower back. Every brush of his hand through the thin cotton separating their skin made her pray for courage. The intimacy of the contact jolted her into motion. She wormed closer. And ended up sitting in his lap, her head resting on his shoulder. He smelled nice, like a summer night, tinged with hints of gasoline and oil from his motorcycle. Warmth and strength surrounded her when he held her in his arms. "Save the hard stuff for Becca."

"I don't think so." The possessiveness in her denial surprised them both. "She's gotten enough *hard stuff* from you as far as I'm concerned."

Luke laughed, his head tilting back to rest on the horrible old-lady floral print of her hand-me-down couch, which the previous tenant hadn't bothered to lug down the three flights of stairs. The tan column of his neck tempted her to bite him, to mark him in some way. "Okay, not all of the hard stuff. And I was *trying* to be subtle, you know. Though with you on top of me... Sorry, not a lot of choice there. No room to hide what you do to me."

"I like it." She purred, in need of a distraction. It had been forever since she'd wanted a man like this. Not since the early days when she'd regarded Brad as her savior. Was she making the same mistake again or was this special? She had to find out. "C-can I kiss you?"

"That's supposed to be my question." He dragged his fingertips along her cheek then her jawbone. "I'm trying not to pressure you."

"I've been thinking about how you taste since Saturday." She licked her lips, eliciting a groan from him.

"Same goes." One second he was relaxed and still. The next, he struck. His hands buried in her hair, spearing into the tresses. Luscious waves overflowed the space between his fingers. She'd always liked keeping her hair long. It seemed he appreciated it too. "Does it bother you for me to hold you like this?"

Brielle drew in a deep, steady breath when he guided her face first one way then the other, kissing her cheeks. Unused to a man asking for feedback, she hesitated before responding, "Not really."

"That sounds too much like a yes for me." He started to untangle himself from her.

"I meant that I'd much prefer it if you'd hurry up and give me my kiss already." A boldness she'd never before experienced flourished inside her. Something about Luke encouraged her reckless side to tiptoe out from the deep, dark hole it'd been cowering in for her entire life.

"What the lady wants..." He didn't bother to finish. Instead, his mouth covered hers, transporting her to a world filled with sensual delights.

The wet heat of his lips brushed against hers, barely there at first. He increased the intensity little by little. Butterfly kisses became a smoldering attempt to persuade her to open for him. When she complied, his deft tongue sneaked past her teeth, teasing her until soft cries bubbled from her throat. Peppermint chilled and sweetened his advance, tempting her to escalate their exchange from light and lingering to brash and boisterous. Answering groans from Luke encouraged her to peer into his wide, oh-so-blue eyes. From here, she could spot the flecks of silver brightening his irises.

Could she really affect him—a smart, kind, wealthy, funny, sensitive and extra-gorgeous man? She tried it again with similar, if elevated, results.

Finally, the need to breathe overrode her desire and curiosity.

Luke gasped right along with her. They looked like fish out of water. "Brielle."

It was nearly impossible to answer when he performed an encore, sucking on her bottom lip. A tiny nip capped off the light suction.

After a bit, she managed to pry herself away from him. "Yeah, Luke?"

"You officially have my permission to kiss me whenever the hell you feel like it. As often as you like." They leaned in simultaneously, meeting in the middle for another round of making out. Had she ever been given a gift as precious as this? She didn't think so.

Brielle climbed to her knees, straddling Luke, so that every molecule of her body could align more precisely with his. They strained together.

Wonder overwhelmed her.

She indulged in the foreign sensation as long as possible, drawing away only to fill her lungs with air.

He nuzzled their noses together. "You know, one great way to reduce anxiety is by burning it off through physical exertion."

Hell, it already felt as if she'd run a marathon with no training. Her chest was tight and her breathing ragged. Arms and legs wobbled, shaky and weak. Being vulnerable was not her strong suit. So she fell back on her trusty friend, humor. "You want to try Zumba at this time of night?"

Thick lashes on lowered lids did nothing to disguise the hunger banked in Luke's stare. After a timeout, he said, "Hmm. You're right, that's probably not the best idea. Another good technique is anchoring. An easy way to think about it is that you're training yourself to associate lying in your bed with good things about to happen instead of bad things. Focus on pleasure, not dread or panic, to break the cycle that you've gotten stuck in."

"That sounds like heaven. But I'm not sure if I'm ready for anchoring yet." She shivered in his hold. Parts of her gave the all clear, most of them residing below the belt. Meanwhile, her brain shouted at her to take things slow and steady. She'd only earned herself more issues by jumping from the frying pan to the fire with Brad. No need to repeat that performance.

"It doesn't have to be about sex, Brielle." The steam practically rising from him proclaimed it could be, though. Tempting.

"How else?" She tilted her head, attempting to focus.

"You replay a happy memory. Think about it over and over while making a gesture. Like putting your hand over your heart or touching the tip of your middle finger to the pad of your thumb." Demonstrating, he caressed her sweetly. "Becca would talk to you while you were doing this. She'd guide your experience and help set the parameters. Essentially, she'd put you in a trance if your mind was receptive. That's not necessary. It does seem to make the tool more effective, though. After a while, you would come to associate the gesture with the feelings. Then, when faced with a panic situation you'd repeat the gesture and recall the calmness, happiness or pleasure."

She blinked. It sounded too good to be true. For so long, her mind had only been capable of horrible tricks, not clever ones. Besides, she didn't have something other than this moment strong enough to consider anchoring. The vision would have to be powerful to overcome her fear. Even she could see that. Some of her euphoria bled out, leaving room for exhaustion to creep in.

"Brielle?"

"I'm too tired to think about all of that," she mumbled as she collapsed on top of him. His chest rose, sure and steady beneath her once more, and the beating of his heart under her ear enticed her to close her eyes. The circuit he drew across her shoulders, along her ribs and back to the beginning soothed her.

Under it all, she yearned for more. Though banked, the fire he'd lit in her still burned. Maybe they could compromise. "Any objections to making a happy memory I could use later?"

"Sounds like a plan to me," he murmured as he eliminated the gap between them by nudging her chin up and reclaiming her mouth.

Drowsiness gave way to the heaviness of arousal. She perked up as he hugged her to his chest. Would he be disappointed with the most she could give tonight? Torturing him wasn't her intention. "You don't mind, right? Will you be...okay?"

"Does it feel like I'm unhappy right now?" For the first time, he leveled a look at her that said she might be crazy. "I'm positive this is where I want to be and what I need to be doing at this moment in my life."

"Why do I get the feeling you're never uncertain?" She patted his cheek.

"I'm not. Usually." A frown twisted his lips. "With you, that's another story. I won't risk hurting you. So I'm not quite sure of the best course of action. You fuck with my perspective. Have from the very first moment you scooted down the grocery store aisle and into my life. That's why I called Becca in to help. Then again, I'm positive this has the potential to be the most extraordinary relationship I've ever had."

"Do we have a relationship?" She tilted her head.

"We will, if I have anything to say about it." Luke's hand sank lower on her back until he cupped her ass. She shivered. "Do I need to persuade you?"

Her mouth opened to refute the ridiculous claim, yet

nothing came out. Because he chose that moment to dip his fingers below the hem of her nightgown and touch the bare skin of her thigh. Thank God she'd shaved. Following their first kiss, she'd upped her regimen from alternating days to every morning, just in case. Funny, after all this time, she hadn't been looking for someone.

And now he was here.

His other hand gravitated to her chest. He massaged her breast through the purple-polka-dot material of her pajamas while his head dipped, allowing him to dust more kisses over the hollow of her collar bone. Then lower to the top swells of her breast just above the fabric there.

When the fingers of his first hand wandered upward, prodding at the edge of her panties, she gasped.

"Brielle? Should I stop? Do you need to talk through this? Happening so fast. Just feels right." He seemed to struggle to say more.

"Less chatting. No thinking. Lots more of that wiggly thing with your tongue and the poky thing with your finger. Right now." She grabbed his lapels and refused to let go. If she was going to chase a tiger, she might as well pull its tail.

Luke didn't disappoint. He slid the crotch of her utilitarian, white-cotton briefs as far to the side as he could make the fabric go. The damn stuff might as well be a chastity belt for all it budged.

"Here, let me help." She lifted up enough to strip them off and fling them away.

Then Luke contorted his hand until she poised on the edge of a life-changing decision.

While he paused, she didn't. She lowered herself onto him.

Both of them moaned when his finger pressed into her. Slickness guaranteed his thick digit didn't cause her any discomfort. The moment he breached her, he sprang back into action.

"Jesus." He kissed the spot below her ear, setting off

fireworks in her system. “You’re tight. And hot. Soft. So damn smooth.”

His finger retreated then spread her wetness around her lips and clit, making her slippery. Each time he touched her, he slid and glided over sensitive flesh. She whimpered and clung to him, afraid of letting go now that she’d found him.

“I’m not going anywhere, Brielle.” He growled against her temple.

“Let me touch you too.” She squirmed until she could jam her hand between them, roving down his solid chest to the even harder ridge of flesh beneath the denim shielding him from her.

“Not yet,” he winced. “It’s not going to take much. I’ve been dreaming of this for days. Hell, weeks.”

“Me too.” And of sleeping, safe, in his arms. But he didn’t need to know that. No reason to frighten him off now.

And then she couldn’t speak, even if she’d wanted to. He examined all of her, tracing her valleys and folds, stimulating every inch of the area between her legs as effortlessly as he riled her heart with his innocent nuzzling against her mouth. Sweet kisses blended with the pure passion swelling inside her, reaching dangerously near her heart.

Reverence flowed through his caresses. He manipulated her body as though it was delicate and priceless, yet with enough finesse to have her seeing stars. A second finger enhanced his exploration. He filled her with probing strokes of his hand.

When she arched in response, she mashed their bellies and chests together.

“Off.” Her request was garbled by another drugging kiss.

“What?” He paused, as if afraid to move. Attentive to her needs, he appeared to evaluate her request.

“The jacket. The shirt. Off. Now.” She crumpled the ultrasoft fabric of his T-shirt in her fists and waited not so patiently for her demands to sink in. Understanding, she gave him a second to think past the lust fogging their minds.

“You’d have to be at least a millimeter away from me for me

to shrug out of this thing." He laughed at her affronted stare.

"Never mind." She settled for sliding her hands beneath the cotton and gliding them up his sides. Full yet proportional muscles met her seeking fingers. She traced the bold slashes of them, which angled over his ribs.

"That's what I thought." He locked a hand behind her neck and drew her in for another series of bold smooches that nearly distracted her from the swirl of his fingers over her pussy. At least for an instant.

Tension gathered inside her when she realized how gently he coerced her into ecstasy. Though passionate, he invoked an efficient, liquid grace as opposed to the brute force and speed Brad had relied on to get her off...in the rare cases she'd found satisfaction at all.

Everything about this man was different. Beautiful, though she doubted he'd appreciate that thought.

"Stop thinking so much." His command held no ire, only coaching. "Go with it."

Taking his advice, she retracted her hands until they landed on his waistband. She popped the top button of his jeans then ripped his fly apart, loving the sound of his zipper unknitting.

Their hands tangled for a moment, until they found the way they fit together best. Before long, she had reached inside his pants, finding him bare beneath. "You rebel." She grinned.

He bit her bottom lip in a teasing warning.

She hardly noticed with the heft and steel of him overfilling her palm.

Until he upped his game, inserting three fingers inside her and massaging her clit with one of his knuckles. Dexterity was a skill he'd obviously mastered.

Brielle's body clenched around him, inspiring a simultaneous moan.

"You're close, aren't you?" He breathed deeply. "I can smell you. I can't wait to taste you. Soon."

A shiver racked her. No one had ever offered to do that to her before. Her fingers squeezed him when she tightened. He groaned and thrust his hips, insinuating himself deeper into her hold.

The trust he gave her, to cup him like this, filled her with power. On top of him, with all the say, every decision at her mercy, she sank lower, burying his fingers in her as deep as they could go. Abandoning grace, she rode his hand, maintaining her grip on his cock. As she rose, so did her fist.

Within seconds, they both verged on climax.

"Brielle. Are you with me?"

"Completely."

He stared into her eyes for a long moment, then sealed their fate by engaging her in a deep, sensual kiss. The combination of the open longing in his eyes, the gentle pressure bestowed by his mouth and the urgent tensing of his body beneath her combined to rocket her into orgasm.

Rapture went on and on as she strangled his hand, hoping he understood how much the exchange meant to her. No one had ever cared so much about her satisfaction. Not in sex. Not in life.

Grateful happiness exploded from her, leaving her sated and replete in the wake of the rush outward.

Between her fingers, he stiffened further. His cock jerked as he joined her, flooding her hands with every bit of the molten desire he claimed to have stored for her alone.

Finally, she got her wish. He nudged her to the side and stripped off his jacket and T-shirt, using the fabric to wipe her clean. First between her legs and then her hands. The sight of his naked chest was enough to inspire several aftershocks.

Neither of them could gather the energy to do much more.

They collapsed in a sweaty heap, still placing gentle kisses wherever they could reach.

A long while later, Luke asked, "Are you okay?"

"Amazing." She yawned. "Sleepy too."

"Change of scenery is another tactic for breaking the patterns leading to recurring nightmares." They stretched out on the couch. He hovered above her, resting on one elbow while he brushed damp strands of hair from her brow. "You could try sleeping here. Any rest is better than none and this seems pretty damn comfortable to me."

"Great." Brielle grinned. "Because I don't think I can move."

"You're welcome." He wiggled his eyebrows.

She buried her face in his light chest hair as she laughed softly.

"Luke," she whispered, "will you stay?"

"Yeah, you're stuck with me." He kissed her gently, scooped his arm beneath her and rotated them both so that he rested on his back and she draped over his chest.

Roaming fingertips, which skimmed across her shoulders, turned her boneless. She allowed herself to go limp, accepting whatever may come.

The nightmares didn't revisit her.

At least not that night, with him by her side.

Chapter Seven

"Knock-knock." Becca gave Brielle a verbal heads-up before she peeked around the corner of the cubicle. "You know, someone should really question guests before letting any old hooligan in here."

"What in the hell is all that?" Satin, silk, lace and tulle erupted from Becca's grasp.

"Dresses." The perky psychologist grinned. "I figured you should have a few choices, though, personally, I think the light blue halter mermaid would look fantastic on you. Plus it will complement Luke's eyes."

"Are you even speaking English?" Brielle gaped.

"I was never much into clothes either." She slowed down a bit from Tasmanian-devil-in-a-tiara to simply infomercial intense. "Or I guess I should say I couldn't really afford to be. Then Kurt started buying all these pretty things for me, and let's just say he created a monster. Plus, over the past year we've had tons of charity events to raise funding for more Dream Machine research. And you know how that goes, can't be photographed in the same thing twice or people will talk."

"That sounds horrific." Brielle shuddered.

"It's not so bad." A sublime peacefulness crossed Becca's face for a fleeting moment. "There's usually lots of slow dancing. Anyway, I thought maybe you'd like to stop down at lunch and pick one out. You could use my office to change so you don't have to worry about the bathroom here. Luke said it's...challenging."

"That's a nice way to put it." Brielle grimaced. "Sorry, Becca, I told Luke I wasn't going tonight. Congratulations again on your award, though."

"Oh, I know what you said. Luke spent almost a full hour whining to Kurt this morning, wondering how he screwed up. But unlike my husband and Luke—who is a really horrible pouter by the way—I understand why you turned him down. It had nothing to do with chemistry or rejection. No way would you have let him give you a ride to work this morning on his bike if you weren't interested. By the way, I hope he didn't have to stop and pick you up." A corner of her mouth curled into a smile.

"I'll have to remind him to drop me off out back from now on." Brielle couldn't help but laugh. "And no, we didn't sleep together. Er, I mean, we didn't have sex. Not really. It's complicated, I guess."

"Actually, Luke will make things simple for you if you let him. No sneaking required. Look, I realize we're in a weird place considering Saturday." Becca hesitated. "I won't be offended if you tell me to butt out—"

"That's not what I meant. There's no reason to be tight-lipped when it's all going to come to light anyway, is there?" Brielle shrugged as she rose and circled her desk. "Please, why don't you hand me some of those? I'll help you carry them to your office. I feel bad that you've gone to all this trouble."

"Don't worry about that. It's fun to have someone to share with. Since I was away from my sister a few years, and now she's busy with her own college friends on campus most of the time, I haven't had too many chances to do this sort of thing." Becca smiled. "*I'm* asking you. Please come tonight. I'd like you to be there, and I'd love to see Luke as happy as Kurt and I."

Brielle could relate. "I've never done something like this. Ever."

"Wouldn't you like to? Just wait until you see the trunk of Kurt's car. It's full of shoes. You can ride over with us and surprise Luke. I can't wait to watch his jaw hit the floor."

Becca seemed so proud of herself, Brielle didn't have the heart to ruin her fun. Oh yeah, and she would kill to thrill the man who'd held her nightmares at bay through the second half of last night. She fingered the exquisite material of the beautiful blue dress Becca offered. "Okay, I'll try. I just don't know, though. I think you're shorter than me without those crazy heels, thinner too. Bitch."

They both cracked up.

"We're not that different, you'll see. It'll work. You have a great figure. A bunch of these are stretchy and some I hemmed myself so we can undo the no-sew tape really easily."

Brielle relented. "All right. I'll come down at lunchtime if you really don't mind."

"Fantastic." She leaned in for a one-armed hug, squashing some of the dresses between them.

Sunset painted the city an array of pretty colors. Glass buildings reflected streaks of citrus hues from orange to yellow with a few pinks splashed about. Bright lights dotted the skyscape, mixing natural illumination with fluorescents.

Brielle should know. She concentrated on the twinkling to distract herself from the tiny car they flew through the streets in. Focusing on the outside calmed the anxiety that built inside her despite the relaxing soft jazz, which floated from the speaker hidden in a door or the back of her seat somewhere.

"Becca, would you mind cracking your window a little?" She tapped the other woman on her shoulder.

"Are you too warm? Kurt usually freezes me with the air conditioning, so I have it set on something less than arctic."

"You ladies have no idea how good you have it in those almost-nothing dresses. Try wearing a full suit and jacket in the middle of summer," he grumbled, still with a smile. No doubt he approved of the tangle of crisscross straps and delicate yet tasteful strips of emerald silk that tied his wife up like a Christmas present he probably couldn't wait to unwrap.

Brielle fanned her face. "Sorry, no. The temperature is fine. Although if you're uncomfortable, Kurt, I could live with it cooler. I'm just having a hard time catching my breath back here."

"Honey, you should have said something." Kurt glanced at her in the rearview mirror. "I forget sometimes how small this car can seem. Luke's always bitching because his long damn legs fold up to his chin when he rides in it. Says he loses all his cool points, grunting and groaning as he tries to get out with some semblance of grace."

Now that she knew him, she could imagine him saying it. How he would sound, the bold smile he'd have on his face and the way his eyes would crinkle a tiny bit at the corners as he made himself the butt of a cosmic joke.

"Next time you can sit up front." Becca pushed a few buttons. The covering on the sunroof slid back and then the glass lifted. The extra pane helped Brielle see more of the clouds and the breeze was enough to splash her cheeks without disrupting the stylish half-up, half-down curly hairdo Becca had crafted.

"I'm sure Luke won't let her out of his sight next time. Good luck riding on his bike in a dress like that, though." Kurt smiled at his wife. "Maybe he'll be forced to give up that ridiculous thing after all."

"How can you guys be so confident this is a good idea? Are you sure he's not going to mind me showing up unannounced?" Acid churned in her stomach. She folded her hands over the gurgling in an attempt to still the nervous reaction.

"I've known the guy since we thought girls were icky." Kurt shifted smoothly as he wove between traffic and zipped through a yellow light. "He's had about a hundred and forty-seven crushes since then. Never once did I believe it was the real deal. Hell, I didn't used to think there *was* such a thing. Maybe partially because I'd see him 'fall in love' over and over, only to change his mind once the infatuation wore off."

"You're not making me feel a heck of lot better." Closing her eyes didn't help the dizziness starting to spin her world around. "I don't do *this*. I've only ever been with one man, for Christ's sake. I'm way out of my league. Maybe you could pull over and let me out. I just saw the Red Line bus. I can take that straight home."

"Way to go, Kurt." Becca slapped his thigh lightly. "I think what my misguided husband is trying to say is that Luke is different with you. He's cautious. Taking things slow."

"We've only really known each other for half a week and already he spent the night. You think that's slow?" Brielle's voice rose an octave.

"It's more like, he's giving you space. Usually, he'd be flirting and weaseling his way into your good graces." Kurt paused as if considering how to explain himself. "He's afraid of messing up and more concerned about doing the right thing for you than he is about getting what he wants in the short term. I couldn't believe he backed off so easily on convincing you to join us tonight. It's very...not his style."

"And somehow the fact that he didn't fight me about not coming makes you think he wants me here?" She leaned forward, bonking her forehead on the back of Becca's seat. "You people are more fucked up than I am. Crazy-ass psychologists."

"In the immortal words of Alfred E. Neuman, 'It takes one to know one—and vice versa'." Kurt grinned, and for a moment she could picture him and Luke as teenagers, huddled together over a *MAD* magazine. One dark, one light—both kids. They would have tempered each other. Could she and Luke find the same balance?

Desperately, she hoped so.

They overflowed the car with laughter.

By the time she'd caught her breath and dabbed a happy tear from the corner of her eye, carefully so as not to mess up the magic Becca had worked on her makeup, Kurt had swung into the valet line at an opulent hotel Brielle had admired from the grungy bus windows.

How had her life changed so drastically in just a few days?

She unclipped her seat belt, but Becca waited for Kurt to round the hood of his sleek sports car. After handing his wife out, steadying her on her heels at the start of the red carpet and kissing her cheek, he slid the seat forward then reached in for Brielle.

"You're going to do great. Luke's going to let me off the hook for the favor he did me last year." Kurt took her hand and squeezed gently. "You look beautiful. Enjoy tonight, have fun and don't worry about anything. You're perfect the way you are."

As pep talks went, it ticked all her worry boxes.

"I can't believe I used to be afraid of you." Happy for his support, she ducked out of the tight doorway. "You're really pretty sweet under all that serious crap."

"Why thank you, Ms. Norris." He shifted her grip to his elbow, extended the other to his wife then led them both toward the wide-open doors. Cameras flashed in their faces as the guests of honor made their way inside.

Brielle tried not to shy away from the lights and pasted a faux smile on her face.

Kurt joked with reporters about his two gorgeous dates.

Through the lightning bursts, she caught sight of a tall, blond man up ahead. He leaned over, facing away from her.

"Luke," she called out before thinking better of the overzealous display, frankly sans manners.

When he whipped his head in their direction, he angled his body toward her. And that's when she saw the woman he'd just kissed on the cheek. The cute, young lady draped over his arm exactly as she and Becca were on Kurt's.

"Oh shit," she balked. Stopping dead, her hand yanked free of Kurt's elbow.

Of course, Luke wouldn't attend alone. Eligible, successful and sexy, he'd brought someone else. Another date. One of the *zillions* of girls he'd crushed on.

How could she have been so stupid?

"Brielle, don't." Kurt reached for her. Becca hadn't noticed and kept walking as she waved to the crowd. Tugged forward,

Kurt left a gap between Brielle and the happy couple.

A reporter stepped in the chasm between them, hoping to snag a quote for his journal article. "Dr. Foster, congratulations on your achievements. Could I ask—"

"Just a moment, please." He tried to break through. When he lunged in her direction, irrational terror gripped her throat.

Brielle, get in the closet.

"No!" She stumbled backward. Her borrowed heel caught in the fancy cobblestone pavers as she stepped off the runner. The crowd staggered away from the drama.

Always causing problems.

"Kurt, don't chase her," Becca intervened, granting Brielle the instant she needed to escape.

She abandoned the shoe where it stuck in the ground and bolted. Uneven strides didn't add to her dignity. At this point, what did it matter?

Foolishness had already reached all-time highs.

She gathered her full skirt and darted for the sidewalk.

Up ahead, a flash of gray emerged from the alley. Skidding to a stop, Luke blocked her path.

Shit. Crap. Damn.

"Brielle." He held his hands out, palms facing her as if she were a wild animal. He didn't attempt to encroach on her space.

"Let me go, Luke." She sniffled, horrified she'd add tears in public to the list of faux pas she'd committed.

"No way in hell." He tested out taking a teensy step forward. "I mean, you're free to do as you like, but I'd appreciate it if you'd let me explain first. Please."

She shuffled away. "Your date is waiting. Don't make her feel awkward. I'm sorry I ruined your entrance. Your night."

"Sweetheart, Elsa is not my date." He shook his head so vehemently she might have giggled at another time. He looked like a big, shaggy, huggable dog when his blond hair swung around his head.

"You could have fooled me." She cringed. "I saw how you

looked at her."

"Like I care for her?" The affection she'd witnessed returned. "I do. She's clueless. And adorable. And part of our family."

Brielle's heart cracked a little more with each term of endearment. "Then go back to her. She obviously means something to you."

"Yeah, no shit." He actually rolled his eyes. "She's Becca's little sister. Believe me, she's not mature enough for any real man and I'd never think of her that way."

"What?"

"You heard me. *You're* the woman I slept with last night, Brielle. Have you forgotten already? If you give me another chance, I can try to make tonight more memorable." He advanced again.

This time she held her ground. "Becca's sister?"

"Yeah." His pursed lips made it seem like he'd sucked on a lemon. "And now I have the ridiculous image of her and me burned into my occipital cortex. Thanks a lot."

Brielle dropped her face into her palms.

"Are you laughing or crying?" he asked softly.

"Both." An undignified hiccup accompanied her response.

"Okay. I can work with that." Luke sidled closer. "I'm going to hug you now, all right?"

She nodded without meeting his gaze, afraid of what she might find there.

For a few seconds, she needed to steal comfort before admitting she'd royally screwed up a terrific thing. She murmured into his chest, "I'm sorry."

"Nothing to apologize for." He rubbed her bare back below the ends of her curls. "Your assumptions were logical. I can't fault you for that. I'm telling you right now, though, whatever this thing is between us isn't some casual affair for me. I've had plenty of those."

Her flinch separated them just a tad.

"Before." His tone held some grit now. "This is different. For us both, I think. I hope. It's something special and I plan to see where it takes us. Are you game?"

"I think so." She clutched his shoulders, hoping she didn't wrinkle the fancy fabric covering their broad span. "But I'm clearly not much good at this shit. Too bad for you. You should have picked better."

Laughter rumbled beneath her cheek. He dropped a kiss on the top of her head. "I couldn't have found someone more flawlessly flawed than you."

"You're nuts." A puff of air passed her lips. "Luke?"

"Yeah?"

"What's jabbing me in the back?" She had barely noticed the discomfort in his hold.

"Oh." When he released her, she regretted mentioning it. Nothing was worth encouraging him to let go. "Sorry. It's your heel. Let me guess, Becca lent you these monsters?"

"Huh?" Dazzled by his nearness, and the relief flooding her system, she didn't realize what he referred to at first.

Luke sank to one knee at her feet. "Lean on me."

She did as instructed, placing her shaking hands on his shoulders. "What are you doing? Don't mess up your pants."

"Shush for once." The skirt of her dress *whooshed* as he swept aside the waves of material that expanded outward from her knees down.

Gaping, she didn't resist when he lifted her bare foot from the pavement, which radiated heat after the long, hot day. He placed a kiss on her ankle then slipped her abandoned shoe into place. "Love the nail polish."

Thank God Becca and she had taken time to exchange minipedicures while waiting for their hair to set.

"Thank you." She stared into his eyes and hoped he understood. Unwilling to take the chance he might not, she put a finger beneath his chin and encouraged him to stand. "I can't tell you how much I value your patience and empathy. I don't know what I did to deserve you."

"You're welcome." A soft kiss followed, showing her exactly how much he meant it. "And you don't have to *do* anything. You're human, Brielle. Entitled to love, compassion, forgiveness and tolerance. Just because you've lived with barbarians who didn't freely give you those fundamentals, doesn't mean you weren't worthy of them."

"I—" She couldn't think of a single response to adequately convey the bliss that erased the last of her doubts and fears. Reaching up, she touched his cheek with the tips of her fingers.

"Shh." Another kiss spared her from responding. This one held a lifetime of longing and, from her side, hope. "You don't have to say anything, Brielle. I feel it too. This chemistry. You do the same thing to me. By being you. Besides, if we don't cut this crap out you'll either have no makeup left—not that I think you need it—or I'll say to hell with the award ceremony and whisk you straight to my place for a more in-depth demonstration of my personal philosophies."

"Maybe I could get a rain check on the whisking and your personal stuff?" She nibbled the inside of her cheek as she peeked up at him.

"This is going to be the longest couple hours of my life." With that, he swiped at her cheeks using his thumbs, then claimed her hand, interlaced their fingers and led her inside.

Chapter Eight

Brielle lit up the room. Any initial awkwardness she'd suffered had faded before the appetizers made their appearance. Luke grinned as she joked with Becca's sister, Elsa. The pair had hit it off right away when Elsa proclaimed she only wished Luke had the hots for her and declared Brielle a superlucky bitch.

Elsa seemed to amuse Brielle with her frivolous *issues,* just as she did Luke. It was refreshing to find someone whose worst day consisted of a broken nail or a mediocre grade, even if they didn't realize how fortunate they were.

Yet another thing he and Brielle had in common.

Kurt and Becca did everything but supply him with a stash of condoms. He didn't doubt for an instant that, if he asked, they'd run to the gift shop in the lobby between courses to stock him up. Their approval meant more than he'd realized. So often had Kurt treated Luke's dates with polite aloofness that Luke hadn't realized the difference between that standard response and true endorsement.

As dinner plates were collected and coffee served, Becca grew quiet. Brielle noticed right away, impressing Luke with her perceptiveness.

"You're going to do great," Brielle reassured the young doctor before Kurt could beat her to it. "Your introduction speech sounded awesome when you rehearsed it earlier. You had it down pat. Although, you still haven't explained some of your statements to me."

"I'll leave Luke in charge of that." Becca grinned. "If there are things you don't understand after Kurt's segment of tonight's presentation, your date can fill you in. Who knows, maybe you could find the Dream Machine useful? It's an option, Brielle. Please think about it. Kurt's invention gave me everything, made all this possible. I'd advise you to include a session as part of your treatment plan."

Voice pitched low, the suggestion didn't carry to the rest of the guests at the table or those mingling nearby. Still, Luke scooted his chair near to his date so he could drape his arm around her shoulders. The instinct to protect her roared to life, surprising him with its intensity.

Could she handle facing her fears? He'd verged on suggesting the same thing last night. Believed as Becca obviously did, that the outlandish technique was actually a sensible solution.

If Brielle was strong enough to make the request, he'd help her get through the intense therapy as best she could.

Creamy skin beneath his wrist tempted him to touch. Her hair slipped through his fingers, as soft as silk.

Brielle leaned into his caresses. She glanced up at him with a tentative smile.

"You don't have to decide right now. Listen tonight, learn, and we can discuss it Saturday. After you've had some time to really consider your options." He looked first to Brielle, then to Kurt and Becca.

They all nodded.

"And now we'd like to welcome the recipients of Elembreth University's prestigious faculty award. For Most Influential Research of the Year, please show your support for Doctors Foster and Foster as they make their way to the stage for the keynote address."

Spotlights swung in their direction. Although they lasered in on Kurt and Becca, all Luke could see was the way they limned Brielle's profile, haloing her in a bright, golden glow.

She cheered for his friends, a heartfelt *whoop* slipping from her lips above all the polite clapping. He joined right in, adding a sharp whistle to the clamor.

Kurt glanced back and grinned.

Brielle cursed the third cup of punch she'd chugged during Becca and Kurt's presentation. She'd felt the need to clear the dryness parching her mouth while they described an experiment so risqué that even their clinical depiction couldn't mask the underlying tones of sexuality. Poor Elsa had winced her way through the hour-long, detailed account of her sister's sexual awakening at the hands of her mentor, and now husband.

After the speech, which had given Brielle plenty to mull over, the floor was opened for the dancing Becca had promised. Classic Sinatra and Martin crooned by the live performers provided plenty of opportunity for Luke to sway, dip and twirl her around the ballroom. Mostly, though, he tucked her tight to his chest and rocked in time to the beat.

She followed his lead, and he never steered her wrong. They glided effortlessly between other couples and the tables on the fringes of the space. After a while, she'd closed her eyes and allowed him to guide her on feel alone.

Two songs later, she couldn't delay another moment.

Brielle blinked at the sparkles cast by the triple-tiered chandelier above them, then went to her tiptoes to lay a smacking kiss on Luke's cheek. She gave him a wink. "I'm sorry but I've got to hit the ladies' room."

"I was wondering...since you haven't gone all night." He tucked a stray section of hair behind her ear. "Are you afraid?"

"Nope." She smiled. "Becca did some recon earlier, during her nervous-pee phase, and reported that the facilities are enormous. Mostly I was concerned about wriggling out of this contraption."

"I could help you with that." His pupils dilated.

"I have no doubts." A smirk crossed her lips. "What if we see how talented you are later?"

"That's a challenge I'm willing to accept, Ms. Norris." He

tickled her.

"Ohmigod." A squeak escaped as she jerked away, laughing. "Don't do that or I'll spring a leak. Seriously."

He grinned. "Why don't you take care of that while I start the process of making my goodbyes? By the time you're finished wrestling with that dress, I should be able to wrap up so we can take this party somewhere a hell of a lot more private."

"Are you sure I'm not interfering with your duties?" She hadn't realized until tonight how much more responsibility he had than the average professor. He wasn't just the owner of his practice and a member of the university's Psychology Department. Hell no, he was the head of the whole shebang, which meant another layer of obligations.

And he was well respected, if the slew of people he'd introduced her to, and their warm reception, were any indication.

Several of them who'd stopped by their table had commented on the fact that he'd decided to take on casework again. She'd have to ask him more about that later. It seemed she wasn't the only one going through a major life transformation. Their internal chaos had collided last weekend. Yet he'd put her first ever since.

"Positive. Now scram." He spun her around one last time, then tapped her ass mostly discreetly with the flat of his palm. Desire warred with the rest of her biological needs. Maybe she could talk to him tonight. About things she'd heard of... The things Brad hadn't understood.

There was so much to explore.

"I'll be quick."

"Counting on it." Luke wrapped an arm around her upper chest from behind. He drew her to his torso, letting her savor his erection against her lower back as he whispered in her ear, "If you're not back in five minutes, I'm coming in after you. My patience is running out."

Brielle angled her head to buss his cheek before breaking free and scurrying toward the hall despite the shoes torturing her feet. She prided herself on her speedy work. Happiness had her so preoccupied, she didn't hesitate on the threshold of the women's bathroom.

Fantasies of all the wicked ways she'd like to experiment with Luke floated through her mind while she nearly sprinted back to him. A lot of the other attendees must have had similar plans after listening to how much more fun the psych department was having than every other area these days. The line for the valet snaked through the lobby, spilling into the hall. It blocked the foot traffic. She dodged a few people loitering as they waited their turn.

One man wouldn't budge. He didn't get the hint as she attempted to slip past. "Excuse me, could I get through, please? I'm not cutting. Just trying to go back into the ballroom, promise."

He didn't chuckle at her joke like Luke would have.

"Who're you?" The slurred question put her on instant alert. Warning sirens blasted through her mind.

"Nobody important. Just here as someone's date." She smiled, trying again to evade the stranger. When she stepped left, he staggered in the same direction, cutting her off again. "You must have me confused with someone else."

"Do not." He pointed a crooked finger at her chest. It looked as if it had been broken and set badly. "Saw you sittin' next to that ungrateful slut. Rebecca." Except Rebecca sounded more like *wa-beh-ah* when he massacred her name.

Too many memories—of her father, her ex and their friends—poured into the void where joy had pirouetted moments before. Her knees locked up, causing her to totter backward when the guy invaded her space.

He took one step, then another.

"That award should have been mine. They'd never have had the balls to go through with it unless I'd helped. Not even a fucking mention of that, was there?"

"I'm sorry, I didn't catch your name so I can't say." Brielle glanced around, trying to find a way to evade the astringent smell of hard liquor and the man it wafted from. She'd had enough drunk bastards in her life to diagnose his condition as hammered to black-out proportions.

Brielle searched frantically for an escape route, but didn't want to cause a ruckus. Not when so many of these people had seen her with their leader. Poor behavior on her part would reflect on him. The car line had shuffled forward enough that no one noticed her plight. She thought she could handle the situation.

She probably could have.

If the belligerent asshole hadn't pressured her straight into the coat check. On such a warm day, no one had bothered with the formality, and the attendant seemed to have abandoned his post. By the time she surrendered her attempt at propriety, the closet closed in around her. Bars stretched from wall to wall, looming ominously.

Her lips parted, her lungs filled and she bumped into a slew of hangers. The rattle of the wire froze her solid. She'd lost the ability to scream for help.

"I'm Dr. James Wexford." He grabbed the door and swung it shut, trapping them inside.

In the dark.

Brielle, get in the closet. You asked for this. You're sick. Lucky I keep you around at all. You'll thank me for it later.

The shout bubbling in her throat cemented there, nearly choking her. Waves of inky blackness that had nothing to do with the lack of light crashed over her, threatening to steal her consciousness. An icy sweat dotted her skin, adding to the tremors ripping through her entire body.

Panic clawed at her.

For several seconds, she teetered on the verge of terror. She tried to recall where she was and Luke's coaching. "I'm okay. I'm okay. I'm okay."

The recital didn't actually pass her lips, though she tried to force it out. Still, she thought it. As many times as she could before the stench of cheap vodka permeated the stagnant air.

Brad's favorite.

Suddenly the rank odor morphed into the smell of her father's corpse, rotting for days as she lay, trapped, feet away.

This time her scream broke free. She wailed for him to let her out.

"Jesus. Shut up. Wasn't going to hurt you. Just wanted to tell you that they're liars. They don't deserve this. I do." Fingers dug painfully into her upper arms, surely leaving bruises. The stranger...Brad...shook her, rattling her teeth. "Stop howling. You're gonna get me in trouble. Not again. Shut the hell up."

Anger thawed Brielle. She lashed out, slashing the bastard with her pretty purple nails. He cursed, and his grip relented.

Pure instinct drove her to seize her chance. She crawled in the direction of the sliver of light, which illuminated the bottom of the door, still screeching for help.

A moment before she reached salvation, the glimmer became a beacon. The doors were thrown open and two imposing silhouettes filled the frame. Crumpling into a ball, she tried to protect herself from the pain to come. They didn't like it when she caused drama.

Brad.

Her father.

"No!" She thrashed and kicked when one of them reached for her.

"Don't, Luke." A woman's directive arrowed through her fear. There were no other girls in the closet. Not unless Brad locked his new one in there too. "She's not seeing you. I'll get her. Everyone is going to be fine."

"I'm not and he sure as hell isn't," someone roared.

"Let Becca work," the second man barked. "Take out the trash with me."

"My pleasure." A shiver ran through Brielle at the steely determination the guys shared.

Bits and flashes swirled around her. Faces, violence, past

and present.

It overwhelmed her.

Brielle curled into herself. She drew her knees to her chin and tried to remember…something…

"You're okay." The pretty voice came again. Very softly. It repeated itself over and over until Brielle began to say it too.

"I'm okay. I'm okay."

"You're safe now. I'm here with you." The litany changed, becoming more complex as she caught on. "I'm Becca Foster. Your friend and therapist. You're not alone and you're not in danger anymore. It's okay to come back to us. You're free. Not trapped. No one is going to hurt you."

"I'm okay?" She tested out the foreign concept.

"You are." The voice warmed. "Open your eyes. The door isn't locked. You can leave at any time. No one's here but us. Brielle and Becca."

"Becca?" Brielle's breathing hitched. "Oh no, what happened? What did I do?"

"Yes, that's right. I'm here. With you. We're safe. Do you understand?"

"Y-yes." The world slowly resolved around her. She levered up without assistance from Becca. The murmur of a gossiping crowd poured in from across the threshold.

"You didn't do anything wrong." Becca inched closer. "I'm going to put my hand on your back. Is that okay?"

Brielle nodded before she realized the other woman might not be able to see her clearly. "Yes. That's all right."

Comfort radiated from the small hand rubbing circles on her shoulders. "Concentrate on slowing down. Your heart. Your mind. There's nothing to run from now. Breathe with me. Like this. Inhale. Exhale. Inhale."

She concentrated on synching their respiration.

When terror leeched from her, the hollowness it left in its wake had her worried she'd implode. Part of her wanted nothing more. "Oh God. What the hell happened? Who was that creep?"

"Someone who's made one too many mistakes. Luke can tell you the details, but I have an order of protection against that slime bucket." Becca seemed like she could use a hug herself, so Brielle obliged. They clung to each other in the shadows, where the patrons buzzing about in the hall couldn't see them. "I'll press charges this time. I swear. He won't bother either of us again. I'm so sorry."

"I'm the one who should be apologizing. I ruined your evening. And Luke's. Everyone will be talking about this. I'll make him look bad." She battled her dress and Becca's arms until she gained her knees. "Hurry. Let me out of here before he comes back. I'll put some distance between us and hope people forget. It was just a few dances. Maybe no one noticed him with the freak."

"Oh, Brielle. Everyone's wondering about the stunning woman who's caught Luke's eye. His feelings for you were evident in his body language. I mean, you were surrounded by experts whose job it is to discern these things. Not one single person will hold the victim accountable for this mess."

A triple knock came softly on the door.

"It's him." Becca patted her hand. "I know it's almost impossible, but try your best not to let the way tonight ended ruin everything else. I could see where you two were headed. It might not be a bad place to forget about all the rest of this bullshit. Please, I couldn't stand knowing I hurt you instead of helping. This was my situation, and I dragged you into it."

"Never." Brielle put her arms around Becca. "You brought me back. You saved me from the darkness."

"You did it yourself. I only helped."

The knock came again, a bit louder this time.

"If we don't let him in soon, he's going to go bonkers." Becca squeezed Brielle. "You don't have to worry with him. He's nothing like your nightmares."

"I'm ready." She drew an enormous breath then braced herself for the distaste or pity she imagined she'd find in his face.

"Come in, Luke."

Slow steps carried him through the wide-open doors bit by bit. In a strangled voice, he called out to her, "Brielle."

His name on her lips did her in. So sad and unsure, the unfamiliar sound dissolved all her boundaries. She'd done that to him. Stolen his laughter.

Tears streamed from her eyes as she cried—full-out sobbed and gasped—for the first time, maybe ever. It couldn't have been a pretty sight. He'd never think of her the same way again. So much had been lost. "So sorry."

"Not your fault." He crashed to his knees in front of her, reaching out but stopping halfway, as if afraid to touch her.

Screw that. She flung herself into his arms, rocking him onto his heels.

He caught her and held tight, wrapping around her like a security blanket. "It's okay, sweetheart. That piece of shit is gone. Kurt's got him. He'll be lucky to make it to jail with just the shiner he acquired as I escorted him to the curb."

"Oh no." Becca launched to her feet. "I can't believe you left them alone. You know Kurt wants to destroy the man already. I'm sure twice as much now. Who's going to keep my husband from sharing a cell with James?"

Brielle shuddered, thinking of how she had split the darkness with the drunk man. She wouldn't condemn anyone to that fate.

"Tell her she can go." Luke interrupted her torrential downpour of tears. "I've got you. No one will lay a finger on you but me."

"O-okay." She lifted her head from his shoulder to meet Becca's gaze.

"Luke, think it through. No way can she ride on your bike. And we're not going to be able to give you a lift. Not for a while. The police will have a ton of questions for us. I can protect you both, tell them as her doctor she's not available for interrogation tonight." Becca put one hand on each of their backs. "I'll call a cab on my way out."

"No need. I thought maybe we'd be shot-gunning champagne tonight. So I reserved a suite. Before Brielle turned me down." He grimaced. "I'm not used to women saying no to me."

"Maybe it will do you some good from time to time." Becca kissed Luke's cheek then squeezed Brielle's shoulder. "Really, I can't tell you how sorry I am this happened. Please, don't let it come between you. I wouldn't be able to forgive myself for causing you a major setback."

"You're in no way responsible for this, babe." Luke gave her a one-armed hug. "I'll call you guys in the morning. First thing."

"Love you."

"Same goes." He never once stopped soothing Brielle. Nor did he attempt to squash her outpouring of grief, which rejuvenated periodically as pockets of terror burst from where she'd stored them deep inside. Instead, he held her, protected her against the assault of years of misery all mashed into one awful release.

"That's right." Comforting nonsense intermixed with delicate kisses and tentative touches rained over her like a refreshing summer shower. "Storing everything up is like swallowing poison. Over time, too much, it's deadly. Get it out."

As he spoke, he rose to his feet, keeping her cradled in his embrace. She curled against his chest, wrapping her arms around his neck. He whispered to her, "Close your eyes, Brielle. Don't open them until I tell you. Can you do that for me?"

She obeyed without responding. No affirmation could penetrate the crying she couldn't seem to stop.

He must have glanced down at her. "That's right. Good girl. You're safe. I have you."

A steady motion made her certain he carried her along the hallway. Concerned voices tried to enter the frail shelter he'd constructed around her. He didn't acknowledge the intruders, didn't stop or allow them to penetrate the cocoon he'd spun for her.

When a false-cheery *ding* rang in her ears, every muscle in her body stiffened. Except the ones controlling her eyelids. They sprang open.

"Keep them closed, sweetheart. Remember?" He must have realized how impossible the task would be. His hand curled around beneath her, covering her eyes. "It's too far for me to carry you, and there's no way you can walk thirty-three flights in this condition. If it helps, know the walls are all glass. You can see lights for miles around. Do you trust me?"

"Yes." She couldn't help hyperventilating when he stepped forward and the sound changed. A little bit echoey, a little bit quieter than the hallway had been.

The sound of the doors shutting had her tensing in his hold. Not again.

He covered the noise and the subsequent chirping of the passing floors by singing to her, the same song they'd danced to earlier. "Strangers in the Night" had never sounded so beautiful, despite the hoarse rasp of this particular rendition. She'd bet he had an amazing voice...usually.

Streams of tears slowed to a trickle as she zeroed in on his lullaby.

Her stomach lurched when the elevator stopped.

"Amazing." He didn't waste any time exiting the car. Kisses peppered her face after he removed her impromptu blindfold. "You're so brave, Brielle."

"Hardly." Hating the congestion transforming her refutation into a nasally whine, she shook her head. "I can't believe I let that asshole get the better of me. I should have stopped him before it got to—"

"Don't you dare do that." Quiet fury from him surprised her.

She wriggled as he approached a room. Balancing her on his hip, he didn't set her down. Instead, he dug a key card from his front pocket and swiped it through the reader. When the indicator flashed green, he flung open the door and strode inside.

"You have no responsibility in tonight's disaster." He didn't bother to prevent the door from slamming.

Brielle cringed.

"And I'm scaring you." He sighed then set her down gently. Shaky fingers scrubbed through his hair then across his goatee. She wondered what he'd look like without the random dark patch. It simply didn't jive with the rest of his gilded features. And neither did his current negativity. "Shit. I'm sorry. I know better, but when I'm with you, I forget about most everything else. Knowing that fuckwad was anywhere near you, it made me see red."

"You cared. You chased him off. You let me out of the closet." A fresh tear welled up. How could there still be anything left inside her to generate the moisture? "You saved me. Thank you."

A feral cry tore from him when the droplet tracked down her soaked cheek. His hand clapped his chest and massaged the light blue fabric over his heart. "I have to touch you. Please, tell me that's okay?"

She shied away from his approach.

"You're not ready. Of course." He stopped immediately. "No pressure. If it helps, I can hold you again while we lie in bed. If not, we can sit and talk. Or you can sleep and I'll watch over you. Whatever you need, Brielle. I'll give you anything."

"It's not that. I feel as though...I'll get you dirty or something."

"Never." Luke cursed beneath his breath. He breached the yawning space between them and swiped the lingering tear from her face with the pad of his thumb. "It's not possible."

"I can smell the alcohol on me." The terror too, she thought. "I can feel where he grabbed me."

Luke bent in half, bracing his hands on his knees for a moment or two. Loud, ragged breaths rattled through his chest before he straightened, all turmoil wiped from his expression.

"Come with me." He held out his hand.

She looked from it to his face and back, then swallowed hard before placing her palm on his. He guided her through the opulent area she hadn't taken time to appreciate yet. Plush carpet gave way to luxurious tiles, marble if she had to guess. Her shoes clicked on the shiny surface.

Luke supported her with an arm around her waist when she faltered, waving her hands to regain her balance. Except with him so near and the horror of the recent events mingling with her endorphin rush from the evening of dancing, dining and laughing, she couldn't quite find her footing.

A red velvet bench accepted her weight easily when he lowered her to its seat. Less delicate than it appeared, it buttressed her in style. She felt for a moment like the subject of an elegant painting. The dress and her surroundings mocked her. An impostor, given the extremes of her misery.

She sat, unfocused, for several seconds. When her eyes missed the sight of Luke, they sought him out. He fiddled with gold handles on what appeared to be a small swimming pool, or maybe an enormous jetted tub, sunken into the floor.

Fragrant foam sprang to life right where the pounding water met the hard surface of the tub. From two unrelenting, punishing forces came something beautiful and refreshing. Could it be that way for her too?

"I can leave you to bathe by yourself if you prefer." He frowned. "Honestly, though, I don't think it's a good idea for you to be alone. And even more frankly, I don't care to be either."

"Stay," she mumbled, barely able to form the request.

Chapter Nine

"Thank you." Luke crossed to her in two strides. He bent, slipping her shoes from her feet, eliciting a gasp and wince. "I'll fix that in a minute. I give great foot massages. But first, this dress."

She stared when he worked the material above her knees. Then he began from the top down, untying and unhooking and unlacing until her breasts were bared to his gaze. Behind him, the rest of the city sprawled, framed in the floor-to-ceiling windows on the opposite side of the bathing pool. "Um, can people see us?"

The squeak didn't have any sexiness to it. She recalled her father's friends, assigned to watch her take the fastest baths in the history of the world. Poor Luke, he couldn't know about all of her quirks. Not yet.

She crossed her arms over her chest, moaning when her hard nipples pressed into her forearms.

"The windows are mirrored from the outside," he assured her. "While I like to show off from time to time, tonight I only care about you and me. No one else is here with us."

Brielle realized he referred to the ghosts of her past as well as the drunk doctor who'd trapped her in the coat closet. She nodded.

"Good." He ran his fingers down the length of her arm until he reached her wrist. Gently, he pried it from her body then kissed each mound before traveling lower. Her stomach flexed when he licked a hot trail around her belly button. "You're beautiful, Brielle. So sweet."

With the sheath bunched around her waist, she had no option but to stand for him to remove it. He helped her up then quickly dispatched the silk, which landed in a pile with a rustle. For a moment, she regretted taking Becca's advice, ditching her underwear to avoid panty lines.

Completely bare, she stood before Luke. Hands at her sides, eyes and heart wide open, she allowed him to judge every bit of her, shivering the entire time.

"Brielle." Her name sounded like a prayer when he uttered it like that.

Luke approached her, but no fear entered her mind.

He scooped her into his arms, kicked off his shoes and waded into the enormous tub, still fully clothed. Half-full, the pool had a water level high enough he ended up drenched from the waist down.

"I think you missed a step in this process." She grinned at him when he set her on a contoured ledge. Once the tub was full her resting place would be submerged yet her head would be above water. Warmth seeped into her bones, helping her relax muscles she hadn't even realized were knotted.

"Welcome back, smart ass." He chuckled as he dropped a kiss on her forehead. "I missed you. Besides, you were cold."

"I could have waited a minute." She sighed, secretly glad for the heat. It helped thaw the frost that had crystallized on her heart.

"No need to suffer." He let the promise sink in. "So you're okay with me getting naked too? Tell me if I cross any of your lines. We haven't talked about them all yet, I know. I don't want to do something by accident to upset you."

"Then strip. I'll feel weird if you don't. *Unbalanced.*" A blush raced up her chest. It was evident in her current state. "And I'd really like to see you."

The powerful stretch and play of his muscles had thrilled her earlier this morning. Had it only been one day since she'd lain in his arms on her ugly sofa?

After waking, he'd roamed her apartment like a jungle cat, stalking to the bathroom and back with efficient use of his glorious physique. While they'd danced earlier, the firm column of his thigh had pressed between her legs, teasing her with his solid frame. It was about time she quit relying on her imagination to fill in the gaps.

"I like that look a hell of a lot better. You can cry on my shoulder anytime, Brielle, but I plan to give you things to smile about more often than not." He sank into the riot of bubbles. The water lapping against his chest plastered his light shirt to his torso.

His hands splashed, breaking the surface as he slung first one sock then the other onto the edge of the tub, far from their resting place. Next came his suit pants. Then a pair of boxer briefs. And finally he shrugged out of his tailored jacket, folding it over the ledge despite its soggy state.

Brielle smiled up at him, crossing her ankles in an attempt to press her thighs together for relief. Knowing not much separated them went a long way toward replacing her lingering fear with desperate need.

He could make her forget. Exchange all her fears for heat. Heal her soul with his gentle touch. Disprove every ugly truth she thought she'd discovered about men and life in general.

Please let her have been wrong about it all.

"Are you sure you want this gone?" He toyed with the top button of his shirt.

"I didn't realize you were such a cock-tease." She raised one brow.

"Well, I'm not. Most of the time. I prefer women, though there were those few experiments in my crazy college days." His easy shrug blew her mind.

"You? With guys?" Eyes wide, she regarded him in a whole new light. One filled with admiration.

"I've tried just about everything, Brielle." Flicking open the top two buttons of his shirt, he spread the fabric so she glimpsed his hard chest. "The club scene, BDSM, voyeurism, group sex in practically every combination. It felt good. All of it. Or most, anyway. I'm not cut out to be submissive. Everything else ranged from decent to 'hell yes'."

"What are you looking for now?" Wrinkles marred her forehead. "I can try to be what you need, but you'll have to show me. I don't know much. Would you expect me to—?"

Luke waved her off. "I'm not trying to shape you into something you're not. That's the point, sweetheart. *You're* what I need right now. The lifestyle doesn't mean anything to me. I tried everything because I was grasping at straws, searching for *something.* I just didn't know that special ingredient was you."

Sitting still became impossible. She shoved off the tiled side and barreled into him, dunking them both below the surface. When they emerged from the deeper section, water sluiced off them. Luke shook his head, spraying moisture in every direction.

Laughter echoed off the hard surfaces of the bathroom, multiplying by the moment. "You never do what I think you might."

"Isn't that the definition of insanity?" She saved him from answering by climbing the trunk of his body, wrapping her legs around his waist and kissing him like mad. While he devoured her, she yanked on his shirt. Buttons plopped into the water.

Bright-white teeth gleamed when he grinned at her urgency.

"I'll sew them back on."

"Don't bother." He shrugged out of the mauled clothing. "I'm going to keep it as a souvenir of our first time together."

"Luke, can we hurry?" She swiveled her hips, rubbing against his thick erection, which nudged her pussy.

"I promised you I'd wash you clean then give you a foot rub. I do what I say." He bestowed several sweet kisses, ignoring any discomfort from his raging cock.

When Brad had gotten horny, he'd fucked her there and then. Delayed gratification hadn't been his thing at all. At least it had been over before she noticed most times. "I figured we'd take it slow. If you're up for it, we could chase away all the things that frighten you. I could make love to you, gently, with candlelight streaming over your smooth skin. Until I'm sure you're okay, and I can let go of what happened downstairs too."

"A singer and a poet? You're unbelievable." She hugged him to make sure he was real and not one of the illusions she'd conjured to keep her sane in the darkness. Just being near him made her feel unsoiled. The minor aches and pains associated with her shoes, or the hold James Wexford had taken on her, dissolved automatically. He was great medicine.

"In a good way, I hope?"

How could he wonder? Did everyone live with a kernel of doubt? Maybe her insecurities did make her normal. "You have a spectacular way about you, Luke. I've never met anyone half as fine. Any other hidden talents I should know about?"

"Well, you haven't heard me play guitar yet. Or felt me fuck." His boyish grin captured her heart.

"I'm hoping to change that soon." She patted his cheek and wriggled in his hold.

A groan reverberated through the space.

"Anytime you're ready, I'm here. At your service." Another series of kisses almost distracted her from her mission.

"Well, it depends. What else do you have to offer? I might want to wait."

"Of course. If you've changed your mind or you're not ready, we can soak for a while. Sit and talk instead. Or just sit quietly. Listen to music. Have a drink. Beat up a pile of pillows with fuckwads' names written on them. Watch a movie. Cuddle. Whatever you need."

Taking a deep breath, she gathered her courage. "That's not exactly what I meant. I'd rather try something else you told me you were interested in, before we get to the main event."

"Like what?" His head tipped to one side as he studied her intently. Had he forgotten? Had he meant what he'd said in the heat of the moment last night?

"If you still want to, I'm curious about you...tasting me." A hard swallow flexed her throat. “I’ve always wondered what that would feel like.”

And it was his turn to act.

Luke trudged through the water, splashing in every direction as he hauled her to the platform she’d abandoned not long ago. “Are you saying no one’s ever gone down on you?”

She looked away.

“Dumb ass,” he muttered.

A flinch jerked her from him. “Is it only for guys?”

“Shit. I didn’t mean you, Brielle. Never you.” Luke pressed her shoulders until she reclined on a ramp fashioned along the side of the tub. He propped her feet on the edge, where it dropped off to the main section of the pool, and positioned her head on a waterproof pillow tied to the top with a nylon cord. “I meant the asshole who abused you.”

“His name is Brad, and he didn’t really…”

“He *did*. And I prefer asshole. Or maybe loser. Or motherless motherfucker.”

“That’s a new one.” She couldn’t help but smile when he picked up steam.

“I’m tabling this for tonight, but Saturday we’ll talk more with Becca to help us stay on track. I can’t be rational when discussing this.” Luke’s hands roved over her body, painting her with suds then rinsing them away. “You’re gorgeous. A masterpiece of nature. You deserve to be worshipped.”

“I wish I could say the same for you.” They laughed together when he paused. “Are you hiding some crazy disfiguration or something? Why won’t you let me see you naked?”

“Huh? Oh.” His shrug made his chest and abdomen glisten where they protruded from the water, which now overflowed the sides of their oasis into the designated run-off gutters. “You distracted me again. Is it really more important than letting me lavish attention on you?”

“Tough call, but yes.” Because what if after he learned

everything, when they worked with Becca, and Brielle maybe let them use the Dream Machine on her, he saw something that caused him to walk away? A memory of him would be the only thing keeping her sane.

"All right, Ms. Norris. Your wish is my command." He put his hands on his hips and ascended the inlaid tile steps on the edge of the pool nearest her. While he rose from the steaming water, he sang in a deep voice that boomed around the room. Though he couldn't be serious for more than five minutes, his self-deprecation couldn't obscure the fact that he actually had an outstanding voice.

"What is that?" she asked.

"My cock?" He paused then resumed his reveal, even more animated than before.

Laughter only enhanced the vision he made. Sleek muscles bunched and relaxed as he performed for his audience of one. And he didn't disappoint. A tight ass perched on powerful thighs that led to sexy calves. She couldn't believe she admired even his feet. When she'd absorbed every nuance of him, she allowed her gaze to roam to his cock.

Wow.

His operatic solo reached its pinnacle. Then he bowed, so she humored him with riotous clapping. "Bravo, bravo."

"It was from *Oedipus Rex* by Stravinsky."

"How very Freudian of you." Another delighted peal of laughter escaped before she could stop it. "You have a very nice sword."

"Thank you, ma'am." He sprinted for the edge. Two steps, a huge leap and his shout of, "cannonball" precluded a tsunami in their pool.

Waves lapped across her breasts, belly and pussy, having the opposite effect of dousing the fire he lit in her. Luke surfaced between her legs. He wrapped his hands around her ankles, making her shift and yearn for more.

"How could I ever be sad with you around?" she asked.

"Kurt tells me I need to grow up and be more serious sometime before I hit forty. So, I've got several good years in me yet."

"I hope you never change." She smiled when he plucked her hand from the water and kissed her palm.

"You know, I don't think I've ever been able to just be me." He nibbled his way up her calves to her knees. "With other women, I've always felt my silly side was unattractive. Not that I couldn't be ridiculous sometimes, it's hard to filter out all my antics, but I guess I kept it separate from the bedroom. And the boardroom. With you, I'm all topsy-turvy. I love that you get me."

"I do." Reaching between her knees, she squeezed his hand.

"So how is it that you know about Freud but not oral sex for women?" He caressed her inner thigh as his hand crept higher and higher.

"I read a lot. In my closet there wasn't much else to do." She shivered, from the memory or the pleasure he imparted, she couldn't say. "But the school library stocks classics and more books about famous psychologists than contemporary sex manuals. And Brad..."

"No need to say more there. Asshole."

"Right." The temptation of his hair was more than she could handle. She ran her fingers through the strands while he situated himself more fully between her thighs.

Luke floated, wrapping his arms around her hips to anchor himself. His back rose from the water, impressing her again with the defined strength there. Carefully, he studied her, using one finger of each hand to spread her lips. He nuzzled the trimmed hair covering her mound, teasing her with the almost contact.

His breath buffeted her sensitized flesh.

Brielle spread her legs wider, arched her spine and invited him to teach her a lesson she'd never forget. Even better, he distracted her from the last bouts of shivers they both had realized stemmed more from her encounter in the closet than the frosty air-conditioning in the hotel.

"You're pretty and flushed." He murmured against her, painting slickness across her using the dew drops gathering at her entrance. "I can't wait until it's my dick filling you, Brielle. It's going to be so good. For us both."

"We don't have to do this." The denial came out stilted and broken. Already he frazzled her nerves, making her go haywire.

"No, but I *want* to. There's plenty of tonight left, sweetheart." He tucked a gentle kiss right over her clit. "Practicing my patience is probably a good thing. Besides, I have a feeling I could eat you all night long and never get tired of the sounds you make, the way you taste or the smell of your arousal. Damn, you're addictive."

This time he extended his tongue, flicking the tip across her opening.

Air rushed from Brielle's lungs in one huge exhalation. She sucked it in again when he firmed his tongue and pressed inward, fucking her with it. He lapped at her, cleaning every speck of her juices from her lips.

"Oh, Luke." She tried to stay still, but couldn't. Sensations bombarded her. All of them fabulous. "So different than when I touch myself. Way better."

A smile curved his lips against her, only bringing her more rapture. "Thanks. Though I'd like to watch you play with yourself sometime. I bet you're soft and timid and gentle. Damn, it makes me hard as a rock to think about."

"Deal," she gasped. "Just don't stop, please."

"I wouldn't dream of it." Another level of euphoria came to life when he sucked on her lips while nudging her clit with his nose. He added a finger to her channel as he migrated upward.

When he closed his mouth around her clit and sucked gently, she screamed his name.

"Yeah, that's it." He tucked another digit inside her, stroking slowly, in counterpoint to the thrust and parry of his tongue on her most sensitive spots. "Here, try this."

Before she could figure out what he meant, he used his free hand to mash a button on the edge of the tub. Jets engaged. They massaged her back and ass. Several also shot streams of water at her chest. The warm liquid flowed over her breasts, teasing her tight nipples. The fluid ran downhill as she lay on the incline. It gathered volume from additional outputs and rippled over her abdomen, then lower still to her pussy.

"Don't drown." Concern for Luke, submerged between her thighs, distracted her for a second. "I don't want to kill the best boyfriend I've ever had. This would be hard to explain."

His laughter blew bubbles against her swollen vulva. He lifted his head, grinning like a fool. "You're hysterical, Ms. Norris. Don't you worry about a thing. I can hold my breath a really long time."

He stole any rational comeback she might have levied when he dove beneath the rapids to continue his demonstration of all she'd been missing. The novelty of his hot, silky tongue and the slightly cooler water rushing around it—not to mention the foreign concept of a man concerned about her pleasure above all else—had her straining to contain her orgasm.

Any other day, she'd have been struggling to achieve climax, not the other way around.

Damn, Luke turned her inside out too.

Her heels drummed on the tile ledge at the end of the waterfall, which cascaded over her. He picked his head up for another breath, grinning when he caught her expression. "I can feel you getting tighter. Hotter. More slippery. Why not just give in?"

"And miss out on this? Hell no." She gritted her teeth, willing herself to last a bit longer.

"What if I promise to eat you every night before bed? Remember the conditioning I mentioned? Would that help erase the worry bugging you as you're falling asleep?"

"Yes!" Brielle hadn't meant to shout. Streams of water combined with the potential for more of this overwhelming ecstasy. The mixture drove her beyond inhibitions or rational thought. Hell, after a release as powerful as the one she felt building inside her, lick by lick, she'd probably crash straight away.

She hoped he wouldn't be offended by her snoregasm. It was really a compliment.

At least she'd decided to always take it as one when Brad did it to her, leaving her unsatisfied.

"Luke." Trying to get his attention, she tugged less lightly than she intended on his hair.

"Careful, sweetheart." He grinned up at her. "I might like that."

"You're going to make me come." She panted.

"I hope so." His grin was infectious.

Had she ever laughed during sex before? "Soon."

"Good." Luke licked his lips. "Because I'm dying to make love to you. And my balls are getting even more wrinkled than usual in here."

"Is it okay?" She clamped her eyes closed, hoping.

"What? I'm just cracking bad jokes. I have no idea if they're extra-wrinkly. Though you're welcome to inspect them and let me know when we're done here."

"Luke!" What the hell was he rambling about? In between sentences he continued to caress her with all the skill and agility of a world-class lover.

This time he rose more slowly, his eyes narrowing. "Are you asking me for permission to orgasm?"

"Yes. Please." She quivered, trying desperately to hang on. Disappointing him was at the very bottom of her wish list.

"Come whenever you like, Brielle." He laid his face on her belly for a second. "Not just now but always. My goal is to give you as much pleasure as possible. You never need to ask. Take what you can. As much as you can. And then I'll figure out a way to give you more."

The paradise he described loomed large and beautiful in her mind. Could he be *that* different? That generous?

Endless possibilities lured her beyond control. She shattered as she rode Luke's face. He followed every jerk and thrash of her hips, sucking hard at first then gently when she began to drift back to reality.

Tingles spread to each extremity.

She slid into the pool beside Luke, floating as every bit of her relaxed utterly.

The extreme highs and lows of the day overwhelmed her, and she took the coward's way out, allowing Luke to tend to her as she wallowed in the ecstasy-induced coma he'd put her in. He gathered her to his chest, humming "What a Wonderful World" to her as he laid her on the area rug and dried her off then wrapped her in the plush hotel towel that had to be as big and thick as all of hers put together.

She pried one eyelid open, grateful she had when she spied him ridding himself of millions of droplets of water. They glistened on him, making her smile softly. Everything about him brightened her world.

"How are you doing down there?" He winked in her direction as he finished up.

"Better," she mumbled. "Way, way better."

Luke laughed. "You're fucking adorable, you know that, right? I hope you don't mind making out with me for a little while. If I don't kiss you, hold you, I think I'll go nuts."

She held her arms open to him.

After collecting her from the floor, he cradled her in his arms then strode through the living area to a bedroom. "Is this a suite?"

"I was trying to impress you," he admitted.

"Totally working." She kissed his pectoral muscle, the perfect cushion for her cheek.

Chapter Ten

Luke stared down at the woman in his arms. A hot mess, she was so ideal for him he could hardly believe he'd stumbled across her. Twice. Engrossed in counting his blessings, he didn't realize she'd stiffened when he laid her on the enormous California king then covered every inch of her with his body, which hummed from pleasing her and the possibility of doing the same for himself.

At least, he hadn't figured it out before she whimpered, "Lines."

"What?" He rose onto straight, locked arms, short-circuiting his little head before his brain disengaged completely. Flooded with the total joy of being close to Brielle, it was hard to think straight.

"Crossing a line." Quick, shallow breaths mashed her breasts against his chest in a too-fast rhythm. Her eyes widened and darted toward the skyline in the window. "Can't move. Can't breathe."

"Oh shit." He rolled off her so fast he nearly fell out of bed. *Super suave, dumb ass.* "I didn't think. It makes you claustrophobic to have a man over you?"

She nodded. "So sorry. I want to. A lot. It's just..."

"You don't need to explain." He settled for lying beside her, tracing her softly arched brows then the prominent cheekbones that highlighted her eyes and finally her lips. By the time he finished, she seemed to have calmed again. "I understand."

"I've only ever been on top before. Like last night, on the couch. I hope you don't mind." She frowned. "I know most men would rather be in control. Brad never objected to letting me do the work."

"Oh no, I slaved away—*long and hard*—to put a smile on that gorgeous face. Let's not go jacking it up now. I think I have a line too. No more Brad in our bed. I might have fooled around with a few guys in my day, but he's not my type. *Really* not."

Brielle didn't laugh, not even a little. That's when he knew things were bad.

"Hey, look at me." He nudged her chin so that she faced him. Still she kept her eyes closed, focused in on herself. This had nothing to do with her and everything to do with the people who had failed to protect her. That was a trend he didn't plan to continue. "Please?"

Thick, dark lashes batted as she fulfilled his request. Languid from her orgasm, she remained mostly relaxed despite his unintentional misstep.

"Damn, you're pretty." He nuzzled their noses together. "I look into your eyes and I forget everything I mean to say. If you watched me at work, you'd know that's not a usual occurrence. Believe it or not, I'm pretty articulate. Have my shit together when it counts."

Finally, she smiled. "You seem to be doing fine to me. And no, I don't suppose they make the screwup the boss."

"Good point. So... Can we try this again?" He hopped from the bed to turn the lights low. The indirect glow rimming the trey ceiling provided enough illumination to permit him to observe her reactions, but left them huddled in a more intimate ambience. One they could sleep in if things went the way he hoped. Then if she woke in the middle of the night, she'd know where she was.

Safe.

With him.

After pulling back a corner of the plush duvet, he lifted her, depositing her slight form on the luxurious cotton as though she was priceless. To him, she was quickly becoming precious. On paper, his obsession might have been diagnosed as unhealthy. Inside, he knew it was right.

The mountain of pillows swallowed her. She looked like a

child curled on her side. Unsure of herself, unaware of her allure, oblivious to the impact she'd had on his life in a few short days. Because now he had goals.

Her—happy, healthy, confident and all his.

Getting there wouldn't be easy. Luke had never shirked responsibility before. He just hoped he'd learned enough along the way to his penthouse office to help the one woman who mattered most. Was he up for the challenge?

He sure as hell would give it his best try.

Goose bumps rose on her arms. Avoiding a look at her tight nipples was impossible. A peek had to suffice before he drew the covers over her. He paused when a series of darkening rings around her upper arm caught his attention.

"Wexford put his hands on you?" Luke kissed each of the finger-shaped bruises that marred her flawless skin. Why hadn't he gotten in a few more punches before Kurt had stopped him?

"Only for a minute." Despite her swagger, she shivered. Her knees pulled closer to her chest.

Luke concentrated on suppressing his fury to be sure her wounds were tended to properly. Most of them weren't visible, but that didn't mean her scars weren't there. The total damage today had wrought far exceeded two fistfuls of purple marks.

"Brielle, I'd like to lie down with you." He kept his statement soft. "Would it bother you if I stayed on the other side of the bed?"

"A little." She peeked up at him through those lush lashes.

"I can take the couch then." Had he read her signals wrong? Pushed her too far, too fast? He should have known better than to complicate matters with sex. But physical contact had seemed to alleviate her mental suffering.

"That would be worse. I'd wonder why you didn't want to snuggle with me after all we just shared." She gnawed on her lip.

"Ah, okay." He crawled in from the opposite side, meeting

her in the middle. "Where can I come to without encroaching on your space? What's comfortable for you?"

"You don't have to walk on eggshells, Luke." She patted the spot beside her. "I have a problem with being confined. As long as you don't pin me down, I'll be fine. Better than, actually. With you nearby, I'll be great."

Staring directly into her eyes, he noticed the slight shift in them. "What is it?"

"Hmm?" Odd, was she pretending to misunderstand him?

"That little flicker of regret. What was that all about?" He held his hand up, palm out and she laced her fingers with his. Dusting his thumb over her knuckles seemed to soothe them both, so he kept going.

"Wow, you're not kidding. You're good at this." Her admiration hardened his cock despite his best efforts to will it flaccid. Of course, at the worst possible moment the contrary organ was raring to go.

"Do you want to answer me?" Only now was he realizing how often she deflected conversations when they hit too close to home. "You don't have to, but I'd prefer if you'd respect me enough to say that instead of dodging."

"You won't get mad at me if I don't feel like sharing?"

And like that it clicked for him. Even she didn't realize how often she evaded heavy topics. It was simply a tool she'd adopted to avoid difficult situations. When faced with an irrational man, no answer was likely to put her in a good position.

"Nope." He progressed to kissing their layered knuckles. "Your feelings are yours to disclose or not. I'm just being nosey I suppose."

"I guess it's only fair, since you treated me so well." She practically purred. "I was thinking it sucks that I didn't bring any condoms, and that if I ask you and you have some, it would mean you planned to sleep with someone else tonight since you didn't know I was coming. Then I decided it was better not to ask because I didn't want to look like a jealous bitch."

"Oh. That's a lot of thoughts in a nanosecond." He grinned. "And yes, I have condoms. But only because I was intending to drive over to your apartment and seduce you as soon as I could sneak out of the award dinner."

"Does that mean you still hope to use them?" She gripped his hand tighter.

"It depends. You've had a rough evening. Will sex help or hurt?" He kissed her cheek. "I was banking on it calming your mind. If I'm right, you might already be relaxed enough to sleep. So, there's no rush. Our first time can happen whenever it's right."

"I can't imagine sex with you being detrimental. Ever." When she leaned forward, taking initiative to kiss him, his heart stood up and cheered.

"I'd like nothing more than to make love with you, Luke." She stared straight into his eyes as she admitted her need matched his. "At the same time, I'm embarrassed that it scares me. You know, to be beneath a man. Even you."

"Brielle, I know plenty of positions. There's a lot more to sex than missionary or cowgirl."

"Show me?"

Resisting an offer that sweet would have proven impossible.

Luke dove beneath the covers, heading straight for her toes. He had a promise to keep. With a kiss on each of her arches, his massage began.

"What are you—? Ohhh," she moaned.

His thumbs pressed into the pad of her foot then rubbed down to her heels, working out all the sore spots that were a side effect of her sexy shoes. While he tended to her, he couldn't stop himself from tasting her skin again. Nibbles, licks and kisses on her legs had her mewling in less than five minutes.

By the time he worked his way up her fine ankles to her calves, her fingers twitched on the sheet above his head and the smell of her arousal perfumed the air beneath the sheets. If it was up to him, he'd go for a rematch, teasing her with his mouth until she unraveled.

It seemed she had something different in mind when she wrapped her fingers in his hair and tugged softly. Jesus, he loved it when she did that. Only thing better would be when she dug those sharp little nails into his back while he fucked her.

He stared into her eyes as he lifted his mouth to hers. Kissing Brielle was like nothing he'd done before. She anticipated where he'd go, and what he wanted. Or maybe they needed exactly the same things. Their lips locked. Her hand wandered from his sideburns to the major stubble now filling out his facial hair.

"Prickly," she tried to mutter into his mouth.

"Should I shave?" He smiled. "It was part of my dark period. But I think those times are over, now that you're with me."

"It just doesn't seem to fit with you at all. I think you'd be even more handsome without it." She scratched his chin, nearly making him groan. If he had a tail, it'd be wagging. The damn beard *was* uncomfortable. Tomorrow, he'd surprise her. Then he'd show her the difference, his smooth chin less abrasive as he went down on her again.

For a long while, they enjoyed simple pleasures—kissing, touching, laughing. But all too soon, the need for something deeper prodded him to action. His hand slipped lower, cupping her breast. He pinched her nipple gently, rolling the hard peak between his fingers.

Brielle squirmed against him until their legs intertwined. Her pantyless pussy rode his thigh, spreading evidence of her arousal along his quad. Tentatively, she reached out to stroke his side. Though somewhat ticklish, he held still for her exploration. He loved that she felt comfortable enough to seek the sensations she craved.

The light drag of her fingertips over his muscles had them both ramping up.

After she'd petted his abdomen, she advanced. Her wandering hand gripped his ass, holding him in place as she shimmied closer until they were pressed together for the full length of their bodies. His erection nestled into the softness of her belly.

"You feel...substantial." She nipped his lip when he laughed. "Hey, that wasn't some make-your-head-bigger bullshit."

"Keep biting me and the head's going to get bigger for sure." His hips flexed, showing her just what effect she had on him.

"Then maybe you'd better put it inside me." Reaching between them, she cupped her hand around empty air, a tiny fraction of an inch from actually grasping him. "Maybe I'll have a chance at taking all of you if we expand together."

"We'll make it work, Brielle. However we have to." Silent promises arced between them.

"Let's start tonight," she whispered.

"Are you sure?" Luke refused to risk injuring her further.

"Make me forget." In the artificial twilight, her eyes glimmered. Pain, loneliness, fear and sadness radiated from her. For a hint of time, her shutters flew open and he could see just how badly she hurt. Screaming in agony, his empathetic nature whisked her away from the present and everything in the world that would dare to fuck with her happiness.

He slipped his hand beneath the pillow and removed one of the foil packets he'd stashed there earlier.

"Does that make-a-wish pillow work for winning lotto tickets and ice cream too?" Attempting to peek under the cushion, she exposed the pale column of her neck. "I might need some later. You know, since I don't smoke either."

"Sorry, no." He kissed her while he ripped open the packet and rolled thin latex over his erection, a little concerned to find it didn't fit quite as easily as usual. "But I am capable of calling room service."

"Okay then, you're on." She shifted until his covered erection nudged the opening to her pussy. The contact made her clench the muscles there, which hugged his cock.

"I'd rather be in." He flexed.

Luke penetrated the outer circle of her pussy. Resistance met his light pushes against the moist folds of her core. Damn, she was tight.

"Don't chicken out now." She grabbed his ass, pricking him with sharp crescents that sank into his skin. The muscles below approved of her rough handling. They contracted, shoving his hard-on a tiny bit deeper.

He wrapped his hand around her knee and lifted, spreading her wide before him. After aligning his shaft, he fucked, mostly using his hips. This time he tunneled an inch or two deep. "That's better."

"Much." Brielle sighed.

"Is this okay?" He monitored her for signs of distress.

"Perfect." A soft smile accompanied her response. "Thank you for making concessions. For me. And my drama."

He couldn't prevent the growl that rumbled through his chest. Or the companion thrust that worked him farther into her channel. She rippled around him as if intending to distract him from the lesson he planned to teach.

"I watch enough reality TV to know there's something a hell of a lot more legitimate than bullshit going on here." He cupped her cheek in his palm. "Your fears are valid. And yes, sometimes they define you. Over time, I think that will change. But I'll take you any way I can get you and be glad for the chance."

"Part of me thinks I'm dreaming when you say things like that. Except, I only have nightmares. You are real, right?" Her lashes fluttered closed as he retreated to the verge of falling from her clasp. Then he returned, plunging an inch or two deeper than before.

"Maybe I'm not doing this right." A chuckle mixed with a groan when he ground them together. "It feels pretty damn corporeal to me."

"Do it again so I can be sure."

They both moaned when he bottomed out. She took all of him, holding him completely within her.

"If it's a fantasy, it's one I wouldn't mind being stuck on repeat." Brielle kissed him, the hand not pinned by her body roaming everywhere she could reach, as if memorizing every bit of him.

"Even if I can't always be this gentle?" Luke worried he might snap in the face of her temptation. Concentrating, he kept his strokes even—short and smooth—when he began to fuck her. Soaked, she made it effortless for him to glide within her.

"Yes!" She shouted when he slid home. By feeding her more, inch by inch, he'd helped her adjust remarkably well. Somehow Brielle always did. Flexible, resilient and tough—she awed him. "More."

Luke couldn't deny her when he craved the same thing. Their position limited his thrusting movement, but opened the door to a sensual dance choreographed to feature grinding, the press of flesh on flesh and precise placement of his pelvic bone. He enjoyed not having to separate from her even a tiny bit.

"Is this enough for you?" He rotated his hips.

"Too much more and I think my head might explode." Humor sparkled in her eyes. Blended with passion, the combination intoxicated him.

"I know what you mean." Kisses distracted him for a minute or ten. "I think my fate is sealed. You feel amazing."

Brielle rubbed against the full length of his body like a cat. Her breasts teased his chest and the softness of her stomach caressed his.

When he shifted slightly, lifting her leg higher, she gasped.

He froze.

"No!" She looked at him, eyes wild. "Don't stop. Not now. Do that again."

"Like this?" Luke experimented. It was obvious when he tapped her G-spot. She moaned and arched in his hold.

Relentless, he stroked her again and again. The superb placement for her, unsurprisingly, worked wonders for him.

Cries filled the room as Brielle surrendered herself to rapture. She stopped thinking and simply reacted to the ecstasy he delivered. When he feared he couldn't hold back a moment longer, she stiffened. Her eyes flew open and her gaze clashed with his.

She didn't ask for permission.

Instead, she took and gave freely. And when her body spasmed around Luke, she pulled him along with her into a pool of endless euphoria that rippled outward from where their bodies intersected.

He poured himself into the condom, shuddering in her arms, which tightened around him and refused to let go.

A long time later, Brielle hadn't stopped staring into his eyes as if he mesmerized her half as much as she did him. Wonder reflected in her gaze.

"Aren't you tired, sweetheart?" His fingers combed through her hair.

"Exhausted." Eyelids drooping, she wrestled the slide into unconsciousness.

"Afraid to sleep? I'm right here. I have you. I swear."

"I don't want anything to ruin how I feel right now." She kissed him, making him wish he had supersexual powers of recovery. "Go to bed. I'll be okay."

"I'd rather stay up and talk in that case." Luke rubbed their noses together. "Hold that thought, okay?"

He twisted, picking up the phone. "Good evening. Yes, morning, you're right. Could you bring a bottle of champagne and a big-ass ice cream sundae to room 3347?"

Brielle giggled behind him.

"Are you a vanilla kind of girl?" he asked over his shoulder. "Or would you prefer another flavor?"

"You tell me." Her stare dared him.

"Some of both, please," he responded. "Don't bother with a

little whipped cream on top, either. We'll take the whole can. Thanks."

She looked at him and burst out laughing. The sight and sound fascinated him. It had him wondering just how much time they had before the staff knocked on their door.

Screw it. Semi-melted ice cream never hurt anyone.

Maybe this connection growing between them made him more than a mere mortal after all.

Dessert tasted delicious.

And when Brielle surrendered to sleep, it was with a smile and a bit of chocolate sauce on her face. She didn't stir until long after daybreak.

Chapter Eleven

Brielle peeked beyond the edge of her curtains. A squirrel dashed across the space beneath the oak tree in the courtyard. She abandoned her post at the window for the interior of her apartment. Funny how it had never seemed so quiet—empty—until Luke's laughter, charm and sexy body had occupied the space then gone missing.

Ignoring the disappointment zinging through her, she put together a strategy for surviving the night alone. Since Luke wasn't there to ply her with hot fudge and orgasms by the baker's dozen, she couldn't count on ultimate relaxation to guarantee her a dream-free slumber.

This morning she'd woken to sunshine.

Groggy but calm, blissfully unaware of any shenanigans her subconscious might have been pulling while she slept. Unfortunately, it had been the unrelenting banging on the suite door that had roused Luke and stolen him from her clinging grasp. The cold left in his swath had stirred her as well.

After questioning them both separately, and then together, the detectives—Mason and Ty, they'd insisted she call them—had documented the nasty bruises on her arms with an endless series of photographs. Each exposure had seemed to agitate Luke more until he growled, "Enough," through clenched teeth.

They both signed affidavits and agreed to testify against the ex-Doctor Wexford, who was being charged with assault and violation of an order of protection.

Around noon, Luke had dropped her off at work. Thank God Becca and Kurt had her covered. They'd notified her boss of the incident and that she would be late. Hell, Luke had encouraged her to take the day off, but she felt crappy enough for her lack of responsibility, never mind the fact that her apartment held no solace at the moment.

Brielle had sworn to keep stoic when Luke had regretfully informed her of his packed schedule. With the delayed start and his extended caseload, he projected he'd finish his paperwork sometime after midnight if he was lucky.

She'd already consumed so much of his precious time. She hadn't dared to appeal for more. They both knew she'd likely still be up then, or soon after. Maybe he'd simply needed a break. Some space from the intensity they'd generated. Or maybe he could tell she was holding back still. She found it hard to believe he carried this same yearning for her.

Every second ticked by as slowly as the tender strokes he'd employed when he'd fucked her to sleep the night before. Hardly moving, he'd introduced her to an entirely new flavor of sex. One that was more about emotional interfacing than basic physics.

Quality versus quantity.

If only she had some way to repay him. In one week, he'd taught her more about herself than she'd reasoned out in the last decade. Seeing things from his perspective had radically altered her outlook. From this vantage, things looked so different.

Her phone rang

She dashed for the cheap plastic beside her bed. When she reached the device, its screen didn't display Luke's name and number, but an unlisted one instead.

Brielle couldn't imagine anyone contacting her at this time of night unless it was Luke. She figured it was a wrong number and let it go to voice mail. Before the caller could have bothered to leave a message, the thing rang again.

Maybe it was Luke's office.

Damn, why hadn't she thought of that? She flipped open the phone and pressed it to her ear. "Hello?"

No warm voice chased away her fears. Instead, scratchy

laughter assaulted her.

"Who is this?" She gathered her anger, at what was probably a prank or maybe a drunk dial gone wrong, in an attempt to stifle the instinctive fear that raced up her spine.

"Don't call here again," she snapped before disconnecting.

Brielle rubbed her neck, sure she'd never fall asleep now. She wandered into the main living space and double-checked her door was locked. Along the way, she spotted a blaze of color.

The flowers Luke had sent her cheered her whole kitchen. Each time she cruised past in her pacing circuit, she paused, smelled the riotous blossoms, then sighed before repeating the pattern. Her disappointment tinged with nerves ensured she'd be up all night. At least she wouldn't have to face nightmares.

After dozens of laps, she glanced up from the bouquet and her gaze landed on her new favorite recipe. Cooking was a skill she'd mastered in her seven-year sentence at Casa Brad.

Ah, that wasn't fair. She was ashamed to admit she'd been hiding from the world behind those bars. The precise measures and rules of chemistry that governed culinary pursuits had helped structure her life and give her control. Of something.

Maybe she'd enroll in a few classes in the evenings and take her hobby a little more seriously.

It was time to try something different.

A few things even. Instead of waiting for Luke to come to her, why not give chase?

Who could resist America's Test Kitchen's brown sugar cookies? Oodles of sweetness, crunchy on the outside, gooey in the middle, with browned butter for a rich nutty flavor. Absolute perfection. Sure, they were finicky and time consuming, but well worth the effort.

Besides, if she made some for him, she could taste-test a couple herself. Benefits all around.

It wasn't like she would be going to bed anytime soon.

With a huge grin plastered on her face, she snagged her apron off the hook beside the pantry and started laying out the ingredients in precise order.

"Hi." A timid finger wave accompanied Brielle's greeting.

"Good morning, Brielle. Can I help you?" Kurt had regressed to the epitome of professional. Was it because he was sitting at his e-fucking-normous desk or because Luke had confided a change of heart?

Stop being so paranoid.

"Is Becca around?" Shifting from foot to foot beneath his definitely odd gaze, she wondered if she should bolt. Maybe this had been a bad idea.

"I'm here." The muffled response grew louder. "Hang on a second, I...uh...dropped something."

Brielle rolled her eyes when the cute therapist popped out from beneath her husband's workstation, licking her lips. "Seriously, you two!"

"Well, it is lunchtime." They both laughed.

She slapped her hands over her eyes lest she be blinded by the syrupy affection oozing from them both. Sweeter than her cookies, it made her teeth ache. Envy threatened to turn her a very unattractive shade of green.

"Were you just stopping in to chat, or did you want to go out for lunch or something?" Becca approached, frowning slightly. She ran her fingers lightly over the long sleeves of Brielle's blouse, inappropriate given the heat. Neither of them mentioned the unsightly state of her arms.

"Actually, I kind of had a favor..." Nibbling her lip, she wondered again if she was making a mistake. *Be bold, Brielle.*

"Sure, no problem." Becca smiled.

"You don't know what I'm going to ask yet." Her head tilted as she considered the woman's genuine willingness to help.

"Spit it out, honey." Kurt rested his chin on his fist as he gauged her reactions. His scrutiny unnerved her.

"I was wondering if I could get a ride over to Luke's office. I would take the bus, but I can't make it there and back in an hour and a cab—"

"Is out of the question," Becca cut her off. "No need. Luckily, my boss owes me one. So...I'm taking a break."

Kurt laughed. "Fine. You girls have fun making mischief, ambushing my poor slob of a best friend. Make sure you tease him, Brielle. A lot. He doesn't stand a chance."

"Will do. And here..." She reached into the tote bag on her shoulder. "A thank-you present. For Wednesday night. And for lending me your wife."

"Mmm. I like the way that sounds."

"You pervert." Becca laughed.

"What's this?" Kurt accepted the plastic sandwich baggie Brielle handed him.

"A sample of the cookies I baked for Luke."

"You *made* these?" One of the circles had already been stuffed in his mouth and bitten in half. Even a logical man like Kurt couldn't argue with scrumptiousness. "Like from scratch?"

"Hey, I want a taste. I'm chauffeuring fresh cookies across town. I deserve to know what kind of quality we're talking about here." Becca crossed the room, again her shoes were tall enough to be stilts, and accepted the morsel Kurt fed her. "Holy shit, Brielle. These are better than the ridiculously overpriced stuff the lady on the corner of Henderson and Lane sells. People would kill for these."

"Luckily for you, I enjoy cooking. Maybe I'll decree Friday Treat Day from now on." She smiled wide.

"I guess I'll just have to burn more calories to afford snacks like these." Becca whistled innocently.

"I can help out with that. As long as I have cookies to give me enough energy to keep up with you." Kurt spanked his sassy wife.

"Um, you know I'm still standing here, right?" Brielle couldn't believe he'd done that. And Becca hadn't run, or gotten pissed. In fact, she seemed to enjoy it, sidling closer to her husband for a sugary kiss.

"Uh huh." Becca shook her head. "Let's get going so you can spend as much time as possible *delivering your cookies.*"

They headed out of the office together. Before they made it to the parking lot, Becca asked, "Do you have any more spares in there? I'm serious. Those rock."

"Of course." Brielle withdrew another baggie, and didn't mention it held the ones she'd intended to have for her midday meal after they got back. "Thanks so much for doing this. Is it dumb?"

"No no no." Becca shook her head vehemently as she backed out of Kurt's spot. "It's a fantastic surprise. He's going to love it."

The ride over passed quickly as they chatted about everything and nothing. Talking to Becca was effortless. Would tomorrow bring awkwardness, especially since they'd seemed more like friends than therapist and patient these days? She truly hoped not. The foundation they'd built guaranteed Brielle would be able to share more easily than she could have with a stranger.

When they neared, Becca formulated a plan. "Parking out front is a disaster. I'll drop you off then circle around to the supermarket a few blocks east on High Street. Call me when you're ready to go and I'll pick you up right where I let you out. You probably have about twenty-five minutes if you want to make sure we're gone for no more than an hour."

"Got it." Brielle saluted. Anything to hide the nerves roaring to life now that she could see the glistening chrome and glass of Luke's tower.

"Here we go." Becca pulled over, ignoring a few honks in the process. "No time to second-guess yourself now. Get out of here, lady. Make sure he thanks you properly."

"I'm on it." She smiled as she hopped from the vehicle and strode into the lobby.

She'd crossed halfway to Mrs. Allerton's desk when she realized she'd made it through the revolving door without even thinking about it.

"First try." The mature woman raised her eyebrows. "Dr. Malone is pretty darn good, isn't he?"

"You have no idea." Brielle's smug smile told the whole story. She didn't care.

Excited and on edge, wasting precious time didn't sound wise. Past the Ficus tree, she paused. Ten minutes was a huge chunk of her twenty-five ration. She'd much rather spend that time trading cookies for intel. Like whether or not Luke intended to come to her place again.

Tonight or any other.

Six deep breaths—hands on knees—and a serious pep talk later, she raced to the elevator before she could change her mind. Fortunately, the mass exodus from the building toward greasy goodness and the bitch at the café meant that Brielle would have the car entirely to herself heading up.

The doors opened. She had to try three times before she could force her legs to carry her forward, as if she were walking the plank. "I'm okay. I'm okay."

She imagined being in Luke's arms again, his warm hand over her eyes. She closed them and put her palm over her lids. The trip seemed to take forever.

Each chirp of the elevator sounded like an alarm to her. She counted them, praying for the end to come quickly. Darkness encroached on her excitement. Panic loomed near. But she focused on slowing her heart rate, steadying her breathing, and she kept telling herself she was fine.

The doors slid open, releasing her from hell.

Hot damn.

Brielle practically tumbled out of the elevator and down the hall toward Luke's office. Her heart dropped when she peered through glass, the waiting room, and more glass to find the space behind his desk empty. Oh no, what if he'd gone out? How dumb that she hadn't thought to call ahead. Her shoulders slumped.

Just then his administrative assistant looked up. She smiled warmly at Brielle and pointed down the hallway.

Craning her neck, Brielle peeked around the corner. And drank in the sight of Luke's long, powerful frame, leaning against the wall. His ankles crossed as he checked his watch. Oh, Mrs. Allerton! She'd given Brielle away.

Sneaking up behind Luke, her heart was in her throat. She expected him to bust her at any second, but she made it within arm's reach. Damn, he must be preoccupied. His height made it difficult, but she rose to her tiptoes and put her palms over his eyes from behind.

A startled jerk later, he spun around and captured her in his arms. "Brielle."

A response became impossible when his mouth crushed down on hers. So she told him through her kiss just how much she'd missed him. When both of them struggled to breathe, they broke apart. Flushed. Eyes wide. It seemed the attraction between them grew stronger by the second.

That's when she noticed. "You shaved!"

"You took the elevator!" he said at the exact same time.

They both nodded. Then laughed.

Luke bundled her into an enormous hug. "I'm so proud of you. Damn, Brielle. It hasn't even been a week."

"I had good motivation. I have to go soon. Becca's waiting outside. I just wanted to give you something…" Okay, and she'd wanted to taste the brown sugar on his lips.

"Did the police drop off the additional documents? They called me about them earlier. I *hate* administrative crap." He dragged his hands through his hair.

It might have been polite to stop staring at him, but she couldn't manage it. With his smooth jaw exposed, he was so damn handsome she could hardly form a coherent thought.

"Brielle?" He stroked her cheek softly.

"Sorry." A wry grin tugged at her lips. "No. Not paperwork. I didn't know there was anything else we had to do for that."

"I guess I missed initialing a page or something." He shook his head.

"Actually, I sort of made you something." She winced, suddenly wondering if her gift was lame. Totally high school. No choice now but to go forward. Reaching in her tote, she withdrew a box wrapped in crinkled foil, the best she could do to dress it up.

"What's this?" His eyes lit up as he shook the package slightly. "Do I smell...? Are these cookies?"

Grinning, she nodded.

"Wait just a second. I haven't taken a break all day and it was a triple-cup-of-coffee sort of morning. I also need to wash my hands before I dig in. You can make yourself comfy in my office." Brielle laughed when he practically bounced from foot to foot. "Take care of my cookies a second longer. Actually, here, would you take my phone too? In case the cops call while my hands are full?"

A peal of laughter escaped her.

He kissed her again then whispered, "Be right back."

She stayed rooted to the industrial carpet until he was out of sight, pushing through the men's room door with a wink in her direction. Still beaming, she headed for his office, a little nervous about barging in with the admin right there.

"Good afternoon. You must be the 'lovely, amazing, exquisite, funny and sweet' Ms. Norris. I've been hearing all about you. I'm Heidi. Go ahead and make yourself at home. I take it you saw Dr. Malone in the hallway?"

Brielle blushed as she nodded.

"Thank goodness. He's been grumpy all day. Impatient. Very unlike him."

"I'll see what I can do." She giggled at the other woman's knowing smirk. "I brought him some of these. Try one?"

Heidi plucked a cookie from the overflowing box. She moaned as she tasted the creation. "Oh yeah, that should do the trick. *Have mercy.*"

The fancy-ass phone in Brielle's hand began to buzz. She nearly dropped the gadget as she juggled both it and the foiled container. "Excuse me."

She stepped into Luke's office, set the cookies down and tried to figure out how to answer the damn thing quaking in her hold. Her basic-feature phone had a simple green TALK button. This contraption's screen showed a gorgeous woman in a box, which jiggled in time to the pattern of vibrations.

Brielle tried poking her in the eye. A glowing circle surrounded the picture with a flashing arrow pointed in a clockwise direction. She traced it with her index finger.

"Hello?" A faint voice surprised Brielle. She held the phone up to her ear, but the exasperated lady was going off. "Jesus. Are you there, Lukey-poo? I listened to your heavy breathing last night. Wasn't that session enough?"

Just before Brielle began speaking, her voice was stolen.

Maybe *Lukey-poo* hadn't been so delayed yesterday after all.

"Luke!" the woman bellowed before continuing, "Come on, baby, tell me where you want to meet up tonight and we'll get the weekend started off right, as usual. I knew you'd get tired of your new toy soon enough. Please tell me you weren't slumming it with the crazycakes from the student paper. She's not even that pretty."

Tears prickled Brielle's eyes. Oh. Hell. No. She wasn't about to do this again.

"Hey, asshole, I'm in your pants," the witch on the other end of the line cackled. She must have thought Luke had butt-answered. "I can't give you another of my spectacular BJs through the damn phone, you know."

Disgusted, Brielle punched the END icon. She never would have talked to Luke like that. What was it with guys? Maybe they got off on that shit.

Just like Brad, Luke had opted for some slut who was easy, disrespectful and crude.

You didn't exactly resist very hard.

A lightning bolt of agony struck her point-blank in the chest. She tossed his phone onto his desk and spun on her heel. As she passed the coffee table, she plucked her pathetic box from the glass furniture's gleaming surface.

Fuck that.

Brielle stormed from the office, desperately trying to convert misery into rage.

"Ms. Norris?" Heidi stared at her flushed face and balled fists.

"Tell Dr. Malone he can forget about eating any more of my damn *cookies*."

The woman sputtered and may have attempted to diffuse the *drama*, but Brielle didn't care. She burst from the pretty etched glass waiting room and marched to the elevator.

The sight of the doors had her stomach lurching. Luke's voice and the memory of his false comfort were the last things she could use to bring her peace now.

Furious at them both, she abandoned the wait. Besides, some action might help alleviate the bitterness pumping through her veins. She bolted for the stairwell, not a moment too soon.

As she yanked the heavy door open, a flash of blond hair appeared through the bathroom door. Luke whistled as he turned the corner into the hallway. Grinning, he probably gloated to himself about having his cookies and eating them too.

The exasperated groan that emerged from her half-closed throat gave her away as she ducked into the stairs and began running.

"Brielle?" Luke's fading question leaked into the stark space. By the time he peeked inside, she'd descended two or three flights. She convinced herself that the ragged gasps busting her lungs were due to being out of shape rather than being short on hope.

Flying through the lobby, she ignored Mrs. Allerton's

attempt to hail her. “Dr. Malone would like you to stay.”

Brielle shot her an incredulous look.

Mrs. Allerton’s feeble involvement trailed off when she caught sight of the silvery trails running down Brielle’s cheeks. She shooed Brielle away. “Men. Such assholes.”

Brielle sniffled as she passed without slowing. The door spinning around made her dizzy. Unsure if she could handle it at the moment, she drew up short.

“Go. He’s coming for you. Hurry.”

“I can’t.” Stuck, she looked over her shoulder at the elevator. The neon numbers counted down. Just a few floors left until it reached the ground floor.

Mrs. Allerton pointed. “There’s a side exit to High Street. It’s a loading dock. Wide open.”

“Th-thanks.” Scrubbing her face, she dashed for the area behind the lobby. The pretty finishes of the high-traffic area gave way to cinder-block walls and the guts of a major building. She saw cracks and chips where before there’d only been pristine marble. Inside the grand architecture was just a structure.

She ignored funny looks from the guys unloading supplies and hopped off the concrete landing into the parking lot, her tote banging against her hip. Stupid cookies.

Sweat began to glisten on her skin as she jogged in the direction Becca had indicated, looking for a grocery store. Right there, by the edge of the sidewalk, Kurt’s sleek sports car waited. Through the windshield, she noticed Becca on the phone.

“Shit,” she mumbled as she folded herself into the moderate front seat. She pushed the chair back all the way and rolled down the window, despite the heat beading drops of perspiration on her brow.

Air. Open. Fresh.

“She’s here,” Becca ratted her out.

Brielle shot her a nasty glare she only half regretted.

Until Becca said, "No, Luke. I won't pass the phone to her. This is between the two of you. As her counselor, I can't get involved. You know I'm already crossing lines left and right. I promise, she's safe. The rest is out of my control. Though if I had to offer you some advice, I'd tell you pursuing too hard right now is risky. Damage has already been done."

Closing her eyes, Brielle let her head crash against the headrest.

"I'm hanging up now, Luke. I love you. Goodbye." Becca's phone gave a terminal beep. "Ack. Um. Do you want to talk about it?"

"Nope." She barely managed to sputter the single word. How could she explain all that had happened in the past fifteen minutes?

Incredible wins and losses rattled her.

"That's fine." Becca backed out of her spot. "Use this time to collect yourself, if you're going back to work. Just remember that every fight isn't the end of the world. You can disagree and resolve your conflicts later, when you're free of the initial emotion. Better decisions are made then too."

"Not going to change my mind on this one." Brielle scoffed. "Playing second string is not my game anymore. I deserve to be with someone honest. Someone faithful."

"What?" The car lurched a little as Becca reacted. "You think Luke was playing around on you? I can't believe he'd do that. He's completely fascinated with you. In fact, probably to a concerning degree."

"He slept with some skank last night." She groaned. "Someone even skankier than me."

"Brielle, you're not—"

"I am. I let Luke fuck me Wednesday night. A bunch." She knocked her forehead on the frame of the car.

"Even after the incident with Wexford?" Becca sounded surprised.

"Yep. Looks like it doesn't take much..."

"I'm guessing that's far from the truth." A warm hand landed on her thigh. "We can talk about it more tomorrow, but I don't agree with Luke's decision there. He should know that you'd need space."

"For the record, I didn't want any." Brielle sighed.

"He still should have known better." She hesitated. "Because, otherwise, you might associate him with your healing or your terror. I can't say I'm surprised, or that I would have done anything different in your shoes, but the speed at which everything is happening poses some risk. Not to mention starting a new relationship during a period of major change in your life. I personally believe what you two have is worth it, but it could definitely make things trickier."

"Why couldn't you have mentioned that about a half hour ago?" She clutched her chest.

"You wouldn't have believed me anyway." The young doctor sighed. "Will you promise to come see me for tomorrow's session?"

"I think I'll need to more than ever after today."

"I'm glad you're not shying away from therapy. Don't worry about Luke. When it comes to that, I'll tell him he's not welcome to join. And if you need to talk any other time, you know where to find me." Becca mumbled, "This is going to be tough. I feel like Kurt and Luke will end up in at least one brawl. I'll make sure to have the frozen peas ready for black eyes."

"Speaking of... Would Kurt mind if I ate in his car?" Brielle cracked open her eyes.

"Probably. But this is an emergency." Becca sounded so serious.

Maniacal laughter wafted up from Brielle's core. "I have enough cookies for us both. I took Luke's back."

"Damn, you must have been pissed."

"Still am, Becca." Three servings of brown sugar did little to help. But at least her stomach quit rumbling. "This might take another round of baking to fix."

"Whatever works for you, Brielle."

"Right now, I just need quiet. And space. I'm sorry."

"You have nothing to apologize for." Becca left her alone, as she'd asked. But, if anything, the silence only widened the hole in her heart. "Tomorrow, though, you're on the hook."

Brielle glanced away from traffic to test a tentative smile.

No dice. "Great. Sounds like fun."

Yeah, just like root canals.

And later, when a single black rose was delivered to her office, placed directly on her desk this time, she assumed it was Luke's way of telling her things were over.

Brielle went into mourning.

Chapter Twelve

Luke couldn't stand another second of the Brielle-mandated solitude. He swung one leg over his bike and unclipped his helmet. He'd given her time to calm down. To think. To sort through what had happened on her own.

Eleven o'clock at night—yet she still hadn't relented and called him as he'd hoped.

Damn it, he had a sweet craving.

For the millionth time this hour, he pressed Redial. Two short bursts before Brielle's voice mail kicked on assured him that she hadn't bothered to listen to the messages he'd left her periodically this afternoon.

Whether intentionally or not, he must really have hurt her for her to hold out so long. He'd assumed full responsibility. He should never have given her his phone. Not with all the old data in there. In fact, after she left, he'd scoured his address book, deleting every single one of his just-for-fun lovers. Talk about a statement. His attitudes had changed overnight. Or over lunch, last weekend.

He paused by the wildflower beds and plucked a daisy from the bunch. A cheery flower for a bright young woman. For an unsteady heartbeat or twelve, he considered playing She Loves Me, She Loves Me Not until he realized it would destroy the whole thing.

Maybe it was better not to know, and to simply enjoy what he could, while he could.

Yes, he had to follow his gut. The damn thing screamed for him to go to her. Stubborn, she'd rather prove she was terrified by preparing for a siege than admit—to herself or to him—she might have made a mistake, as if he cared either way. After her cheating ex, he didn't blame her for jumping to conclusions.

Even incorrect ones.

Luke gathered every bit of his legendary patience and the talents he'd honed over a decade of practicing active-listening techniques. He couldn't stand to fuck this up the time it mattered most. The problem was that staying impartial would be impossible when he really wanted to toss her over his lap and spank her for assuming the worst.

Somehow he figured that might be the wrong approach.

He glanced up at her window, the only one that had been bright a few nights ago. The lights were on, and just then a figure passed in front of the pane. The hazy silhouette wasn't much to go on but he could tell. It was her.

Brielle.

Stairs passed beneath him in a blur as he charged up to her place. In his haste, Luke nearly knocked over a scruffy dude hanging out on the second-floor landing.

"Watch it, fucker."

"Sorry, man." Luke held his hands out. Preoccupied with Brielle so close and yet so far away, he didn't bother to question why the guy was loitering. He skirted the ill-tempered man and headed up the next flight of stairs.

With Brielle's door looming in front of him, he restrained himself, managing to impart a very timid knock. Well, it came out sort of normal. At least it wasn't the pounding he might otherwise have launched.

It didn't surprise him when she refused to answer.

Artificial stillness from the other side of the cheap, dinged-up hollow-core was too absolute to be real. "Brielle. It's me, Luke."

As if she couldn't guess.

Hell, maybe she couldn't. Though he hadn't seen any evidence she'd made friends here yet, he hadn't specifically asked and she hadn't mentioned anyone significant. The thought began to make him sweat. What if she didn't need him?

"Please, will you open the door? I'd like to talk to you. To explain what happened earlier today. I know Sandy hurt you—"

Brielle whipped open the thin wood separating them. "Stop. I don't care for my neighbors to know every detail of my business."

"Then you should probably let me in so we can speak in confidence." He edged toward her apartment.

"I don't think so. I'm not interested in hearing excuses." Frown lines disfigured her forehead and tugged her full lips into a pout.

Not now, he warned his cock, which twitched in his ripped jeans.

The warmth and light streaming from her home began to fade as she closed him out again. He jammed his foot in the gap.

"So now you're going to force your way inside?" Her chocolate eyes hardened. "I knew you were just like the rest."

"Shit." He yanked away as if scorched. Holding his hands up, palms out, he took several steps back until his shoulders bumped the wall on the opposite side of the hallway. "I'm nothing like them, Brielle. I'm willing to do what it takes to prove it to you. If that means walking away right now, I will. I don't want to, but I'll respect your call. You're in charge."

"Why do I get the feeling that was too easy?" She peeked around the doorframe, surprised and interested.

"Because I'm not giving up on us." He folded his arms. "You can kick me out, but I'll keep coming around. Unless you can look me in the eye and tell me you don't give a shit about everything that's happened this week. If it was just some random fun to you..."

"You know it wasn't." Her quick denial buoyed his confidence.

"Not for me, either." Luke grimaced. "Before I go, I have to say I'm sorry one of my casual affairs impacted you. I won't forget that something meaningless ruined something treasured.

I'm done with those days."

"A little too late to decide that now." Brielle couldn't hide the tremble of her lower lip, no matter how hard she bit it to keep it from wobbling.

"I'd already kind of made up my mind about empty sex." He scrubbed his hands over his face, surprised to find it smooth again. Ah, that felt better. Stupid goatee. Never had been right for him. Brooding didn't suit him as well as it did Kurt, either. Action held much more appeal.

"Just needed one last go-around to work it out of your system?" Disgust tinged her question. "Well, too bad, Luke. I'm not the kind of girl who puts up with disloyalty anymore. I deserve better."

Her conviction filled him with pride. She'd come so far, so quickly. "Damn fucking straight you do. And if I'd violated your trust, I wouldn't have bothered to come back here tonight. I would never cheat on my girlfriend. I never have. Not in all my life. The women I slept with for fun knew it was nothing more. Hell, most of them aren't looking for anything permanent either. Pretty things, hot sex—that's enough for them."

She blinked.

Luke seized the opportunity to sway her. "It was fine for me too. But not anymore. I want the real thing. The kind of love Kurt has for Becca. It's powerful. Life changing. I can't believe that fucker found it before me. But you were worth waiting for, Brielle."

Her jaw hung open. Still she didn't utter a peep.

So he went for the kill. If she didn't believe him, there was nothing more he could do. He let truth ring in every single heartfelt word he spoke. "I swear to you, Sandy is nothing to me. A fun time. One I haven't bothered with in months. Last night, I wanted to talk to you, but I hoped you were sleeping soundly. I wrapped up around two in the morning. Still, I kept my phone in bed with me in case you needed me. I had my hand on the damn thing and I must have hit some buttons when I rolled over onto it."

"You're telling me you sleep-dialed some ex-bimbo? Did you have narcoleptic phone sex too? She rattled on about your heavy-breathing session last night. *Last night,* Luke. Not months ago." She swallowed hard as she looked away.

"She's a smart-mouthed lady." Luke grimaced. "She was giving me shit about snoring into the phone, despite her yelling at me apparently. I didn't even know I'd done it until I called her back after I found my phone on my desk, her number in the recent calls, and you missing from my office."

"I'd hardly describe the things she said as ladylike." Brielle turned her nose up. She looked so damn cute he could barely stand it.

A door opened down the hallway and an elderly man poked his head out. "Ms. Norris, is this guy bothering you? I can call the cops if you want."

"No, Mr. Carter. It's okay. Luke was just leaving." Brielle glared at him.

"I wasn't." He stood firm. "Not unless you make me."

"Brielle," the older man called again.

"We'll be quiet. I'm sorry for disturbing you." She tried to placate him.

"Are you kidding? This is more interesting than *Jersey Shore* reruns any day." He gawked at them. "But I think you should let the poor guy inside. You've got his balls in a bind."

Brielle looked from Mr. Carter to Luke and back. Then she burst out laughing.

The sound lightened Luke's heart.

"Please, Brielle," he tried again, "I won't hurt you. You don't need to be afraid."

"I know that." She grimaced. "At least not physically. I believe you won't lay a hand on me."

At least not in anger, he thought.

"He better not, or I'll kick his ass. I was in the navy back in the day." Mr. Carter butted in again.

"Jesus. Fine." Brielle flung open the door and stepped

back. "Get in here so we can finish this. I'm not saying you're staying, or that I forgive you, but at least we can have a civilized discussion before we say goodbye."

"Thank you, Mr. Carter." Luke grinned at the older man, wondering what he could give the guy for Christmas.

"Don't muck it up." He shot Luke a salute then disappeared inside. The blaring TV came on a few seconds later, guaranteeing their privacy despite the thin walls.

Brielle slumped with her back against the elevated portion of the kitchen counter, which formed a bar on the living room side of the island. Exhausted from her predawn bake-a-thon, and the catastrophe with Luke this afternoon, she couldn't bear to stand up straight.

Why did he have to look so damn sexy all the time? The sadness etching grooves into his jaw only enhanced his appeal.

Sunshine with a hint of shade.

Anger flared. How could she be such a pushover? A few tiny, hardly believable excuses and she longed to launch herself into his arms.

"Damn, it sucks when you look at me like that." He scrubbed his hands through his hair, rearranging yet not ordering the tousled mop. "I wanted to be your hero, not another guy who let you down. I messed that up in less than forty-eight hours. I may be dumb, but I'm not a jerk. Nothing happened between Sandy and me. At least, not yesterday. You were the only woman I was dreaming about."

"So what you're saying is that I'm so dull, I knocked you out and caused you to snore uncontrollably?" Despite the turbulence churning the air between them, she couldn't suppress the silly side he evoked in her.

"Holy cow." He tugged on the ends of his hair. "No. That's not—I mean, more like a twelve-hour day on the heels of our sexfest drained me dry."

When she choked on a laugh, he caught on.

"Wait. Was that a joke? You're *teasing* a dying man?" He clutched his gut and staggered in a horrible mock croak worthy of an old spaghetti western.

"Hell yes." A smile snuck on to her face. "It seems only fair that you suffer as much as I have this afternoon. And last night... I fucking missed you, Luke. Like hell. Meanwhile, you were off snoring over the line to some ridiculously beautiful woman."

"Ah shit, Cookie. I missed you more." He took a tentative step forward.

Brielle couldn't find her voice to command him to stay put.

"Do I at least get one last wish before you put me out of my misery?"

"That depends. Will you go home if I say yes?" She propped her hand on her hip. If she didn't oust him soon, she'd cave. In truth, she believed his story, even if she feared she might be the most gullible person on the face of the planet.

Relief swamped her twice over. Her judgment hadn't been completely skewed. And he seemed oblivious to the less-than-flattering article in the student paper. Brielle had Sandy to thank for alerting her to the cover photo of Luke toting "a troubled employee" out of the coat closet. She'd worried the exposure might have contributed to his change of heart.

After she and Becca had returned from their delivery-gone-wrong, she'd cleared every copy from the plexidispenser outside the Franklin Building. If Sandy hadn't tipped Luke off, Brielle sure as shit wasn't about to open another can of worms.

"I'll leave if you still want me to. Just let me hug you first. It tears me up knowing you were upset because of me." He held his arms open wide. The sincerity in his gorgeous eyes squashed her resistance.

She didn't flinch when he approached, slowly, placing one foot in front of the other until her nose touched his chest.

"Put your arms around me, Brielle?" The uncertainty in his question was a first.

She hated it.

If nothing else, she was sure about how she felt for this man. Maybe that was all that mattered. And just then she realized he needed to be embraced as much as she did. Always the life of the party, the advanced-class clown...

A lot of his life had been spent seeking attention. Affection might be what he'd really required all along. The poor substitute couldn't sustain him forever.

How many women had bothered to look beyond his affluence, intelligent wit and pure adorableness to the lost boy she had sensed all along?

This part of him was what drew her. A kindred spirit to the girl in the closet.

She couldn't forsake him after he'd helped her unlock the door and start emerging from the shadows.

Brielle turned her face and leaned forward so that her cheek rested on his chest. She looped her arms gently around his waist.

Timid Luke vanished so fast, she wondered if she'd imagined that facet of his personality. He engulfed her in a bear hug, nuzzling his nose into her hair and breathing deep. "Sandy's nowhere near as lovely as you are, by the way."

"Nice try." She patted between his shoulder blades. "I saw her picture on your phone, remember? Besides, she said so herself."

"What?" He drew away just far enough to peer down at her then frown. "You realize, whatever the hell she spouted off, it was just a cover for her jealousy, right? Never again. The contact is deleted, along with the others like it. I told her not to bother calling. Ever. Those days are over. I swear to you."

Her frozen core thawed a bit more in the face of his fiery reassurance.

"Does this mean we're dating?" Her fingers tightened on his back. "An exclusive couple?"

"I thought I'd made that part pretty obvious." Luke growled

softly in her ear before nipping the lobe. "Yes. Get used to introducing me as your boyfriend."

"It seems like a tame label for...this." A shrug rocked her against his chest.

"It's whatever we make of it. I do have one question though." Luke fisted his hands in her hair and used the resulting pressure to angle her head back to stare into her eyes. She loved the firm hold he had on her, promising he wouldn't let her go. "Since we're mostly good here, may I have my cookies now?"

"Well, first off, I'm sorry to say Becca and I put a pretty big dent in them when I was trying to replace you with trans fats galore." She licked her lips, watching his stare track the muscle's progress as it wet her mouth. "And second, I think I'd like you to make a meal of me before we serve dessert."

He didn't need to be asked twice.

"I've replayed Wednesday night in my mind a million times since you climbed off my bike the next morning." He slid his hands up her rib cage until they locked beneath her armpits. Then he plucked her from the floor, carrying her as if she weighed nothing. "I keep wondering if it could have been as good as I remember."

"It seemed divine to me." She recalled his singing and splashing before he got down to serious business. Was it always like that for him? Fun paired with heat. "Clearly, I'm nowhere near as experienced as you, though."

Luke aimed toward the dinette table she'd squashed into a nook where the kitchen and living room overlapped. He shifted her to one hip while he removed the glass shield of a hurricane lamp she'd rescued from the Sunday flea market. Then he transferred a candle and the antique marbles she'd used to make a colorful centerpiece out of the found art.

When he'd set the components carefully aside on the bar, which he could reach by merely leaning, he placed her on top of the rickety butcher-block-topped furniture. She squeaked, "Is this going to hold?"

“I wasn’t planning on climbing on top of you.” He rested his forehead on hers. Sitting with her legs spread around his torso, the growing length of his erection stole her concentration. “Unless you’ve changed your mind about that?”

“Can we start with a kiss?” She ran her hands from his tight pecs to his rock-hard abdomen. The wall of muscles rose and fell unevenly with his breathing.

“It would certainly be the best *amuse-bouche* I’ve ever had.” Leaning in, he dusted his lips over hers so gently she felt prized.

“I don’t know what that is, but it sounds nice.” Especially if it was anything like the teeny-tiny, emotion-packed kiss he’d just bestowed.

“If therapy isn’t too draining, I’ll take you out to dinner tomorrow night. To celebrate. Our first-week anniversary.” They grinned at each other. “I’ll show you then.”

“Sold.” She didn’t have a lot of free brain cells to record his trivia at the moment. “I’ll try to pay attention better then.”

“Unless I can talk you into sharing my side of the booth, in which case I can think of better uses for your concentration.”

Brielle laughed. “You can try, Dr. Malone, but I am a very proper kind of woman. I would never fool around with you in a public place like that.”

“Or on a kitchen table?” He swept her arms from behind her, spilling her onto her back.

“Certainly not.” A sigh puffed from her lips when he began to work her tank top up her belly, kissing every inch he exposed below the hem. “Well, maybe, if you keep doing that.”

A flick of his tongue resulted in goose bumps along her arms. Her spine arched, lifting her midsection from the table. He slid his arms beneath her, supporting her so she rested in his hold.

Pausing his ascent, he skipped to her mouth once more. “I can’t go more than thirty seconds without tasting you.”

“I thought I was the slightly cracked one of this pair.” She dodged his flurry of loud smacking kisses as best she could.

"Maybe we both are. Who's to say? I know one thing for sure," he whispered as he stared into her eyes, maybe deeper below the surface. "I'm crazy for you, Brielle. Please don't ever shut me out of your life. I'm sure things won't be smooth sailing every moment, but we can work anything out if you'll talk to me."

"I got scared." She looked at the ugly light fixture instead of at him.

"I know. Me too." Luke covered her lips again. He really wasn't kidding about this kissing addiction they both seemed to have developed overnight.

Prepared to make some smart-ass remark to ratchet down the intensity, she changed her mind when he licked her bottom lip, encouraging her to part for him. There really wasn't any choice in the matter.

Brielle went lax, allowing him to lead wherever his heart—or destinations farther south—took them. A brush of his fingers over her breast inspired a moan.

"You're not wearing anything under this are you?" He circled the hardened point of her nipple through the thin material. Next he repeated the gesture between her legs. "Or this?"

"Nope. It's too hot for underwear."

"You can say that again." He shook his head. "Or better yet, *you're* too hot for them."

The need to move against him overwhelmed reason. She spread her legs, propping her heels on the edge of the table. Splayed before him, she invited him to take a taste by reaching down and stripping off her half-lifted top.

"Damn." He bent down to kiss her breasts, plumping them with his broad hands so he could get the best vantage for his lips on her nipples. Despite the heat, she shivered when he sucked on first one, then the other. His tongue lapped at the crinkled skin around the peak, making her eyelids droop and her pussy clench.

Brielle fisted the cotton of his V-neck at the shoulder seams and tugged. The material slid up, partially covering his mouth. They both groaned when he pulled off her breast with a wet smack to discard his T-shirt.

His chest amazed her all over again. She recalled licking whipped cream from the valleys between his flexed abs. He reminded her of an action hero, but one with a sense of humor and brainpower so impressive he didn't have to flaunt it.

A wicked grin spread over his face. "Thank you, Ms. Norris."

Blushing, she averted her stare. "I hate that I'm so obvious to you."

"You can't tell exactly what I'm thinking right now?" He tilted his head.

"I mean, I can see you're..." She waved a hand in the general direction of his crotch, where a thick bulge had distorted the front of his jeans.

"It's more than that, Brielle." He lifted one of her feet and kissed her ankle. "I'm so grateful you let me in. Tonight. At all."

His hands glided ahead of his mouth, caressing her leg on either side of her knee and then up her thighs. When he reached the thin fabric of her shorts, he skipped to the waistband. Drawing soft lines along the edge, he kissed the sensitive spot behind her knee.

"You're really good at this." She gasped. "Show me what to do for you."

"Enjoy. That's all." This time he sounded as though he'd run up her stairs all over again. He tucked his hands inside her shorts and tormented the skin below her belly button, just skimming the top of her mound and the trimmed hair there.

He rotated his hand, cupping her.

Brielle arched into his hold, pressing tight to his palm. His fingers curved, the tips taunting her, on the brink of penetration.

"Enough teasing." Luke withdrew, making her cry out. She didn't have to suffer long before he whipped the material away and appraised her, bare, laid out like a feast prepared in his honor.

He bent at the waist to kiss her. Though their bottom halves weren't touching, she reveled in the press of his chest on hers. Halfway through the exchange, it stalled out. Luke lifted up a bit as though he were doing a pushup on the table. "Is this okay? I'm not scaring you, am I?"

It took her a second to reengage her mind. "Oh. Because you're over me? I guess not."

His smile encouraged her.

"I like the way you feel. Don't stop, Luke."

Chapter Thirteen

"You got it." Along the way back to her mouth, he dallied. First, he dragged his parted lips over her shoulder then along her collar bone before meandering up her neck.

Brielle canted her head to grant him better access. She shivered, loving every instant he explored. When he discovered a particularly sensitive spot just below her ear, she cried out. Her entire body flexed and hummed.

Next thing she knew, her fingers had twined in his hair as she directed his talented tongue to exactly the right location.

He seemed to key in on her reaction, suckling lightly at first, then harder when they both came to the realization that she preferred a bit of sting along with the stimulation.

"You know," Luke whispered as he paused to catch his breath. "If I keep this up, you'll have to wear your hair loose or everyone will see my mark on you."

"I'm certainly not ashamed of this." She stroked his hair.

"Me either. I just thought I should warn you I'm about to paint the proof of our liaison on your skin."

"Why does it sound like you like that idea?" Wonder added to the pleasure he conferred. He didn't just *not mind* if people knew they were fooling around. He actually considered advertising it.

His possessiveness should have terrified her, a big-time turnoff. Somehow it was different, though, from the vile ownership Brad had deemed his right.

"I do. I'm so fortunate I can hardly believe it. A seriously lucky bastard."

This was honor and glorification of a symbiotic exchange. Not an iron-fisted ruler branding his chattel. His consideration only enamored her further, placing her fully under his spell.

"Do it." Brielle gulped when he surrounded her throat with his long fingers, positioning her.

"You're sure you don't mind being mine?" The pad of his thumb swept over her parted lips.

"Not if you're mine too." A fierce urge overcame her when he peered into her eyes.

"For as long as you'll keep me." Luke shocked her by placing his compulsion on hold. He released her then lunged forward, bracing himself above her and inclining his chin to offer himself for her indulgence.

Brielle bit her lip instead. "I feel like a vampire."

"A sexy vampire?" he chuckled.

"Gross. Drinking blood is not my thing."

A strangled laugh gushed from him. "I thought all girls were into that crap, aren't they?"

"I prefer doctors." She applied her mouth to the vulnerable area over his carotid artery.

"Harder, Cookie." Luke presented himself more fully, pressing against her open mouth. "I want something that won't fade quickly. Something that lasts."

His wishes vibrated her lips and thrilled her, inside and out.

Happy to oblige, she dedicated herself to kissing him, suckling the salt and night air from his skin. If only it was as easy as this to guarantee their future. Maybe after tomorrow's session, he'd change his mind. If so, he'd have one hell of a hickey to remind him of the promises he'd made and broken.

Brielle rubbed the flat of her tongue over the spot, soothing it before she withdrew, grinning.

"I bet I can do better." He devoured her smug smile in an exhibition of what was to come.

She couldn't believe just an hour ago she had been moping, convinced she'd never experience this rush again. And here they were. She hoped she never had to go without his brightness.

When she tapped on his shoulder, he disengaged with a groan. Tipping her chin up, she enticed him to put his boasting to the test.

Pressure developed into an almost-pain that was really a gluttony of rapture. She writhed on the table, causing the uneven legs to skip and the surface to rock.

"Oh my God. What are you, part Dyson vacuum?" Brielle squirmed, trying to get closer or put some distance between them, she couldn't say.

"Hold still." Luke's murmur garbled due to his mouthful of her neck. He banded his hands around her waist and forced her to comply.

She jerked, but couldn't escape. Though she tried to elude his grasp, she couldn't. Her breathing went spasmodic and she clawed at his back.

But just as he recognized that he'd tripped her panic button and began to retreat, something else in her gave way, venting all the terror and combined yearning. A barrage of sensation rained down on her. She flew apart, shattering into a million dazzling shards. Surprised, both of them simply rode out her orgasm, staring directly into each other's eyes.

"Oh, Cookie." He finally came back to life, blanketing her then peppering her with a mix of sweet and fiery kisses, caresses and hugs. "I get it now. You're scared of yourself."

"Wh-what?" Shudders still racked her as the ecstasy continued in endless waves that only grew again as he petted her.

"We can talk later." His grin seemed fit for the big bad wolf. "I know exactly how to help."

"You do?" Flames scorched her from the inside out. Her release had triggered more need, more sensation. More of everything.

"Uh huh." He stood up sharply, making her whimper and reach for him. "Don't worry, I'm sure as shit not leaving now."

He only went far enough to unbutton his jeans then rip the zipper down. Kicking out of the denim left him naked. Apparently, it was too hot for him to wear underwear too.

His cock bobbed, hanging long and low as the heavy weight of his erection dragged it down against his thigh. Another few seconds and he'd taken a condom from his back pocket, ripped it open and rolled the thin latex over his length.

"That was amazing, Brielle." He notched the fat head of his dick at her entrance. "I've never been so damn turned on. I've seen women who could do it from pain, sensual whippings, or breast play, but not bondage. A woman who can come just from being restrained… God!"

"Don't forget the neck thing." She felt less like a freak when she detected the awe in his tone.

"That wasn't what pushed you over the edge and you know it." He inserted himself deep inside her with one long, smooth shove that joined them completely.

She winced.

"Still sore from the other night?" He paused.

"Not enough to stop."

"No chance of that." He folded over her. "But I could go slow. Gentle. Take you to bed and make love to you for hours."

"Don't you dare." She bit his shoulder. "Fuck me, Luke. Now."

"It wasn't enough, was it?" His pelvis ground against hers, stimulating her clit.

"Not even close." She attempted to retain a shred of dignity by refusing to beg for more. She'd never been insatiable before. He didn't make her ask.

Luke stood up straight, wrapping his hands around the tops of her thighs. He used their angle, spread around his hips, to ensure leverage as he tugged her to the brink of the table.

Her hands splayed on the painted white wood, which she'd refinished herself to hide years of scratches, water stains and other abuse. A little touching up could do a world of good, she'd found.

"I won't let you fall."

Secure in his grasp, she relaxed, allowing him to plow deeper on his next series of thrusts. From his new angle, he could screw her relentlessly. Deep, hard and exactly as she needed in that moment to banish the last of her fears—both of losing him and of the ghosts of her past.

Every inch of him was used to best advantage in this position. She couldn't believe how deeply she felt him prodding her, rubbing the undulating walls of her pussy from the inside. He reached every ache and massaged the rings of muscle clasping around his intrusion.

Brielle's legs hooked over his hips, drawing him closer. Her heels rested on his ass, loving the clench of his powerful muscles as he rode her. Not with brute force, but with authority. Controlled and directed momentum ensured this would go down in her personal history book as the best sex of all time.

She didn't know how it would be possible, but she hoped he continued to destroy that record time and time again. Looming above her, he looked like the Greek king he'd sung of in the suite's opulent bathroom earlier in the week. No, he was Apollo—sharing sunrays, medicine, knowledge and poetry with mere mortals like her.

Luke probably would have laughed if he could have read her thoughts. Fortunately, he seemed pretty intent on what he was doing instead. He bent his knees and changed his angle slightly. The upward arch of his hips had her eyes rolling back in her head and her spine bowing.

"Oh, anatomy classes." He grunted. "My favorite part of med school. Probably why I decided to stick with psychology instead of psychiatry after all, huh?"

"Well, you're putting them to good use now." A dead-on plunge connected him with someplace inside her she knew no one had ever reached before. Surely she would remember something that felt like *that*.

"Hang on to the edges of the table." He picked up her hands and placed them out to her sides. "Don't let go."

She might have questioned him if he hadn't chosen right then to ramp up the frequency of his impaling strokes. He banked on her obedience, turning his attention to her chest.

Filling his hands with her breasts, Luke groped her. He pinched her nipples in time to the peak of each journey of his cock. When he added a little swing of his hips every time they locked tightest, she conceded defeat.

Imminent, her surrender must have been obvious.

"Yes." He swooped in, low and near. He smothered her in affection, desire and his healing touch. "Yes. Come with me on top of you. In you. Like this. You can admit you want it. Your body has control of your mind now. Listen to what it's saying."

Brielle hovered on the verge of tipping into orgasm.

Adding the pressure of his lips on hers, he layered yet another sensation on the riot of feelings coursing through her. They communicated on a level beyond speech. Their bodies, their eyes and their souls spoke loud enough.

"Fine," he snarled as he ripped his mouth away. "I'll give you what we both know you need. Don't hate me for this. Please."

It hurt to be so close to flying yet unable to soar.

"Help me," she whispered even as he fucked her—harder, deeper, faster. Still, always with care and her pleasure as his main concern.

Luke stared into her eyes for the span of several more strokes. Then he nodded curtly.

Before she could beg again, he grasped her wrists, brought them above her head and pinned them to the table. The hold was impossible to break. She never wanted to get loose.

A cry—of relief mingled with terror—flew from her throat.

Her entire body stiffened. She went stock-still, and yet he rode her beyond her rationality to a place where only base instinct mattered. And hers trusted him. Implicitly. The ability to hand responsibility to him, to know that he would care for her above all else, forced fantasies to intersect with reality.

This was happening. Luke was real.

Brielle stared into his eyes, electric blue with his own arousal.

Despite everything—the tension between them, their experiment, her irrational fears, his delayed gratification, their short courtship—he smiled in the midst of the storm.

"Go ahead, Cookie." The tender kiss he placed on the tip of her nose was so at odds with the unrelenting rhythm of his fucking and his unshakable grip on her wrists it shocked her system.

Like putting a hot glass dish in freezing water, the contrast made her explode.

This was no quick venting of pressure.

No easy climax to giggle after.

No simple relief.

It impacted every part of her being, and altered the course of her life. Because he knew all her secrets. *Almost.* She couldn't hide her darkest desires from him. And he seemed comfortable corralling them.

In fact, her release seemed to trigger his. She milked his cock as it bulged, growing harder than she thought possible. His stride hitched for the barest second before he picked up steam, rejuvenating the spasms wringing her.

"*Brielle!*" he shouted. With his head thrown back, the purple outline caused by her mouth contrasted boldly on even his tan skin. The proof of her claim triggered a final round of squeezing, which drew the last of his semen from his balls into the tiny barrier between them.

When he'd finished quaking between her thighs, he fell forward. Careful of her reaction, he caught himself on his elbows, leaving a solid six inches between them now that her insulating arousal had worn off.

"Give me a second. Then I'll move." He cursed softly before

whispering in her ear, "That was…the best. Ever."

"For me too." A blush stole across her chest and up her neck. "By a mile."

"Thank you, Brielle. For trusting me."

"Thank you for deserving it." Her hands cupped his smooth cheeks as she drew him in for a long, lingering kiss. They might have gone on that way for quite some time if he hadn't slipped from her body when his cock softened completely.

Both of them groaned. The disposal of the condom distracted him.

"Go ahead. You know where the bathroom is." She pointed toward the glow spilling from her eternal night-light. "I'll grab the cookies and meet you in bed."

"I knew you were my dream girl." He brushed his lips over her forehead before parting with a grimace. "You don't mind me eating in there?"

"Let's just say I like you so much, I'll overlook any crumbs."

She snagged the box off the counter, ripped a couple paper towels from the roll and poured a glass of water big enough to share. Too bad she didn't have something fancier to offer him.

Brielle set her bounty on the floor beside the air mattress. You didn't need end tables if you didn't have a bed frame. Win-win, she thought, trying not to be embarrassed by her spartan apartment.

Stealthy, Luke crept up behind her to land a smack on her bare ass, which her position displayed prominently. "God damn, are you trying to give me a heart attack?"

He hugged her when she stood upright.

Too soon, he unfolded himself and hopped into bed, patting the space beside him. He chuckled as he bounced. "Fun. Now, about my sweet treats. Well, the other ones."

Her laughter echoed off the bare walls as she sank, cross-legged next to Luke.

"No worries, Cookie. I'll be sure to eat every single morsel you feed me." He reclined, crossing his hands behind his head and opening his mouth.

The temptation was too much to resist. She straddled him. Then dipped her index finger between his lips. His eyes darkened as he sucked on the tip. A chill ran up her spine.

Before they got too far from the easy intimacy they were sharing, she selected a pretty damn perfect-looking circle of brown sugar yumminess and flew it toward him in a ridiculous loop-the-loop he tracked with his stare. When it got within range, his homing appetite engaged and he chomped it from her fingers.

She adored the way he practically inhaled it. The fussy recipe had been worth the work to see his eyelids lower and hear his stomach growl its approval. After he'd packed away a half dozen, graciously offering her a bite, he grew serious.

"Brielle, we need to discuss what happened earlier." Luke's soft statement still carried a wallop. It reminded her that the real world was right outside these barely there walls, waiting to ambush them.

"I'd rather do this." She shifted back and forth across his lap.

"Cookie—"

She put her fingers over his mouth, smiling when he kissed them. "There's plenty of time tomorrow, isn't there? With Becca...and Kurt. They mentioned the session could take all day, especially if we opt for the Dream Machine. That's a lot, Luke. Maybe more than I can handle. Can't we just enjoy tonight?"

Because she feared that after all her cards were on the table, he might not feel the same way he did in this magical moment.

Brielle wasn't ready to let go yet. She might need this memory to be her anchor through lonely nights ahead, so it needed to be spectacular. At least, no matter what, she would have this time to remember.

"Okay," Luke conceded, proving again his innate intuition. Pushing then wouldn't have gotten him anywhere. "Tomorrow."

"Thank you." She leaned down to kiss his left pec, over his heart, before she asked, "Do you have any more condoms?"

"A whole pocketful." He sighed. "I guess I'll just have to have another snack while you're fetching them. You know, to get my oomph back."

"Maybe next time I'll make chocolate chip but substitute Viagra instead of M&M's." She laughed at his horrified expression. "Just kidding. Clearly you don't need any help in that department."

When Brielle squirmed on top of him, they both groaned. His cock lengthened between them, nearly ready. "I'll be right back. Don't go anywhere, Luke."

"I'm not planning on it anytime in the next century."

She intentionally remained in his line of sight when she bent at the waist to retrieve his stash.

"You're lucky you're not in spanking distance. It's not polite to tease, Brielle."

Her toes curled in the worn carpet. Maybe tomorrow he'd find out she might like it if he made good on his threats. Until then, she'd stick to exploring this magnetism between them.

"Did you miss me?"

"You have no idea." Luke bundled her into his arms, chasing away the chill even a few seconds away from him allowed to creep in.

Together they began to replace her bedtime anxiety with something a hell of a lot more delightful.

Chapter Fourteen

Brielle clutched Luke's shirt as they rolled into the parking lot of the Franklin Building precisely at ten o'clock the next morning. He eased the streamlined, black and red metal of his motorcycle into the spot beside Kurt's car. So he could hear her over the roar of the obscenely loud, powerful motor, she yelled, "Maybe we should go around the block?"

"We've already circled the thing four times, Cookie." He turned the key on his bike, deafening her with the silence and his much quieter response. "It's now or never. This isn't as scary as you think, I promise. We're just going to talk. Unless..."

"What?" Her heart skipped a beat.

"It's all up to you. You're the boss, remember?" Luke hung his helmet from the handlebar and rotated his torso as much as possible to look at her. "You've been so aggressive in taking strides this week. I'm impressed as hell. I feel like you're open to change. If things go really well, I suspect Becca might suggest using the Dream Machine on you."

"She already mentioned it at the banquet." Brielle shivered. "But not today, right?"

"I'm not your doctor." He winced a tiny bit. "I can't say what treatment plan she'll prescribe. However, any psychologist worth listening to will let you draw the boundaries. If anything is overwhelming or frightens you, we'll stop."

"And it's necessary for both Becca and Kurt to be there?" Though she'd come to see the stern doctor in a new light this past week, he still unnerved her a bit.

"Again, it's going to be your call ultimately. Especially since we're approaching this as a couple, having them both involved could be helpful. So...why not take two for the price of one?"

"Because too many quacks spoil the cookies?" She softened her snarkiness with a smile and hug.

"True, most times. In this case, though, Kurt would be invaluable. He created the Dream Machine. If it comes into play, I would recommend taking his expert advice." Luke returned her squeeze with one arm. "He's a good man. My best friend. I wouldn't let just anyone get involved in something so important. To us both and our future."

She kissed his cheek before climbing off the bike on unsteady legs. "Okay. I trust you."

"I'll be with you every second." He cleared his throat as he joined her on the pavement. "Actually, that's not my call either. If you ever want me to leave the room, just say so. I'm here for you, whatever you need. Even if that's space."

The last of her trepidation thinned out like haze on a blazing day.

Brielle gave Luke a proper hug then held out her hand. They walked up the sidewalk together, fingers linked. It felt funny to be here yet not be going to work. She guaranteed she'd remember him beside her each time she passed this way. Without him, it would be lonely. She admired flowers in the beds she'd walked by dozens of times without noticing.

Everything seemed more vivid with him by her side.

She used her ID badge to gain entrance then trudged up the stairs, a fraction of her unease returning.

"It's okay, Cookie."

"That's a completely ridiculous nickname." She latched on to his welcome distraction.

"Would you prefer Booger Bear?"

"You wouldn't!"

"How about Honey Bunny? Snookems? Muffin? Sweetypie? Dewdrop? Snuggle Pups? Dumpling? Chickadoodle? Diddums? Toots?"

"I will knee you in the nuts if you call me Toots." Her

laughter made it hard to appear mean. "And you seem to lean toward a really high ratio of food-based endearments."

"When my stomach's happy, so am I. Sugar Puss?" He wiggled his eyebrows.

"You know what, Cookie is terrific." Brielle clutched her gut, about to pee her pants from cracking up. "And so are you. Thanks for distracting me."

He paused with his hand on the handle of the Fosters' practice door. "Are you ready? Should I open this?"

"Let's do it, *Buttercup*." She nodded and prepared to step into the office.

Becca sat on the couch in the waiting room, staring at her iPad. With her legs crossed, she swung one foot, complete with another wicked heel. Even still, when she stood she was no taller than Brielle. "Good morning."

"Missed your old spot?" Luke filled Brielle in. "Her desk used to be right there when she was Kurt's intern."

"It seems like a whole different lifetime." Becca's faraway gaze disappeared with a shake of her head. "Actually, I was reading the digital edition of the student paper. Trying not to wake Elsa's ass up to explain herself right now."

Luke glanced between Becca and Brielle.

"Oh, it was your sister who did it. That's right, I forgot she told me she was a photojournalism major." Brielle's stomach sank. She'd tried to ignore the paper since Sandy had drawn her curiosity. Her hopes Luke wouldn't see it were about to be dashed. "I guess that makes sense. I wondered who could have identified me."

"What am I missing here?" Luke stilled, growing quieter.

"Elsa wrote an extremely dramatized article for the front page of the paper. About the award banquet and the 'most exciting part of the dull evening'. Her insensitive phrasing painted you as a badass avenger and Brielle as a helpless victim. It's horrible. Outrageous. And rude beyond belief." Becca squared her shoulders and stood directly in front of Brielle. "I'm so sorry. I will talk to her. She doesn't understand the impact of her actions sometimes."

Kurt strolled in from his office across the hall. "When are you going to stop cleaning up her messes? She'll only grow up when she's forced to deal with consequences on her own."

"Now is probably not the best time for this discussion." Becca crossed her arms and stared at her husband.

"I'm not criticizing you." He came up behind her and rubbed her shoulders. "I understand why you're so protective of her, you know that. But she's got to take the training wheels off sometime, even if she crashes every once in a while. One of these times it will be someone less understanding than Brielle that she offends."

"Maybe that's a good plan." Becca sighed. "I hate to put you in the middle, Brielle, but would you mind sharing with Elsa the way Luke's...uh...whatever she is, used the article as a weapon against you? Elsa has to be more careful. And objective. You are not crazy. And our presentation was *not* dull."

Brielle laughed.

Luke didn't.

"Why am I just hearing about this now?" He glared at Kurt.

"I texted you last night, but you didn't answer." The knowing smirk he leveled at his best friend held a hint of approval.

"I was busy. Plus I made a bunch of calls during the day. And I left my charger at home. My phone's dead." He scrubbed his hands over his face. "Maybe *I'll* talk to Elsa."

"It's a thought." Becca nodded. "She follows you around like a puppy. Part of me wonders if that had something to do with her less than flattering depiction of Brielle."

"It's over now." Brielle laid her fingers on his forearm when he tensed.

"I'll take care of it." He assured them all.

"Hey! You shaved." Becca changed the subject, lightly smacking Luke's bare cheek. "Thank God. I hated that goatee. It looked horrible on you. And so weird, how the drapes didn't match the curtains."

"What?" Kurt tilted his head. "Baby, that's really not how the saying goes."

"Well, yeah, but both were on his head. And still different colors." She poked Luke in the stomach. "A medical miracle."

"Gee, thanks. Way to make a guy self-conscious." He hung his head. "I thought you were supposed to help us out today, not cause more issues."

"I'll do my best." She waved for them to follow her deeper into the office. "If I don't put you to sleep with my *boring* methodologies."

"Oh, Elsa is really in trouble." Brielle giggled.

Luke clasped her hand. "I wish you'd told me about the article. And Sandy. If I still had her number, I'd call her and let her know we're no longer on each other's Christmas card lists. Forget just not speaking or seeing each other anymore, this is over the line. I won't stand for people hurting you."

"And that's why I didn't see any reason to share." She rested her head on his upper arm as they headed into Becca's room. "I already knew you'd protect me. I didn't need you to prove it or get upset. And I was hoping it would just go away without causing you too much drama."

"I'm starting to dislike that word." He stared at her. "*You* didn't do anything. Wexford did. Elsa did. Sandy did. Not you."

She nodded.

"Good." He led her to a seating area.

They shared the plush leather couch. "Wow, this is a bit different from Kurt's office. I love all the colors."

Light poured in from giant windows. A small yet tidy desk in antique white was surrounded by purple walls and tasteful modern art in complementary hues. Becca took the seat beside where Brielle and Luke settled in. Kurt dragged the desk chair beside his wife and sat, straight, not resting against the ergonomic mesh backing.

"Thanks." Becca smiled as she looked around. "I really feel at home here."

"I can't believe you used to wear black every day and never let your hair down." Luke clicked his tongue against the roof of his mouth. "I didn't believe Kurt all those times he swore there was a vibrant, sensual woman lurking in there. Of course, he's never wrong, is he, that asshole?"

"I hid it well." Becca shrugged. "Sometimes it's hard to escape the patterns that once were survival tools."

Brielle leaned forward. "You? You were like me?"

"In some ways, yes." Becca nodded. "I repressed a lot of myself in order to reach my goals. I had a pretty backward childhood, where I assumed the parent role for both my mother and my sister. I can see that now. I understand where you're coming from. Though to be honest, you suffered a lot more outright abuse than I did. And still my upbringing impacted every facet of my life. So much so that I didn't realize the extent until Kurt helped me unravel it all."

They reached out at the same time, finding each other without looking.

"So you think it's possible that I could learn to control my fears?" Brielle hadn't realized how much she'd worried that Becca might contradict Luke's optimism.

"I'm certain of it." She nodded. "I'm not saying that it will be easy, or that it will be quick, but there are a lot of things for us to work on. I don't have the answers any more than you do. We'll find what's effective for you. Together. I know it's unorthodox, this tangle of friendships between the four of us, but I think it could be a benefit. If you disagree at any time, if the intimacy is hurting rather than helping you share, just say so and we'll find someone well qualified to replace us."

"I like my team of specialists." Brielle smiled, squeezing Luke's hand. "I can't imagine going through this with a stranger. I appreciate all your help. I hope you know that."

Kurt smiled at her. "I suggested to Becca this morning that your eagerness could work in your favor. Normally, we'd see a patient like you once a week or once every other week for an hour, depending on a variety of factors. Not the least important is their endurance. The things we discuss will be draining. It's not easy to examine everything you have taken for granted for so long. Your mind takes shortcuts to be able to process the overwhelming amount of information we sort through each day. When you start inspecting those foundations, you're expending energy on even the simplest things."

"I slept more this week than in the past month, I think." As if on cue, she yawned. "And still I'm tired."

"That could also have something to do with...us." Luke rubbed her back. "I should have let you rest more last night."

"I'd rather be sleepy." She grinned. "I'll be okay."

"That's the attitude I'm talking about." Kurt picked up where he'd left off. "I think you might respond better to intense therapy, rather than stretching things out. Tell me if I'm off base, but I think you're the kind of person who goes on attack. You've made up your mind to kick this thing so now you want to act. It would put you on edge to wait a week to discuss what we do today again, wouldn't it?"

"I hadn't thought about it." She considered, then nodded. "Yes. You're right. Damn, Luke, I see what you mean about him."

Becca put her head in her hands. "Don't encourage his ego, please. However, I do agree. I believe you'd naturally keep working on your own, unguided, and I'd rather be there to assist you along the way.

"So how do you feel about a traditional session from now until lunchtime? We have some basics to discuss, especially regarding your father, your ex and their treatment of you.

"After that, I'd like to start filling your toolbox with different techniques for navigating tricky situations. Even the best outcome won't eliminate those momentary panics or prevent you from encountering triggers out in the everyday world. So we can try anchoring. Luke told us he mentioned it to you. We'll attempt putting you in a trance and tying your memories to a gesture for you to use in times of high stress. I have some other tricks up my sleeve to teach you too.

"Then we can take a break, go out to dinner, enjoy the evening as two couples who are friends, not doctors and patients. Relax a bit. If you're up for it afterward, I'd like to use the Dream Machine on you tonight."

She'd known it was coming, but Brielle still swallowed hard. "After what I saw at the banquet, I'm a little nervous. Would I have to sleep here? Alone?"

"The tool works best without outside influence," Kurt responded. "Isolating stimuli will help us get a good read without distortion."

"He's saying yes," Becca translated. "During the original research gathering, Kurt slept with me. I was spoiled. But he was really stacking the deck in his favor because he knew my underlying desires centered around him, after that fucker Wexford snuck in here and used the machine on me without my consent."

"He did?" Brielle shuddered. "I'm surprised Kurt didn't kill him."

"I might have." A coldness settled over the doctor. "Luke stopped me. I was tempted to let him do the trick Wednesday night, but I figured I should return the favor and keep him out of jail. You're welcome."

She patted Luke's thigh when he tensed.

"In your case, we don't have a baseline yet." Becca kept them on track. "I think it's best if you sleep alone tonight. Now, with that said, we'll all be here. Just monitoring from the laboratory, not sharing the room or the bed with you. If something goes wrong, we'll be right there. Don't worry about that."

Brielle looked to Luke, questions swirling in her mind. "Will you all see what I dream about?"

"Yes." Becca hesitated. "Unless you aren't comfortable with that. But I frankly feel like having friends in the know, people who can and will help, is in your best interest."

"You could just tell me what you're worried about." Luke took her hand and rubbed his thumb over her knuckles. "It would save a step."

"I-I can't." Brielle clamped her eyes against the image of Brad dragging her by the hair. It was too terrifying to say aloud. Too embarrassing to admit she'd let him do that to her. And after last night, Luke already knew she liked it. She'd asked for it. How would he feel once he realized just how fucked up she was?

"Don't force her, Luke." Becca stopped him with a palm up. "I know you want to take away her pain, but this isn't the way. Think of her as any other patient."

"He can't, baby." Kurt came to his friend's defense. "That's why we're going to help him. So he doesn't make some of the mistakes I did. It's impossible to separate logic and emotion when you're dealing with someone you love."

The *L* word shocked Brielle. Certainly he meant *care about.*

Luke didn't correct his friend.

"This isn't going to be easy," Becca said again. "But we're in it together, the four of us. I think those are pretty good odds."

Brielle took a deep breath. "Okay then, let's dive right in. What do you want me to talk about first?"

Chapter Fifteen

The next several hours seemed both endless and instant.

By the time they broke to order Chinese food, Brielle had recounted most of the garbage she'd piled on Luke the first day they'd met. Had it really only been a week ago?

Becca had listened intently, while taking notes. On occasion, she'd asked questions for clarification or offered reassurance. Kurt had let his wife take the lead, sitting back, steepling his fingers over his svelte stomach and observing with a focus that left Brielle a tiny bit unsettled.

This retelling was easier for her. Maybe because she'd rehashed it all so recently, maybe because she knew the three people in the room and had come to think of them as friends. Most likely, because of the man who'd clenched her hand as she recounted life at home, her attempts to break free and how she'd hidden at Brad's house for years.

That part got to her a little. Okay, kind of a lot.

Luke's knee bounced as she choked up over how much of her life she'd wasted. If she'd come to her senses sooner, maybe things never would have gotten so out of hand. And that's where Becca had stopped her, telling her that she'd managed the best she could under the circumstances. But had she really?

Looking back had no value. Only the future could be changed. And she was committed to doing just that. So much that she'd slipped easily into the hypnosis Becca put her under. Brielle had never really believed in that phenomenon, but the quiet monotone the young psychologist had used had quickly put her mind to rest. If that counted as a trance, she'd been there.

Brielle had been aware of her surroundings, including Luke's slow and deep breathing next to her. Still, she'd felt distant and open to absorbing the suggestions Becca planted in her unguarded mind. They'd settled on putting her hand over her heart as the trigger for the anchored memories.

Luke's smile, his mastery at bringing her pleasure, the way they could laugh together even in the face of adversity, the certainty he would rescue her if another Dr. Wexford ever crossed her path—all of those things combined to become her shield from negativity and fear. Each of the three doctors had cautioned her about tying her happiness to external sources, like, say, a man she'd only known a sum total of one day for each year she'd spent in Brad's clutches. Or one day for more than every two years she'd lived in her closet.

Yet, the bond growing between them, and the feelings it evoked were strong enough to counteract decades of misery.

Afterward, they'd spent a few hours discussing other techniques for managing anxiety and desensitization to her phobia triggers. At one point, she'd even managed to open the door to Becca's closet and step across the threshold with the door open. She'd stood there for a solid thirty seconds before memories encroached on the present.

The moment her hand flew to her heart, blasting the terror clawing at her with rays of sunshine and hope, Luke had dragged her out into the light and his warm, welcoming arms. He'd held her tight, running his hands up and down her back before burying his fingers in her hair and kissing all her lingering memories into oblivion.

They'd gotten a bit carried away until Kurt cleared his throat and declared it was time for dinner. Luke hadn't bothered to listen, continuing to make out with her until the last of her tremors had morphed into bonelessness.

Hours later, that lassitude had only grown. After strolling past several crowded restaurants that set her on edge, given the freshness of her anxiety from the day's sessions, they had settled on one of Becca's favorites. It quickly became Brielle's too. A large, open deck granted them views of downtown and excellent people watching.

Conversation had flowed effortlessly about music, books, movies, school, jobs, mutual friends and aspirations. Brielle had admitted she'd like to take cooking classes someday when she could afford the tuition and the time to attend.

"If those cookies you made yesterday are any indication, I think you'll do really well in the culinary arena." Kurt patted his stomach. "I'm stuffed, but I think dessert might be in order now that you've got me thinking about those sweet treats."

Luke handed her the menu. "Anything that catches your eye?"

She considered trying the lemon raspberry cheesecake. "I would only be able to handle a few bites. I don't want to waste it."

"Split it with me then?" He scooted closer on the bench seat. "I'll return the favor for you feeding me cookies in bed last night."

"So I guess there's no hope there might be some left?" Kurt scratched his chest with his middle finger in a not-so-subtle message to his best friend. "Sharing is caring, you know."

"He probably has a point." She rested her chin on her fist, peering between Becca, Kurt and Luke.

"Hey. Whose side are you on, Cookie?" Luke peered at her.

"Well, I mean, he has shared his *wife* with you." Brielle laughed at the alarm on the men's faces. As if she would be upset about something they did before they'd met her. It might have been awkward, butting in the middle of their history, but it wasn't. Not after all she'd revealed to them today.

Besides, they accepted her as part of Luke. Her admission to their club was free when she accompanied him. Would it still be if their relationship soured? Could she measure up to those special times the trio had shared? Luke gave her every indication she did. Maybe even exceeded them, though the magnitude of that idea blew her mind.

Afraid to bank on continuing to satisfy him, she reserved her judgment for after they'd gotten to the heart of her issues. What would he say when he knew about the darkness at her core?

"I'm definitely going to need dessert, and maybe another glass of wine, if we're going to talk about this. Friend to friend. No doctors at this table." Becca flagged down their waiter and placed her order. Luke requested a slice of cheesecake.

"Shouldn't we ask for two forks?" she suggested.

"Nah." Luke waved her off. "I'd rather you eat from mine."

His decadence made her groan. "Remember, you have to sleep alone tonight too, buddy."

"Don't remind me." He winked at her. "Ever get it on in the back of a tiny sports car before? Maybe they won't notice."

"I'm pretty sure there isn't room for me to tie my shoe in that thing. You'd have to be a contortionist to give a blow job in there."

His eyes widened. "We could try."

"It's possible." Becca flicked an imaginary piece of lint from her sleeve.

Brielle laughed. Genuine curiosity got the best of her. If they were willing to talk... "I've never done anything very adventurous in the bedroom. Well, not before this week anyway. So, what was it like to be with two guys?"

Both Luke and Kurt leaned in to catch her answer.

"I'm not going to lie. It was phenomenal." Becca looked pretty smug as she explained. "I mean, if it were two random guys, I'm sure it could be fun. But when it was the man of my dreams and a man we both respect and trust...well, that's a recipe you can't screw up. They always made me feel precious. I think what I adored the most about those times was how safe I felt and how beloved. I could lie back, knowing they would attend to everything, or I could take whatever I pleased, and they would cheer me on.

"Plus it's a pretty great place to be when once just isn't

enough and there's another guy waiting to go. Sometimes they'd take turns until I spent so long coming that one orgasm led to another and another with no break in between. I was so spoiled. And I relished every minute."

Kurt tucked a strand of hair behind her ear. "We can look for someone else if you still need that, baby."

"I think I'm ruined now." She smiled. "I can't imagine anyone other than you and Luke. There's no one else I'd trust enough."

Brielle couldn't have explained what drove her to speak before considering the ramifications of the stray thought that popped into her mind. Maybe the exhaustion creeping over her after a long, draining day. Maybe the glass of excellent zinfandel she'd had with her grilled chicken. Or maybe honest desire she felt comfortable enough to express in the company of close friends. But once she put it out there, it was impossible to take back. "Maybe we can arrange a trade sometime. Two for you. Two for me."

"You wouldn't want to scratch her eyes out for touching me?" Luke sounded a little hurt by her suggestion.

"Of course I would, but maybe I could sit on my hands, or go first so that I'm too worn out to attack her or something." She blushed. "Sorry, I shouldn't have said that. It's been a hell of a day."

"No no." He put his arm around her shoulder. "Never be afraid to tell me what you're thinking. You just...surprised me. Again. That's all."

"Frankly, me too." Kurt scratched his chin. "But the idea has merit."

Becca laughed. "Oh really, Dr. Foster?"

Her husband was dead serious when he said, "Yeah. I wouldn't have a problem pleasing her if it meant you get what you need in exchange."

The stiffness of Luke's body faded and he leaned forward. "Sorry, Brielle. I guess I forget you haven't done all the wild things I have. If I were in your position, I'd be curious too. Just because we met at different stages of our lives, doesn't mean I don't want you to experience everything you wonder about. I just hope that in the end, you're still satisfied with me. I've done it all, and I'm certain. You're what I want."

"It was just a thought." She took his hand and squeezed. "Everything between us is so new. I think I'm just off balance. My whole life is different today than it was a week ago. It's making me reconsider everything I thought I knew."

Before he could respond, the waiter returned with their indulgences. If only all cravings were so easy to satisfy, life might be less complex.

"I'll give you anything you need." Luke plucked the fork from the table, scooped up a bite of cheesecake drizzled with chocolate and held it out to her.

"Thank you." She accepted his offering, cleaning the tines with little licks. "Mmm."

"Oh yeah, this might not be a bad idea." Kurt grinned at his wife.

"Not to be the Debbie Downer, but I think there are some other things to put in order before Brielle starts getting fancy. It worries me a little that she and Luke are already… Well…" Becca waved her napkin in their direction.

"The timing was not ideal," Luke agreed. "But what in life is? I'm just glad we found each other. I think it was meant to be. She came to me for help. We'll do this together. Both of you too. We're all in it now."

Their commitment and concern for her in all its different forms touched Brielle. She dabbed at the corner of her eyes with the quality linen napkin. When had she ever eaten dinner somewhere that didn't have paper? And now, twice in one week.

She opened her mouth. Then closed it again.

Finally, she realized they were all looking at her. Smiling.

"All I can say is thank you. It's not nearly enough, but it's all I can give." She held each of their gazes for a few seconds. "Really. Thank you."

Kurt looked to Luke. "I can see why you fell hard. You are so screwed. I can't wait to watch you make a fool of yourself. Just like I did."

Becca snapped her napkin at her husband, laughing. "Behave yourself."

"Make me." He dipped his finger in the raspberry sauce garnishing her plate then stole a taste.

"Don't make me take you back to the laboratory." She blushed. "Then again, I think you might have liked it when I bossed you around."

"I think I did too. Maybe we'll have to try that again sometime." Kurt's eyebrows rose as he looked to Luke. "Will you stand backup to make sure she lets me loose this time? Unless you just want to check out my naked, trussed body again. I am pretty sexy, or so I've been told."

"Holy shit, Becca." Luke covered his eyes. "You've created a monster. I'm never going to get that image out of my brain."

"Maybe I can help." Brielle came to the rescue. She leaned over and whispered, "Becca and I could put you in his shoes instead. I'm pretty sure the two of us could replace your memories with something far hotter. Only fair if we're each going to have both of you guys someday."

"Ohhh-kay." Luke took an enormous bite of their dessert then fed her one twice as large as the first. "Everyone hurry this course along. We might need a little private time before setting up the Dream Machine."

"Sounds like a plan." Kurt stared at his wife.

Becca gobbled her treat.

Brielle slid their plate toward Luke. She'd rather have what he was serving any day.

Chapter Sixteen

Luke gritted his teeth from his post in Kurt's laboratory. He peered through the newly installed one-way mirror into the tiny bedroom, hardly worthy of a freshman dorm. Without windows, it couldn't be comfortable for Brielle.

"Do we have to leave her in there alone?" He glanced to Kurt, who was busy adjusting knobs and dials on the latest, more sophisticated version of the Dream Machine.

"Is it you or her who's having the hard time with this?" Kurt stopped what he was doing and crossed the tile floor so they stood shoulder to shoulder.

On the bed—which took up the majority of the space in what had been Kurt's study while he completed his research, often working late nights—Brielle shifted, trying to get comfortable. Becca perched on the edge of the mattress, attaching diodes that would measure her patient's vital signs.

"Personally," Kurt said as he elbowed Luke in the ribs, "I think it's hot. My wife, your girlfriend, in bed together..."

"You would, pervert." He grunted. "Probably reminds you of getting it on with Becca for the first time during the original Dream Machine experiments."

They observed Kurt's new wife placing the sticky radio transmitters on the back of Brielle's neck, on her upper chest and at her wrist. When she drew a harness from the hermetically sealed bin beside the bed, Brielle's eyes grew wide.

"Yeah, that's the doozy." Kurt adjusted his junk. "Becca's doing a great job of coaching Brielle through this. It makes me hard to see how fucking great she is at working with patients."

"As long as you're not sporting that wood thinking of my girlfriend wearing your damn vaginal probe." Luke grimaced.

"It's bad enough she's already considered letting you jump her bones."

"That bothered you." His best friend didn't ask. He also didn't look Luke in the eye.

"At first. Yeah." Luke pressed his hand to the glass, wishing he could touch Brielle. Talk to her. In private. "I mean, it's different with her, Kurt. I'm playing for keeps."

"No kidding." The smile that crept over the mad sex-scientist's face was genuine. "You love her already."

"Look at you, acting like an expert. Jesus. A little over a year ago, you didn't believe such a thing even existed." Luke hoped to deflect Kurt's too-accurate intuition.

"Even a genius can be wrong occasionally." A shrug accompanied his shit-eating grin. Still, he never once took his stare off his wife. "I'm not trying to discourage you. If it's the real thing, and you damn well know it when you feel it, then you're a hell of a lot smarter than me for admitting it right away. Protect it. Her. So nothing can take this shot at happiness away from you. You deserve it, Luke. More than I ever did."

"Uh, wow. That's a lot to digest." Luke clapped his hand on Kurt's shoulder.

"I have to admit. She's one of the bravest women I've ever met. Look at that." He pointed.

As if Luke had blinked.

On the opposite side of the damned glass, Brielle shimmied into the leather loops that would trap the vaginal probe inside her while data about her dreams, maybe her fantasies, was collected overnight. She managed to pull it beneath her loose nightgown, supplied by the Dream Lab, without showing too much skin.

Too bad.

As though she could sense his thoughts, she turned, lifted the hem and flashed him her bare ass.

"Whoa," Kurt murmured his appreciation. "Nice tush."

"About that..." Luke gulped, even as Becca laughed and clapped in the other room. "If that's what she really wants, and Becca's okay with it, I won't say no."

"There's a world of difference between your permission and actually enjoying the show." Kurt shook his head. "No. I won't do it under those circumstances. It's asking to fuck up some major feelings. If you get to a place where *you* want it too. Come talk to me."

"Bastard." And he was right too.

Neon green lines began to track across the screens that littered the data collection booth. Kurt rushed over to take notes. He hummed as he ticked off each sample of biometric data. "Your girl is holding up, Luke. She's calm. Heart rate and blood pressure are stable. Her breathing is in the upper-normal range. And her pussy is hot as hell. Tight too."

"Quit that." Luke punched Kurt in the biceps when he smirked.

"Hey, just the facts." He held his clipboard in front of him to ward off future attacks.

Becca rose from the bed, dimming the lights. She knew better than to douse the space in total blackness. She waved to Brielle, who returned the gesture then angled her face toward the mirror and blew Luke a kiss as if she could sense exactly where he stood.

"Goodnight, Cookie. Sweet dreams." He pulled up a chair and tried to get comfortable. It was going to be a long night.

A scream pierced the glass-and-concrete wall, startling Luke from sleep.

He'd nodded off with his cheek pressed to the one-way mirror, smooshing his face into a wrinkled mess he was sure Kurt had snapped a photo of with his smartphone. He'd probably see it on Facebook later with an obnoxious caption all the doctors in the psych department could chime in on. He laughed, not minding taking one for the team.

He blinked, trying to generate some moisture in his dry eyes. After staring at Brielle sleep for hours, he must have eventually caved to exhaustion.

Another scream had him bolting to his feet, realizing what had woken him. “Brielle!”

Becca was right behind him.

“Her readings are shooting off the chart.” Kurt shouted from his station in the laboratory. “Abort the collection phase. Wake her up, Luke.”

As if he planned to let her suffer.

“Careful! She’s going to fight you.” His friend filled him in as he crossed the handful of steps to Brielle. “I’m watching her dream. She’s trying to escape a guy before he stuffs her in a closet. Hurry, Luke. Get her out of there. Becca, hang back.”

Brielle thrashed, crashing through the paralysis usually associated with REM sleep. “No. Don’t put me in there. Don’t leave me.”

Luke’s heart broke as he tried to rouse her from the nightmare of her father’s house.

“I take it back. I didn’t mean it. No! Don’t put me in there. Please. No.” She clawed at him as he shook her, trying to bundle her into his arms. Then she went limp before punching and kicking the air. “Let me out. Don’t leave me like this! Brad!”

Brad? What the fuck? It was her father she’d escaped by running into the closet, only being trapped at the end, after he’d been shot by some druggie or bookie. Not the man who’d kept Brielle as some wounded pet he could take advantage of whenever he felt like it. Right?

His stomach fell through the floor as he realized she hadn’t divulged all of her past trauma. What else hadn’t she told him about?

“Cookie, it’s me. Luke.” Worried she might injure herself, he pinned her arms to her side despite the cries emitting from her when he restrained her completely. “You’re safe. I’ve got you.

Come back to me, Brielle. Please. Wake up."

Caught in the horror, she didn't respond.

"Try something else!" Kurt shouted from the next room. "It's bad. God, it's bad."

Unsure of what to resort to when shaking her and calling to her didn't work, he followed his instincts. Softly, he began to sing the first song that came to mind, "I Got You Babe".

Cher's parts popped out of him in falsetto.

If Brielle had been awake, she would have cracked up with him.

Music and laughter were two things she'd never had in her life. Not during the dark period she lay trapped in now. *Please don't let me be wrong about this.* She was suffering every second he wasted.

If his approach bombed, Becca and Kurt would consider him certifiable instead of certified.

By the time he got to the second verse, she'd settled enough for Becca to approach cautiously. No women had occupied Brielle's world since her mother died.

"Talk to her," he whispered just before he kicked into the refrain.

"She can hear you," Kurt called in a more reasonable tone from the other room. "It's working."

On the next go-around, he substituted *Cookie* for *Babe.*

A gasp big enough to suck all the air from the room inflated Brielle's chest. She bolted upright, tearing from his hold and scrambling across the mattress until her back slammed into the wall. Her chest rose and fell at an alarming rate.

Luke didn't abandon the song, though he nearly choked on the lyrics and the misery radiating from her as if it leaked from every pore.

"It's okay, Brielle." Becca layered on her voice. "You're all right. We've got you. Luke is right here. Can you hear him singing to you? Listen to him."

Brielle's lids fluttered open. Her stare locked on him

immediately. "Luke?"

"Hi." He kept humming as he inched closer to her, crawling onto the mattress. When she didn't flinch, he reached for her. The instant his fingertips grazed her shoulder she launched herself into his arms. "I've got you."

"I've got you, Cookie." A hiccup interrupted the line when she parroted the song back to him. "What made you pick that?"

"It worked for Phil Connors in *Ground Hog Day.*" He shrugged.

Brielle blinked up at him several times then burst into a fit of blended sobs and giggles.

"Oh, damn." He rocked her against his chest. "Please tell me this isn't what you're living through every night. All our talks today triggered some bad memories, right?"

No affirmation came from her. Instead, she burrowed closer and began to tremble.

"No more." Cradling her in his arms, he swayed to the melody still ringing in his mind. "I've got you and I'm not letting go. Not tonight. Not ever."

Kurt approached slowly. "I think you might need to, just for a little while. You and Becca should watch the recordings. It was my turn to monitor her. The upgrades to the Dream Machine translate the waves with a delay of just a couple minutes. I saw it all as it happened."

"And you didn't wake us sooner? You fucker." Luke might have thrown a punch if he hadn't had such precious cargo. "You let her suffer."

"We needed answers—fast, thorough, accurate. That's the point of the Dream Machine. It shaves months, or even years, off treatment times. Now we have critical information. One more replay was better than sending her home to live it over and over. Every night. Just like this, except alone." He frowned. "Brielle, you left out some pretty important parts of your story earlier today. We can't help you if you don't share everything."

"I couldn't." She clutched Luke's back. "I'm sorry."

"It's too much for her, Kurt." Becca shook her head, taking Luke's side. "There's no rush. We're pushing her too hard."

"You haven't seen it. You don't understand." Kurt began to pry Luke from Brielle.

"Don't leave me," she cried. "Please."

"Take your hands off of us, right now," Luke growled at Kurt.

The other man relented, finally kneeling on the floor beside them so he could speak to Brielle directly. "You've come this far. Don't falter at the last step. Your fears are unfounded. I swear to you, I know Luke better than he knows himself, I think. He's not going to run. He'll give you what you need. Your ex fucked this all up. He didn't understand like we do. Or he didn't care to help you."

"What are you talking about?" Luke squinted at his best friend.

"Go watch for yourself." He jerked his chin toward the other room. "I'll stay here with your Cookie. Take Becca. Go."

"Is that okay with you, Brielle?" She still cowered in his hold. He hated seeing her so afraid. Maybe Kurt was right again. If they could stop this here and now, they should.

"This is why you asked us to help, Luke." Becca patted his knee. "Trust Kurt. He's neutral in this. Objective. You know he has your best interests at heart too. Come on, let's watch the dream sequence."

"Brielle?" Trying to meet her gaze was impossible when she stared at the floor.

"I'm afraid, Luke," she confessed.

"I know." He hugged her again.

"Anyone reasonable would have been scared of that slime bucket." Kurt peeled one of her hands from Luke's back. "That's a completely normal response. If you hadn't been frightened, that would have concerned me."

Becca met her husband's stare. "I'm going. Luke, are you with me?"

"Brielle?" he asked again.

"It will change how you see me." She sniffled. "I don't want to lose you."

"If he cut out because of that, he wouldn't be worth keeping," Kurt interrupted before Luke could find the right words. "You deserve someone who loves all of you."

A challenge like that couldn't go untaken. Luke pulled away a bit to kiss her forehead. "I want to see, Brielle. To show you it doesn't matter to me. *You* matter, and I l-like you the way you are."

Kurt lifted a brow at his stumble.

This wasn't the time to drop another bomb on her.

"I'll be right back, Brielle," he promised. "Do you want Kurt to hold you while I'm gone?"

"Is that a trick question?" she asked.

"Hell no." Luke frowned. "I'm not trying to trap you. I only want you to be as comfortable as possible."

"Do you mind?" She peeked at Kurt over her shoulder.

"Hanging on to a pretty lady?" He smiled. "Never could get tired of that."

Kurt slid onto the mattress, propping his shoulders on the wall. He held his hands out and Luke lifted Brielle, passing her to his best friend. She instantly curled against him, resting her head on his shoulder.

The fire burning in his eyes had to have warmed the chill her nightmares put in her heart.

"There you go, Cookie." Luke stroked her hair a few times, all the way to where it dangled above the small of her back. "I'll be quick."

He glanced at her when he was a few steps away, then strode back to kiss her cheek before steeling himself to watch whatever it was that disturbed her so greatly.

Night after night.

"You're doing great, Brielle." Becca added her reassurance

before leaving the room. "Will it bother you if I close the door?"

"Not at all." She was surprised to find it was true. Her phobia usually peaked after a particularly vivid nightmare. Maybe it was the change of scenery or being in such great company, but something was different about tonight.

As soon as the door shut, Kurt took advantage of their alone time.

"Here, let's take these off." He peeled the transmitters from her neck, chest and wrist then averted his gaze when she shimmied out of his devious contraption and placed it in the bin beside the bed.

"There, better?"

She nodded.

"Get ready. When Luke comes back in this room, he's going to be furious." He advised her. "Not at you, Brielle. Don't ever get those things confused, okay? He's going to be pissed off *for* you. Big difference."

"Did I bring that on myself?" She hated that she had to ask. Talking to the most practical person of the bunch helped, though. He wouldn't bullshit her or spare her feelings.

"Of course not, and I amend my earlier estimate of how much Luke stands to gain tonight." He wrapped his hand around her wrist and held on. "You're meant for each other. I bet you he doesn't even recognize right away that part of your disturbance from the dream is the curiosity you expressed about bondage, and what effect that might have had on Brad's treatment of you. To Luke, desires like those come standard."

"And you?" She figured, what the hell, she didn't need to be the only one with secrets on display. "Becca?"

"We play that way too." He studied her as if hunting for signs of confusion or disgust. It would be better to know that now, before Luke returned, she assumed. "Frankly, there's a reason you picked the closet as your safe place, before your dad's death stole that comfort from you. Your ex used that terror to mold you into what he wanted. A slave. That isn't what BDSM is about. Not in the least.

"A fundamental part of you still craves that experience. My gut says some of the desire is because you really need someone you can trust that completely, especially after a lifetime of disappointment in the people who should have protected you. Those deficits shaped you into the person I've gotten to know. Part of it is more basic. It's in your nature. Your instinct has always been to seek comfort through focusing internally. Bondage and, to a greater extent, sadism facilitates that process for a lot of people. Becca is like that. It's not my story to share. Ask her. She'll tell you why she loves to be tied down more than most anything else we do together."

"Oh. O-okay," she stuttered, wondering to what extent her new friends dabbled in the forbidden desires she'd tried desperately to erase from her list of cravings. Unsuccessfully.

Why hadn't she had someone like him or Luke to help her understand instead of Brad's manipulative attacks?

An enormous *bang* rattled the wall that separated them from the laboratory. A *clatter* of what sounded like metal instruments bouncing off the tile floor followed. The noise had Brielle jumping in Kurt's hold.

"I hope that wasn't anything irreplaceable." He shook his head. "Our boy Luke hardly ever loses his temper. But when he does...look out. It'll blow over quick, though. Just remember, he's not mad at you. And he would *never* hurt you. I wouldn't have sent my wife in there with him if I had any doubt about that. He's not like the men you've known before."

"He's not mad at me." Maybe if she repeated it a few hundred times, she might believe it.

The door between the two rooms flew open, banging into the wall. Becca cried out in the background. "Calm down, Luke. She's already pumped full of adrenaline. Don't scare her again."

His chest heaved as he looked directly into her eyes. He didn't shout, or even raise his voice. The deadly cold chilled her more than if he had. "Where is that motherfucker? I want him in jail. Or dead."

"I have no idea." She shrugged. "I'm sorry I fibbed to you

about him kicking me out. I just wasn't ready… After that night, when he trapped me in the closet, I knew we'd crossed a line. When I finally got up the nerve to leave it was too late for anything like calling the police. I didn't want to give him a chance to change my mind or twist things around…or worse. I waited until he was out with his new girlfriend, the one he said he started cheating on me with when he realized how fucked up I really am. You know, for wanting to be restrained. I packed my suitcase with some clothes and a couple books and I took off.

"I never looked back. At least not for a few months. And when I finally decided the shelter was right, I should report what had happened—what if he does the same, or worse, to the new girl—our house was empty. I think he must have moved in with her. I know he was behind on bills. He abandoned the place, just like my dad."

"Let it go, Luke." Kurt held her tighter when his friend staggered near. "Only one of those two people has any place in your future. Do right by her. She's who's important."

"He hurt you." All the golden warmth drained from his face, leaving his tan skin a ghastly shade of gray. "I saw what he did. How he manhandled you. How you injured yourself trying to escape. You broke your hand."

"I didn't go to the doctor. It might have been nothing." She tried not to flex the knuckles that still ached when she lifted something heavy.

The stormy blue of his eyes misted over. "And you're wearing bruises again tonight. I should have protected you better. We have to find him before he finds you."

She shivered. "I assumed he was out of my life."

"He is," Kurt cut in, stopping Luke from frightening her with the what-ifs of his overprotective nature. He spit out the rest of his words. "And you aren't responsible for Wexford. If anyone should take blame for him, it's me. I left the door unlocked the night he broke into the lab. I started it all."

"And if you hadn't, none of us would be standing here today." Becca maintained her professionalism best of all three of the doctors. "This is a difficult case. We're all involved, no matter how much we think we're not. Everyone's emotions are in play. I think we should call it a night. We can regroup in the morning to discuss the dream sequences and what our next steps will be. I think this has been a huge unlock for Brielle. It will only get easier from here."

Becca stepped behind Luke. She ran her hands down his arms and unfisted his hands, finger by finger. "She needs you to love her, not fight her."

Maybe he wasn't interested. Did some of his anger stem from disappointment? Brielle might not be what he was looking for. He said himself he wasn't interested in his old pursuits these days. This could be a part of his life he was hoping to leave behind. And here she was, bringing it into play. Because Kurt was right. It was time to admit some of these yearnings she had for bondage—he'd called it—were ingrained.

If Luke couldn't help her, she'd find someone who could. No matter how badly that hurt. She'd spent enough time in the shadows, hiding.

Damn Becca. A perceptive woman, and maybe one who'd shared Brielle's concerns at some point, it was as if she'd read Brielle's mind like an open book. "Dig beneath the rage, Luke. Tell her what the rest of her dream did to you. She needs to hear that you're turned on by it."

"What sick fuck would get hot looking at any part of that nightmare?" His question was tormented.

"Obviously, you." Becca shifted her hands lower and toward the center of his body. When she cupped his crotch, his breath caught. "And her. I saw the readings from the probe, Brielle. I can understand how conflicted you must be when you want something similar and yet a galaxy away from what your ex did to you. You need someone to show you the difference between safe, sane and consensual and...that."

She had everyone's attention now.

"I stand by what I said." Becca took her hands from Luke and strode a few feet deeper into the space until she could look at each one of them in turn. "We're done for tonight. There's a lot to digest. But in the morning, I'd like to suggest a demonstration."

Kurt's whole body went rigid beneath Brielle. Including his cock. She shifted away, a little embarrassed.

"Sorry, honey." He chuckled. "I think I see where my wife is going with this. She's pure mastermind. Nothing makes me hornier than a smart woman."

Luke staggered to the bed and collapsed on the other end. He held out his arms to her. "Come here, Cookie. If you want to."

Brielle didn't hesitate a single second. She kissed Kurt's cheek, whispered, "Thank you," then launched herself at Luke.

He caught her easily, bundling her to his chest. "I'm so sorry you had to go through any of that, never mind all of it."

"I'm just glad I have you on my side now." She glanced away from his eyes to Becca and Kurt. "All of you."

Becca nodded. "You do. And that's why I'm going to propose something outrageous."

Brielle held her breath.

"I want you and Luke to watch Kurt and me together." If she blushed a tiny bit, no one called her on it.

Kurt stalked to his wife, his entire bearing different in an instant. He stood straighter, taller. When he lifted her chin up, he demanded her attention. She gladly gave it. "You'd like to have a formal session? In my laboratory? With your patient observing?"

"Yes, Doctor." The dynamic between them had completely transformed.

Brielle's jaw hung open when Becca went to her knees, bowed her head and folded her arms behind her back. "Will you dominate me tomorrow, first thing?"

"Maybe all day if you're lucky." Kurt nudged her jaw until she peered into his eyes. "I love you, Becca. For being willing to help, however you can. Even if it's deeply personal and makes you vulnerable. A year ago you wouldn't have been able to expose yourself like this. I'm proud of you."

"Thank you, Doctor." She nuzzled Kurt's hand. "It's all because of you. You've earned my trust. Just like Luke will with Brielle."

Kurt shocked them all when he joined his wife on his knees on the floor of the room where it had all begun. "You're everything to me, Becca."

Brielle leaned forward when the two doctors kissed. She caught hints of tongue mixed in with the tender locking of their lips. When Becca tried to tug her husband closer, he captured her wrists, broke their exchange and *tsked*. "Don't get carried away, baby. It's only a couple hours until dawn."

"You plan to get up early, right?" Becca looked to Luke and Brielle with wide eyes.

"It's your call." Luke chuckled at her earnest entreaty. "How does eight sound?"

"A lifetime away." She groaned as she and Kurt climbed to their feet, hands still linked. "I think we'd better leave you two to rest up. There'll be no more Dream Machine tonight. Can you sleep here? The couch in Kurt's office is plenty big enough for us both. I mean, not that I would know."

Kurt smacked his wife on the ass. "Liars get spanked, don't they?"

"Promise?" A grin developed at the edges of her smile and worked its way inward. "My husband has a small penis. He never pleases me in bed…"

"Oh, you're in trouble now." Kurt dragged her toward the door.

Their playful interaction was night-and-day different from how Brad had treated Brielle. Yes, she would love to watch them have sex. Even if it made her a freak.

"If you need us, we'll be right down the hall." Becca looked over her shoulder before crossing the threshold.

"I'll be fine, thanks." Brielle spoke to Becca, but stared into

Luke's eyes. Compassion emanated from them.

"I'll make sure of it." He hugged her again, chafing warmth into her cool skin. "Can you lie down and close your eyes? Or is it like a hangover when you wake up from a dream like that?"

"Usually I can't go to sleep again right away." She slid beneath the covers when he pulled them back.

Luke tucked in beside her, gathering her to his chest. "I don't know how you survived that so long. I swear that's not how things are supposed to be. We'll show you what it can be like. If you want, you and I could try it sometime."

"It's not weird that I still think about those things, even after...everything?" Luke's heart skipped a beat beneath her cheek.

"No." His hands roamed over her back and into her hair, massaging her scalp. "Not at all. How much pleasure did it bring you last night when I held your waist?"

"A lot." She groaned, rubbing against him involuntarily.

"That's all that counts. If it makes you feel good, do more of it. If it doesn't, do less. Or tell me to." Though his erection pressed into her thigh, he didn't attempt to coax her into relieving that need.

Brielle reached for him. He took her hand and wove their fingers together. "I don't think I can right now, Cookie."

"You're really hard," she whispered, thinking of the moisture pooling between her thighs as well. Something about having him hold her, safe, in the aftermath of all that awfulness, called out to her.

"It'll go away." He didn't sound so sure. "I'm still angry, Brielle. At your ex. Your father too. Fate for putting someone as innocent as you in that position. I won't touch you like this, when I'm on the verge of losing control."

His restraint, even in the face of his own discomfort, proved to her again that he was the perfect man to walk beside her on this journey. Emotions welled up inside her and she felt a glad tear roll over the bridge of her nose and drop onto his chest.

Then another and another.

Silently, she cried.

It didn't take him long to notice or smother her in affection. The sweet care he lavished on her only opened the floodgate further. She couldn't say how long she vented her misery while he protected her from the rest of the world. But by the time she finished, not a drop of moisture left within her, sleepiness had replaced panic. Hope had filled in the gaps left by the draining of all her dread.

Brielle yawned between the tiny sniffles lingering.

"Doze if you can." He sounded like he might be close to relaxing too. "It's going to be another intense day tomorrow."

"'Kay" was all she could manage.

"You're incredible, Cookie." He trailed his fingers back and forth over her shoulder then started singing softly again.

"I Got You Babe" instantly became her favorite song. She drifted off with a smile on her face and evaporating tears on her cheeks.

Chapter Seventeen

"Good morning, sleepyheads."

A light knock stirred Brielle from peaceful slumber. Awareness crept in gradually. The mixture of hardness beneath softness made her realize she had been kneading Luke's chest like a kitten for some undetermined amount of time.

"You don't have to stop," he practically purred. "I like that you're groping me even in your sleep."

Brielle shot upright and grabbed a pillow, which she used to whack him over the head.

He laughed and returned the favor.

Like a sunny morning after a storm, all their clouds had lifted.

"What the hell is going on in here?" Kurt peeked over his wife's head at the chaos ensuing. "That's not exactly the kind of mattress gymnastics I thought we might be butting in on."

Luke paused and sniffed the air. His stomach rumbled loudly. "Holy shit, is that breakfast?"

His friends each carried a tray. Becca handed one to Brielle then sat on the edge of the mattress closest to Kurt's desk when he set down a matching meal and slid out the chair there, preparing to dig in.

"Yeah." Kurt forked up a slice of bacon. "Becca figured I'd need some fuel for today's session. She knows me so well."

His wife blushed even as she rolled her eyes. "I know this is a little informal, what with us hanging around in our pajamas and all. I don't expect much about this weekend therapy to be status quo, though. I just wanted to recap yesterday and say I think you're doing terrific, Brielle."

Luke dug into a stack of pancakes, holding out a bite for

her. She gladly took the offering, closing her eyes at the unexpected flavor. "What's on top of those?"

"It's ginger syrup." Kurt hummed as he sampled some of his own. "I love this stuff. Unusual, yet twice as tasty as plain old maple syrup. Sometimes things don't have to be what you expect to be amazing, Brielle. I hope you'll see that today."

"I guess that's part of what I wanted to cover." Becca paused with her orange juice halfway to her lips. "After Luke told me about your past, and you shared the details of your father's death, I assumed I understood the basis of your claustrophobia quite well. However, last night got me thinking."

Luke drew her glare when he whispered conspiratorially to Brielle, "Uh oh, she's dangerous when she really gets going."

"It's not the fear of being unable to escape a confined space that really scares you, is it?" Becca asked.

Brielle sucked in a few deep breaths at the thought of the coat closet at the banquet. "It's not a pleasant feeling to consider being trapped."

"But you didn't have any trouble with this room last night." Becca scooted closer, abandoning her omelet. "Not even after your nightmare."

Luke paused too.

"I think what really terrifies you is a more fundamental schema." She seemed to be excited by the line of thought.

"That means a set of beliefs, Cookie," Luke interpreted for her.

"Yeah, sorry. Tell me if I'm going way out there, but maybe what terrifies you is something along the lines of... *Did I make the right decision?* The part of your nightmare that stood out to me most last night was when you fixated on Brad's accusation that you *chose* what he did to you. The same thing caught my attention in your story about running away and the man in the park who tried to molest you. You *chose* the park and it didn't work out. You *chose* the closet in your father's house. You *chose* to take the elevator to Luke's office...or not. I think you doubt your own judgment. And I can't imagine how difficult it must be to live in constant fear of yourself."

Brielle didn't realize silent tears were streaming down her face until Luke collected her into his lap. Hell, she hadn't cried as much in her whole life as she had in the past few days. She hated being so weak. And so transparent to everyone but herself.

Or maybe Becca was just really good at her job.

"That's brilliant." Kurt sounded in awe of his wife. So maybe it hadn't been so obvious to him either. "I think you're exactly right."

"Luke said the same thing, two nights ago." Brielle barely choked the words out. "He was talking about sex, about holding me down, but...I haven't been able to stop thinking about it since then."

He kissed the wet trails from her cheeks, murmuring reassurance. "I didn't see the big picture like she did. I only thought it was your claustrophobia at war with your desire for bondage. It sounds entirely plausible to me, Brielle. But you have to tell us what you feel."

"I feel like a sweater with a rip in it. Like I'm about to unravel, and I'm not sure what's underneath. It might have been ugly but it's kept me from freezing to death all this time." She plucked at the hem of the nightgown she wore, barely covering her from these three people she would love to call true friends.

"I think that's a pretty good indication that we're on the right track." Luke kissed her gently, tasting of the sharp, refreshing tang of ginger. Unexpected and delicious. "I know it's uncomfortable. Dizzying, even. But you've made so many changes in the past week, that's to be expected."

"Thanks for keeping me from falling on my face." She *thunked* her forehead onto his chest.

"Anytime." He laid his jaw on top of her head.

"So, if that's the case," Becca continued, "I think what we really need to work on, in addition to showing you BDSM practiced properly is not anything like your nightmares, is your self-confidence. You've done an amazing job of picking paths through tricky situations that would have destroyed many other people. Getting you to believe it is a long-term issue we can work on together in sessions to come."

"And for today?" Brielle hoped she knew what Becca would say.

"We stick to the plan." The psychologist winked. "I'm not giving up the chance to show off Kurt. And I honestly believe you'll find it valuable to see that what you want is not the horrible choice you've been led to believe by circumstances outside of your control. It's not a bad decision to submit if you have a knowledgeable, skilled, sensitive and trained partner. Trust what you want. Trust that you've selected the right man."

A weight about as heavy as the bus she usually rode to work lifted from her shoulders. Forcing herself to see the world through Becca's lens changed everything yet again. She nodded and pushed the rest of her cinnamon toast into the corner of the tray.

"Not eating?" Luke brushed a crumb from the corner of her mouth with the pad of his thumb. "Are you upset?"

She sucked it into her mouth, cleaning the slight stickiness from it. "Nah. More like anxious. The positive kind."

"Well then," he declared in a stern voice, "you'd better finish that. Because playing voyeur always makes me horny as hell. Don't expect to sit on the sidelines as if you're watching a movie."

"Why not?" She whipped her gaze to Kurt and Becca. "Is that okay?"

"What you choose to do, or not, is up to you." The redhead smirked. "But he's not lying. Sex as a spectator sport is one of Luke's favorite pastimes."

Kurt shifted in his seat. "Are you about done eating?"

Pancakes flew off Luke's plate at an alarming rate as he forked in the fluffy discs, followed by some eggs, bacon and the rest of her toast. When he realized they all stared at him, he shrugged. "What? I'm in a hurry. And I love breakfast in bed."

"Less talking, more chewing." Kurt wagged his finger at Luke.

Brielle added gourmet French toast to her list of epicurean experiments. Hopefully there'd be plenty of mornings he was around to sample her progress.

He wiped his hands and face, scrunched up his napkin and took the tray to the bathroom. In less than thirty seconds, he'd cleaned Becca and Kurt's dishes as well.

"What are we waiting for?" He put one hand on his hip and tapped his sexy bare toes.

All three of them cracked up.

Brielle climbed from bed and joined him near the door to the laboratory.

"Go ahead and get comfortable." Kurt waved his hand toward the other space. "We'll be with you in just a second. I want to make sure Becca is in the right frame of mind."

"Does that mean strip?" Luke draped his arm around Brielle's shoulder but looked to his friends.

"You heard the lady." Kurt shrugged. "What you do is up to you."

"Today is going to be a good day." He gave a happy sigh, patted his belly with his free hand then ushered Brielle into the adjoining space.

Luke whipped his T-shirt over his head and tossed it to the floor. They hadn't even made it the ten steps to the leather wingback chair in the corner. Brielle recognized the enormous seat from Kurt's office. There wasn't as much space as, say, a bed, but it would have to do.

Any other time, she would have waited for Luke to instruct her. Today, she was a new woman. A bold woman. And she took what she liked.

Brielle came up behind him, putting her arms around his waist. She ran her hands from his taut abs up to his chest. A breath hissed out of him when she played with the hard discs of his nipples, pinching them lightly.

"Maybe I'd better leave my shorts on." His head fell back, exposing the powerful cords of his neck. She wished she were tall enough to suck on them as she had two nights ago.

"I prefer you naked." Power flooded her as she ran her hands down his sides, loving his shiver when she scraped her nails over his toned waist. She didn't stop when her fingers encountered the drawstring of the cotton hugging him to perfection. "Besides, it seems only polite. I assume Kurt isn't going to perform on Becca with both of them fully clothed."

"Guh." Luke's hips thrust when she slipped her hands inside and found his hard-on. The motion shoved his cock through her grip. She smiled against his back when she felt how slippery he was already. Sliding her hand to the base of his erection, she cupped his balls. "You're torturing me, Cookie."

The nickname was a warning. She withdrew before she pushed him too far. God only knew how long it would be before any of them found release. All she could say for sure was that being part of their circle, trusting them to help her and care for her made her far more willing to see where things led and far less patient about getting to the destination.

When he caught his breath a bit, Luke turned in her hold. He stared into her eyes as his head lowered. "Amazing," he whispered just before he sealed his mouth over hers.

"I missed this last night," she murmured when he paused to drink in some air.

His forehead rested on hers and he chuckled. "I guess we should have given them a show first. I'm dying now. There's no way I'm going to make it through their demonstration with you on my lap."

Brielle surprised herself. She shoved him hard so that the chair hit the back of his knees and he sat with an *oomph*.

"Cookie?"

"Cookie monster maybe." She faux growled as she slid into the gap between his spread thighs.

Laughter warmed him. "Hard to be afraid of something as cute as you."

"Even when I do this?" She grasped his shorts and tugged. They didn't come all the way off, but they lodged far enough beneath his ass that she could reach in and extract his cock.

"Okay, now you've got my attention." His erection twitched in her grasp. "What are you planning to do with that thing?"

"Something I haven't tried yet." Brielle licked her lips.

"Oh Jesus." His head hit the chair back. "Seriously. I won't be able to resist your mouth."

"So don't." She smiled a little shyly. "Then again, I've, uh, never really done this before. Brad didn't like anything but straight fucking. I might suck at it."

"That's definitely the point." Luke flashed that lopsided grin and his dimples, visible now that he'd shaved that awful goatee, upped his smoking factor to about five billion and thirty-seven. "It's not rocket science."

She decided the brave new her should throw caution to the wind and go with her gut. Leaning in, she licked the fluid glazing his thick, purple head.

A raspy groan had her pulling off pretty damn quick.

"That was a happy sound." Luke curled his fingers toward his palm in a come-hither gesture. "Do it again. If you want."

He didn't have to ask twice. She teased him a bit more, lapping from the root of his penis to the tip. When she got to the top she put him in her mouth, choking a little when she took too much, too fast.

"You don't have to go so quick. Take your time. Slow feels just as good. Hell, Brielle, I could come on command right now. Maybe it's best you're taking the edge off. I wouldn't want to embarrass myself in front of Kurt and Becca. Or you, for that matter."

His cock slipped from between her lips. She looked up at him and said, "Don't hold back on my account. I don't want you to suffer. And I get the feeling my jaw is going to be sore in just a few minutes. You're kind of...chubby."

Amusement had his cock bobbing along with the rest of his

body. She loved making him laugh and joining in.

This time she savored him as she slid down his length. She paused when he became a mouthful, rubbing the flat of her tongue underneath his shaft to discover the feel of his prominent veins. When her mouth began to ache she rose, spreading kisses over his head, then descended again.

His thighs quivered beneath her palms.

If she could have roared with him filling her mouth, she would have. To know he granted her this much trust and influence over him thrilled her. Out of the corner of her eye, she saw his balls drawing tight to his core. She cupped them in her palm and rolled them around gently.

With her other hand, she encased the second half of his cock in her fingers. Her lips rested on her knuckles and she moved them together, caressing all of him at once.

"Cookie. Stop if you aren't ready for me to come in your mouth." Grasping the arms of the chair, his knuckles turned white. "I'm so close. Going to—"

When she smiled, the slightest hint of her teeth abraded his solid cock. He didn't finish his warning. Instead, his entire body locked tight then exploded. His hips thrust upward, wedging his dick in her mouth an instant before jets of warm, salty come overflowed the space remaining around his embedded hard-on.

She swallowed as best she could, but dribbles escaped and painted her lips with his desire. He quaked and thumped his fists on the chair. Even his toes curled on either side of her knees.

And then he went totally lax, his chest heaving as his belly still occasionally clenched.

Brielle stared at him, captivated by his masculine beauty.

All the while, she rubbed her hands from his knees to hips, calming and soothing him as he recovered from what appeared to be an epic orgasm. Several seconds later, he lifted his hips, whipped his shorts off and used them to clean the remnants of his climax from his crotch.

When he peered down at her, he made a sound that was a cross between a moan and a sigh. "Thanks. You seriously never did that before?"

She shook her head.

"You're going to be dangerous when you have a little more practice." He found a clean section of his shorts, wiped her chin then lobbed them into a pile with his shirt. Next he reached for the hem of her nightgown and peeled it from her frame. She put her hands up to help him free her.

Bare breasted, she felt slightly exposed yet comfortable. When he reached for her panties, she shied away. "Can I keep them for now?"

"You're the boss." He patted his lap. "Will you snuggle with me? I want to taste us together on your lips."

Brielle wondered if he meant what she thought until he tugged her forward. She curled into the spot she fit so well, conformed to his body, and tipped her face up to his.

He devoured her, including the slickness she could feel glossing her lips.

With her fingers resting on his neck she could feel every pound of his heartbeat.

"I usually have a little more endurance than that." He grimaced. "You're just too much for me. I'll make it up to you later, I promise."

She angled his chin up so she could press a kiss to the bold mark on his neck that she'd given him. "I trust you."

Luke inhaled so hard, his chest mashed against hers. "That means everything to me, Cookie."

She tipped her head, sweeping her hair to the other side so that her mark was exposed. He rubbed a circle around the claim with his thumb, staring deep into her eyes before dipping down to enhance the decoration. Now, no one would be able to miss it.

Sometime later, maybe seconds, maybe minutes, Kurt entered the room. "You gave her a hickey? Leave you alone for a few minutes and see what happens?"

Brielle giggled, proud to be his. Luke put pressure on her shoulders, encouraging her to turn. She did, using him like a recliner. Her ass snugged into the juncture of his legs and torso. His semisoft cock fit in her crack, making her squirm. Nudging her legs, he suggested she splay herself with one knee draped over each armrest. The position was actually quite comfortable, so she stayed despite the shyness she would normally have suffered around Kurt. Today she felt as if she owned the world. They'd given her this chance.

One of Luke's arms wrapped around her waist, like a belt, and the other created a band just below her breasts. His hand cupped her even as his forearm took the weight of the other side of her chest.

Her boyfriend made the best seat in the house.

Settling in, she lifted her gaze to Kurt. He had his back turned. A white lab coat covered most of him, but his legs and feet were bare where they extended below the hem. Was he naked beneath the thin poplin?

When he stepped aside, she got the answer to that question and a couple more. Like where was Becca?

While she and Luke had been busy making out, Kurt had placed his wife on the examination table that took center stage in the laboratory. The terry-covered platform contoured to her body and looked fairly ergonomic. She was completely naked and, from the rosy hue of her cheeks, Brielle assumed Luke wasn't the only one who'd gotten some warming up before this exhibition.

"You understand the purpose of today's session, Becca?" With that, Kurt began to educate Brielle.

Chapter Eighteen

"Yes, Doctor." Becca squirmed a little beneath her husband's regard.

"Tell me."

"You're going to use me to prove to Brielle that her fantasies of bondage and other perceived deviant sexual practices are nothing like the abuse she suffered. You're going to show her how a loving Master can mold the experience into one of mutual admiration and pleasure."

"Very good." Kurt petted his wife. He toyed with her hair, using the ends to tease her breasts until her nipples plumped and tightened.

Brielle knew the recap had been for her benefit. She nodded.

Prodding and poking his captive, Kurt tested various parts of her anatomy. Pinching the tips of her pebbled nipples, he shook his head. "Could be harder. I think you're holding out to try my new inventions."

Becca whimpered, but the sound seemed like it was motivated more by need than by pain or misery.

Brielle stared.

"She'd agree to anything if it would get his hands on her," Luke whispered to Brielle. "She trusts him completely. It's beautiful. I've seen plenty of subs in my time. Very few ever reach this level of devotion to their partner. Same goes for Kurt. He can sense her every thought and desire. I used to think it was a little creepy. Until you started tuning in to me the same way."

"I do?" His revelation tempted her to take her eyes from Becca for a second.

"Yeah." He nibbled on her ear lobe. "I hope I can learn the same for you someday."

Her pussy clenched. She wished he would touch her.

Luke's hand disappeared between her thighs. He cupped her mound, pressing on the engorged flesh enough to still the ache, even while his touch inspired a much deeper longing.

"You're doing just fine already." Breath caught in her lungs when he began a circular motion of his fingers.

When their attention winged to the couple on display, Kurt had opened several compartments in the table. He extracted wide black straps, like seat belts, from each of the slots. The material made a distinct *whirrp* as he unwound it from the spring-loaded coils.

Brielle tensed when he extended one over Becca's wrist and clipped it to the table. He did the same to her other arm and then both ankles in quick succession. Though the redhead thrashed in the bindings, she couldn't escape. She'd had no chance to object.

And now she was trapped.

"Let her go!" Brielle couldn't stop herself from shouting the order.

Luke didn't cling. He released her immediately when years of conditioning were triggered by Becca's innocent testing of her bonds.

Brielle rushed to her friend's aid, stepping between Becca and Kurt. She might not be nearly as tall as the doctor, but she was mean when cornered. Half-naked, she puffed up to her full potential and squared herself for confrontation.

Kurt went still. He didn't yell or lash out in any way to punish her for interfering. Instead, he pointed to his wife. "Time to mix logic with your reflexes. Ask her if she needs your help."

Becca blinked from a sensual fog at the intrusion. "Brielle?"

"I'll get you out of here." She picked at the devious clasps holding the belts to the table on the opposite side of Becca's limbs. How the hell did they come off? "We have to leave before it's too late."

"Hang on." Becca didn't sound frightened. She sounded sluggish, as if it was hard to think in her condition. Fear did that to Brielle all the time.

"No, I've got you. Luke won't let him hurt you. Neither will I." She dared Kurt to come closer or buckle the strap in his hand. He didn't budge. Didn't attempt to cage his poor wife any more fully to the—

Brielle shook her head.

Rationality began to override her knee-jerk reaction. "Oh, crap. You're not trying to stop me. You're not keeping her against her will. You're not Brad."

She looked from Becca to Kurt and, last, to Luke. Had she embarrassed him?

"It's okay, Cookie." He stayed still, not encroaching on her space.

"No one's hurting me, Brielle." Becca smiled up at her. "I want to be right where I am. Kurt would never violate my trust. He's giving me what I need. Actually, he's going slow on purpose, taking his time and teasing me until I might scream. But only because I'd like a hell of a lot more."

"You're sure?" Brielle held Becca's hand. The fact that they were both nude, or nearly so, didn't register.

"Positive." Becca squeezed her fingers. "Thank you for caring and coming to my rescue though. You've got big balls, Ms. Norris."

"Anytime. I can take Kurt. I'm a tough cookie." She flexed her nonexistent muscles, trying to lighten the situation.

Luke took his cue to collect her, holding her close and repeating reassurance until she couldn't help but hear him. And start to believe.

"Would it help you to see concrete data, Brielle?" Kurt stopped her when she would have slunk away. "You seem like a very visual person. Sights impact you more than other ways of gathering information."

"What do you mean?" She canted her head as she peered up at the doctor.

"Remember how you wore the probe to bed last night?" He reached out and squeezed her shoulder, not at all upset with her interruption. "I have similar tools that can record and project Becca's responses on the monitor over there. In fact, it makes her hot when we play with it."

"Seriously?" Brielle's eyes grew wide.

"Yes, on all counts." Luke ran his hand down her arm. "Kurt is a brilliant and devious scientist. Let him have show-and-tell with his creations. It'll help you see the truth, and Becca really does get off on Kurt's big...brain."

She bit her lip then nodded. "Okay."

"Pull the chair up, Luke." Kurt directed his friend as he turned to the supply cabinet and rummaged through the contents. "Make sure she can see everything."

Brielle gulped. Could she handle all of it?

"If you're uncomfortable, we can walk at any time." Luke spoke softly in her ear as they resumed their position, but closer.

"I'd like to watch." She took his index finger, wrapping her fist around it. "I'm sorry—"

"No apologies needed." He put his other hand over her mouth.

Brielle kissed his palm.

They gave their attention to Kurt and Becca when the doctor returned with several items in tow. The long, thick dildo in one hand was easiest to identify. He fished around beneath the table, releasing a lever. The platform split at the bottom, allowing him to shove Becca's legs apart, still bound, but spread. He clipped the device to a metal shaft in the base of the table and aligned it with Becca's pussy before speaking up so they all could hear. "The material of this tool is embedded with electrical circuits and more of the radio transmitters for collecting temperature and pressure data, the same as the ones used on Brielle last night."

Brielle couldn't believe she'd been so bold. The thought alone had her squirming on Luke's lap again.

"The screen is now displaying a historical average of Becca's response levels during vanilla sex. We've conducted a large number of trials to ensure the validity of this data." Kurt's lecturing monotone couldn't hide the decadence of what he was saying.

"Yeah, they basically fucked with the monitoring tools on," Luke explained in a hushed voice. "A lot. Then they did it some more with her tied up and stuff like that to compare."

He pointed to a blue line emerging much higher on the screen than the original slash.

"When Kurt puts the probe in her, you'll be able to see how today compares to those two groups. There's a lot at play here. Having us watch could be distracting or it could make her arousal greater. Considering the other times I've seen them together, I'm voting for us turning her on more."

Following his explanation, Kurt flashed a grin in their direction. "If I were a betting man, I'd say you're right. And the winner is..."

A *whir* echoed around the clinical surfaces of the room. Becca moaned and arched off the table as much as her partial bindings allowed. Brielle could see there were plenty more belts Kurt could have used to strap his wife in. Apparently he didn't want to upset their guest.

"Come on, Becca," Luke cheered low and deep. "Show Brielle how much you love an audience when Kurt puts you through your paces."

The orange line that glowed to life on the monitor was nearly off the charts.

"She likes it." Brielle was in awe. She could hardly believe it. Becca. Sane, smart, pretty, fun Becca enjoyed being bound and used where her husband's friend could watch.

"No, Cookie. She *loves* it." Luke huffed. "And we've hardly begun. What's that purple thing, Kurt? I don't remember seeing that before."

Brielle put her hands on the rests and shoved upward, trying for a better view.

"Do you want to go stand next to them?" Luke tempted her, but she didn't want to intrude.

"Come on over, Brielle." Kurt waved to her. "It's important that you don't miss any details."

Lifting her from the chair when she hesitated, Luke carried her to the front row.

"Here, you can check them out." Kurt handed Brielle one of the new instruments. She was surprised by how lifelike it felt. Soft and fleshy.

It was like a shallow purple bowl that fit pretty evenly in the palm of her hand. At the bottom of the vessel, a wheel coated in filaments of the fleshy material kicked on. As it spun lazily, the strands fluttered. The device had a part of the wall cut away in a deep U.

"How do you think of this stuff?" Luke leaned over and put his knuckle against the endless parade of flapping tendrils. "This is going to drive her wild."

"That's the goal." Kurt cracked his knuckles. "I sit in my office and imagine how I might torment her with more and more of this."

"Oh God. It's working." Becca met each thrust of the probe.

Brielle refused to fall behind. "Wait, I don't understand."

"Let me show you." Kurt took the gadget from her, drew a tube of lubrication from his pocket and squirted a daub onto his fingertip. Then he put his slick digit into the bowl, allowing the fibers to coat themselves as they turned, slapping his hand lightly.

Once satisfied, Kurt stepped between his wife's legs, checking the fit of the straps around her ankles along the way. Tight but not biting. He attended to her as if she were a queen and he her subject despite the balance of power supposedly weighted in his favor.

Though Becca was helpless to do anything but entertain his attention, Kurt never once acted selfishly. Every action was designed to maximize Becca's delight. Bound, the pretty redhead still retained plenty of clout.

Luke rubbed against Brielle's back and bottom as they observed Kurt turn the bowl upside down. He whispered, "Don't get scared. She's probably not going to be able to stay quiet when that starts licking her clit."

"Ohh." Brielle could see how that could work. The flexible bowl covered Becca's mound and the U groove in the bottom slid over the metal shank of the dildo probe, which steadily filled, then retreated from Becca's pussy.

Sure enough, Becca gasped and shrieked when the Licker nestled into place.

"Take it, baby." Kurt leaned over her, keeping his hand on his new toy to ensure it created suction and adhered. "It'll be just right in a few seconds."

"Yes!" Becca cried out as she thrust her pelvis upward. The motion forced the probe to misalign on its next return journey.

Kurt reacted quickly.

"Keep still," he commanded in a tone that brooked no argument. He fed the dildo back into her clenching pussy then restarted its forward motion before glancing over at Brielle. "I won't let her hurt herself. I'm sorry, she needs additional restraints."

Brielle looked at Becca. Really stared.

Flushed and desperate, the doctor begged. "Please, don't make him stop. More. I need more."

Brielle took a deep breath. She reached out herself and extracted the belt near Becca's waist. Testing the resistance of the auto-retract feature, she dropped it once, startling herself. On the second try, she handed the length to Kurt.

"Do you want to do it?" He was unbelievably patient with her, given the state of his undeniable arousal. From this angle, she could easily spot his raging hard-on, which protruded between the flaps of his lab coat. Dark hair sprinkled over his bare chest, leading in a very happy trail to his cock.

No one else reacted to their nudity, so she continued on as if she was totally impartial to their beautiful bodies. “I’m sorry, what?”

Kurt’s laugh drew her gaze back to his face. “You guys aren’t exactly making it easy for me to concentrate either. I asked if you’d like to strap her in tighter. I’ll show you how the fasteners work. Just in case… It would actually be possible for you to release her if you needed.”

A nod shook Brielle’s hair around her face a little more vigorously than she’d intended.

The Dream Machine’s creator covered her hand with his. He guided her first to uncover the receptor for the clasp, teaching her the slide-and-twist motion necessary to engage or extricate the buckle.

“Very good.” He nodded as he double-checked her handiwork. “How about one more across the top of her chest?”

The monitors beeped as if they were performing Vivaldi’s “Allegro”, Brielle’s favorite track from the CDs she’d snagged on one of her rummage sale runs.

Becca truly enjoyed this. The equipment sang the proof.

She looked down at her friend, meeting Becca’s gaze fully for the first time since they’d entered this room today.

A smile graced her lips, which were swollen from Kurt’s kisses earlier, Brielle guessed. “I hope one day you can open your mind to experiencing what you crave. It will be worth every bit of the fear and agony the desire has caused you when you are bound and yet free. I promise. I struggled. Kurt guided me to this place. I would be honored to help you find your way here.”

“I love you, baby.” Kurt swooped in for a kiss. Passionate, urgent and gentle simultaneously, their exchange brought to life a combination Brielle couldn’t have quite imagined before.

"They're great together, right?" Luke cupped her chin in his hand, angling her face so that he could share with her.

Though she didn't respond verbally, Brielle tried to communicate her gratefulness with every swipe of her lips over his. This awakening inspired her to reach farther than she'd ever thought possible. For an enduring mate rather than temporary companionship.

Instead of chasing the bull to grab it by the horns, she stood in the center of the ring and declared herself fair game, daring him to charge her. Because she deserved a man who felt for her the way Kurt did for his wife.

After witnessing something so brilliant, most other things paled in comparison.

Except Luke.

When he drew away to evaluate her expression, he beamed. His smile illuminated so much of the blackness she'd swallowed it amazed her.

Harder to believe, she seemed to balance him. To be his counterpart.

"Are you two going to stand there and make out all day? Or do you want to try my spare Licker?" Kurt grinned.

"I knew you were my best friend for a reason. Well, aside from the time you put plastic wrap over the urinal when Doug Blanser slept with my date to the prom." Luke snagged the device from the stainless steel rolling tray then kneeled at Brielle's feet.

"Or maybe how I let you sleep with my wife until you found someone to slay the loneliness that was starting to drive you mad?"

"Uh, yeah. That too." Her golden-haired lover pressed on the insides of her knees until she widened her stance. After peeling her underwear down and off, he nuzzled her mound, breathing deep when he parted her lips with two long fingers. "Before I turn you into a guinea pig, how about I give you something to compare this thing to?"

Luke kissed the top of her slit, weakening her knees.

"Lean here." Kurt positioned her so that her ass rested on the examination table. Then he teased his wife, "I bet you wish you could see them, don't you, baby?"

Kurt's attention returned to her. Brielle couldn't imagine they'd be as interested in Luke's wicked tongue as she was with Kurt's inventions and how he wielded them to tame his wife.

That possibility combined with the wet sounds of the probe fucking Becca, encouraging Brielle to lift her leg and rest it on Luke's shoulder. He buried his face deeper between her thighs, sucking on every engorged valley of her flesh.

She began to shake when he manipulated her clit with his nose while he lapped cream from her lips.

"You're about to make her come, Luke."

Both Brielle and Becca moaned at Kurt's announcement.

"W-wait. Want to try the Licker." Brielle tried to escape, but there was nowhere to go.

"Honey, he's not going to let you off the hook that easily." Luke laughed and Becca moaned at Kurt's declaration. "We don't run a one-and-done operation around here."

Chapter Nineteen

"Huh?" She couldn't think when Luke's tongue circled her—slow, and then fast, and then slow again—before he added one of his fingers to his strumming of her body.

"We're not leaving this room until we've shared a dozen orgasms between us. Luke and I *might* be good for two each. So guess who's going to make up the difference?" Kurt's assumption of control pushed Brielle nearer to surrender.

Luke paused to gloat, "I already had *numero uno*, thanks."

"We only left you kids alone for five damn minutes." Kurt chuckled.

"Just doing my part to reach your goal." His smart-ass remark was slightly garbled as he dove back into business. Brielle adored his sense of humor. It spiked her need higher.

The thought of their semi-private naughty adventures must have driven Becca beyond restraint. She screamed Kurt's name then bucked within the confines of her bindings. This time, the probe stayed in place.

Brielle felt herself slipping toward climax too. The other woman's cries and the knowledge that Kurt had actually used the restraints to keep her safe while pleasing her was too much to combat. She tugged on Luke's hair. When he peeked up, he smiled against her pussy.

She came so hard she should have fallen. Except both Kurt and Luke braced her through the rampage of sensation that stormed her nervous system. Brielle slumped against the examination table, uncaring that her shoulders and Becca's thigh pressed together.

Kurt motioned to Luke, who lifted her into his arms. "That's three. Nice."

A giggle escaped between their lips when he bent to kiss her, sharing the mingled taste of them. Amazingly, she had no doubts she had more to give. Metal clanked as Kurt rearranged the space, extending side panels in the table. One was a kneeling bench and another a padded rest for her arms and head.

“Gorgeous.” Luke nipped her bottom lip. “I want to fuck you, Brielle. While they’re watching. With you wearing Kurt’s Licker.”

“I’m not planning on objecting.” She could hardly believe that hoarse voice was hers.

“Pay attention, up close and personal. I don’t think there’s any way you can miss how special it is when Becca submits to Kurt.”

“Already see that.” She gasped when the world spun around her.

Luke set her on her knees. She instinctively turned her cheek to rest on the upper pad. At that angle, he was right, she had one hell of a view.

“I’m not going to tie you, Cookie, but I’d like it if you would put your arms in the small of your back. Cross your wrists for me. That’s it. You’re completely able to move at any time. If you feel the need, just pull away.”

“I don’t want to.” She moaned and arched her back, flashing him her drenched pussy.

“Kurt, where are your condoms?” Luke’s frantic inquiry had her feeling smug.

“Uh oh.” The scientist froze from where he’d wandered near Becca’s shoulder, petting her and reigniting the fire in her. “I haven’t had to use those in for-fucking-ever. They’ve got to be expired.”

“Rub it in. Crap.” Luke massaged Brielle’s ass, on prominent display. “I didn’t expect this today. Don’t worry, Cookie, I’ll still take good care of you.”

Brielle peered at him over her shoulder. She spent half a

second debating if she was making the right decision before Becca's input came rushing back. Doubting her choices wasn't the way to spend her whole life.

This was good.

This was right.

"Brad used to take me to get the shot. It made my cycle easier so I kept going to the university clinic when my benefits kicked in. I sure as hell got tested for everything under the sun after I left too. I'm clean. If you are..."

Luke covered her in a flash. He knelt with his legs on the outside of hers. "Today just keeps getting better and better. Let me in, Brielle. Skin on skin."

The press of him against the backs of her thighs, the way his belly trapped her hands between them as he leaned forward, his fingers in her hair and his lips at her neck all guaranteed she wouldn't last long before contributing another climax to the count.

And that was before she realized what Kurt was doing.

His groan had her peeking over the full mounds of Becca's breasts to where he tucked his cock between his wife's lips. She continued to grind on the probe while the Licker tortured her.

Brielle could relate when Luke reached around her hip to place the device's twin over her pussy. The material felt too real when it sucked tight to her body. Luke switched on the revolving action. She nearly choked on her tongue.

"Yet another moneymaker from the Dream Lab, huh?" Luke didn't give her time to adjust before pressing his cock against her. Whether her imagination contributed to the sensation or not, he felt hotter. Harder too. He buried himself in her a few inches on each shove. Soon he filled her to brimming and then some.

The combination of his possession and the Licker, mercilessly tapping her where it counted most, electrified her. Instead of a slow buildup of passion, it shocked her, like being struck by lightning. Without warning, she exploded.

"Ah shit. *Yeah!*" Luke tucked close and didn't let her slip from his grasp, or off his cock, as she convulsed. "Four down."

Kurt withdrew from Becca's mouth. He groaned as he admired Brielle's total lack of restraint. Stepping nearer for a better look, his cock glanced off Becca's shoulder. He planted a hand on the table and leapt. Careful not to squash his wife, he placed one knee on either side of her body, leaving him facing her feet.

Before he could instruct her, Becca lifted her head as far as possible and took his balls in her mouth. She suckled them for a few seconds until Kurt lifted up and readjusted. "Too much more of that and I'll come all over you like a fountain."

The monitors went wild.

"You want me to?" He caressed his wife's softly rounded stomach as he stared at his inventions working her.

She mewled, completely at his mercy and loving it.

"Who am I to argue?" Clearly, this was one of his favorite activities. No way could he hide the mask of desire sweeping over his face. With two fingers, he pressed his cock down until it rested in the valley between Becca's breasts. His other hand plumped one side of her chest, smooshing it around his cock.

Luke assisted by reaching over to do the same for the other mound, snugging Kurt's erection between dunes of softness. He hesitated long enough to ask Brielle, "Does it bother you that I'm touching her while I'm fucking you?"

"No." The glide of his cock inside her, now fully inserted, showed her just how much he needed her. "Just don't stop. God. Please."

"I can multitask." He grunted.

Kurt roared when Becca inclined her head enough to lick whatever parts of him she could reach as he rode her chest, picking up steam. Brielle's vantage made it clear the haphazard delight of his balls, perineum and maybe even his ass drove the doctor wild.

The raw lust on Kurt's face as he staked his claim had

Brielle getting drunk on the passion they all shared. When his cock emerged from the far side of Becca's breasts and nudged Luke's forearm, which still secured Becca for his friend, a shock wave rippled through Brielle.

"You like that, huh?" Luke did too if the increase in the pace and force of his thrusts were any indication.

"Yes. Yes." She panted her response, uncaring about her total loss of decorum.

As if their ecstasy fed off one another's enjoyment, Kurt was pushed higher by Brielle's reaction. He threw back his head and growled, "Here it comes, baby. All for you."

He spasmed on top of Becca, his lab coat rustling as he shook. Then pearly white streams poured from him with enough force to blast the first one halfway to his wife's pussy. The strand draped over Luke's forearm. The next shot blasted Brielle's lover full-on. She sighed when the next two or three fell short, dribbling over Becca's breasts and the space in between.

By the time droplets accompanied each flex of Kurt's muscles, he'd moved on to smearing them over Becca's nipples.

"Oh damn." Luke slammed into her now. Combined with the scenery and the Licker, Brielle figured she didn't stand a chance.

But Luke sealed the deal by retracting his arm. He laid it on the side of the table right next to them and licked a swath through his friend's come, which ran in rivulets through his golden hair.

Both Becca and Brielle shattered in unison. The sight too much to bear.

Their shouts mingled and complemented one another, joined by the harmony of Luke's grunts and cursing as he flooded Brielle's pussy. Bare, he scorched her with the heat of his seed, which splattered her still-rippling tissue.

She could feel him overflowing her, and was sad for the fluid squeezing out around his thick shaft when she craved all of him inside her. Rapture stole every trace of rationality. The only thing she could do was experience.

Kurt slithered to the linoleum, bracing himself on his knees as he caught his breath. He puffed as though he'd run an entire marathon in the past three or four minutes. The sawing motion of his hand made it clear he pumped his cock. She was surprised to see the tip of it above the examination table from his post on the other side. Still hard.

"Brielle. So good." Luke covered her back with kisses, stopping only to bite lightly on her shoulder. He held her as his cock began to shrink inside her, spilling more of his release onto her labia and thighs.

"That's only eight. Ladies, you'd better get back to work." Kurt didn't waste any time or allow his wife to cool off.

Luke wrapped Brielle's wrists in one of his hands, reminding her that she hadn't once felt the need to flinch or retract them.

"Can you stand, Cookie?" he whispered. "I'll help you. I'd love to see this. Hell, it might get you fucked again if luck is with us."

Anything that involved Luke's cock in her pussy was good with her.

She wobbled as she stood, but managed to get to her feet—this time facing the table. Kurt was busy disengaging the probe, though he left the Licker in place. "We don't need any more proof of her reactions, do we, Brielle?"

"No, Doctor." She couldn't say what possessed her to mimic Becca's polite address. If the dilating of his pupils was any indication, it'd been the right choice. "The results are obvious."

Becca was wasted. Thoroughly replete, yet about to be pushed higher.

Kurt hummed. "It's going to have to be something good to get her there again."

He prowled to his supply station, taking two latex gloves from the box on the counter. He drew them on with an exaggerated motion. Becca undulated on the table, proving how much she loved his show.

Wondering what debauched creation he'd showcase next, Brielle was surprised when he bypassed cabinets, drawers and even the tools on his rolling cart.

"Sometimes simple is best." Kurt dug in his pocket once more for the tube of lubrication.

"Are you going to attempt what I think you are?" Luke paused his kneading of Brielle's breasts and ass and whatever else he could reach, as though he hadn't been able to put his hands on her enough. Thank God, because she needed more too.

Brielle whimpered, and he recommenced the caresses, keeping her from dipping into a sated catatonia. She nearly begged him to stop, to let her rest, but it was too marvelous to end prematurely.

"Do you think I'm about to show you just how far Becca has come in her training to accept all of my hand inside her?" Kurt's quicksilver eyes flashed his dirty intentions. They glowed as brightly as the supernova featured in the poster hanging outside Brielle's cubicle in the Science Department below them.

She'd never be able to sit at her desk again without remembering this day.

The time her eyes and soul were opened to so many possibilities.

The truth of the matter was that Kurt and Becca didn't need anything other than each other to be deliriously happy. All the trappings and extras were simply bonuses. Sprinkles on a decadent sundae. Something they enjoyed together. A statement of their trust, loyalty and dependability, as well as the total devotion they already exhibited for each other.

Kurt satisfied himself by delighting his wife. She reveled in the attention and the joy it brought him to dominate her completely. Could Brielle give that to Luke?

She glanced over her shoulder. Her boyfriend—she loved thinking of him like that—was mesmerized. Not by Kurt's advance between Becca's spread and trapped legs.

Brielle caught him staring at her own expression.

"I want to show you everything," he explained.

"I can't wait." She touched his cheek. "I just wish there was something I could give you."

"You already have." Luke hugged her to his chest. She was surprised to feel his erection trying to make a comeback. "You impress me more every minute. So much progress. Such a short amount of time."

"He's right about that." Kurt shifted his focus to her for a moment. "It's somewhat incredible actually. I wouldn't have thought it possible when I read Becca's case notes earlier this week. It won't be easy, Brielle. There will be lots of struggles to come. Up days, down days. But I'm sure you're going to triumph."

"We're here to help." Becca struggled to speak. "However we must."

They all laughed at her fake sacrifice.

Until Kurt transformed her chuckle into a groan by inserting his slick middle finger into her pussy while the pinky of his other hand invaded her ass.

"Um," Brielle blushed.

"Yes?" Luke kissed the nape of her neck.

"I thought that was a one-way street." She grimaced at her naiveté.

Kurt nearly bust a gut, triggering more needy sounds from Becca as his hands jiggled within her. "You're so freaking adorable. I swear on my pair of Jung's spectacles that's something Luke would have said when we were little."

Coming to her rescue, Becca must have been able to tell the rosy cheeks Brielle sported had more to do with embarrassment than excitement. "They were really early bloomers. I had no clue either. Then Kurt corrupted me."

"And you loved every second of it." Her husband added a second finger to her ass and two more to her pussy.

"Still do. Will forever." She let her head drop back onto the table as she accommodated his foray into her body.

"Would you like to find out what it feels like too?" Luke grazed his fingertips over Brielle's ass and the cleft of her buttocks. "Just a little. It's not something you want to rush."

"Does that mean it hurts?" A trickle of unease spoiled her curiosity.

"Not if you do it right." He flicked the tip of one finger across her rear entrance. "I won't fuck you there. Today. Not with my cock. But you can take a finger or two. Hell, Becca's about to swallow an entire fist, I think you can handle my pinky."

"What?" Brielle lifted her face in time to see Kurt put all four fingers of his right hand inside Becca's pussy. It didn't seem like she should be quite so...stretchy.

"We've been practicing," Kurt reassured her. "This has been one of Becca's fantasies for a while. She's never gone all the way. Lately, she's come close before she calls mercy."

"Not today." Becca's mouth set in firm resolve.

"That's what you said last weekend," Kurt goaded her.

"Don't like failing you." She sighed.

"Baby, you're doing great." He changed direction in an instant. "I frankly never expected you to take all of me. You're so little."

"More." She strained at her bonds, attempting to bear down on his hand.

Luke reached into Kurt's pocket and swiped the lube. He squeezed a blob into his palm and washed his hands together until the synthetic goop absorbed some of his heat. Then he smeared a substantial portion on Brielle's ass and used the remainder to slick his index finger.

"Take a deep breath, Cookie," he instructed. "When I tell you, let it out and push against me. Nothing too hard. Nothing too fast."

"You're sure this will work?" She shifted uneasily.

"Positive," Luke said at the same time Kurt and Becca confirmed the plan.

Brielle nodded. "Okay. Do it."

Pressure built against her bottom. She flinched.

"Come back here." The strict tone from Luke surprised her. "You're not going to run away from what you want. No more."

The slap of his other hand on her tensed cheek reverberated through the laboratory.

"Careful, Luke," Becca warned. "Not too much yet."

"No!" Brielle shouted.

Everyone tensed.

"That was a 'no, don't stop'. Not a 'no, don't spank me'." She cleared her throat. "Please."

Luke's laugh never got old. The warm sound rained over her like a refreshing shower. Complete with lots of steam and something even more fun than misusing her detachable showerhead.

He imparted another light tap, then a third. When she concentrated on the combination of sting and sugar, sweetness began to outweigh the sparks.

Brielle moaned, encouraging Luke to rub the areas he'd agitated.

Just as she recovered, his finger returned to her ass. "Remember, breathe out and try not to tense up. That will only make it hurt worse."

She followed his directions, her muscles clenching when the tip of his digit wormed inside, animating areas of her she never expected to enjoy. Inspired, Kurt added his thumb to Becca's pussy. He folded his hand so his fingers formed a shape like a shadow puppet, or maybe a duck's bill.

"Breathe with me." Although the doctor spoke to his wife, Brielle synched her respiration with Becca's and Luke utilized the pattern to his advantage as he plundered her virgin hole.

For each exhalation, Kurt worked his hand a bit farther into Becca's pussy. He continued to stretch her with every screw of his fist, which turned as it advanced, working inside the petite woman. She clawed the table now.

"Almost there." Kurt spoke low and urgently to her. "You've got this, Becca. I need to feel you around my wrist. I want to be embedded in you. Permanently."

"Push." She gritted her teeth.

"Yes, ma'am." He granted her wish.

There was a moment when Brielle thought they would be disappointed. Kurt's hand lodged at the mouth of Becca's taut pussy. He stared into his wife's eyes, and Brielle saw him about to quit.

Then his knuckles compressed or Becca's body relented or both. His fist sank into her steadily yet with some degree of resistance, as if it were plunging into a bucket of mud.

Luke groaned almost as loudly as Becca. "I can't stand this."

Brielle wondered what he meant until his cock returned, nudging her dripping slit, wet with the remnants of his orgasm as well as her own. He must have excelled at Twister because he somehow managed to keep his finger, now joined by another, in her ass even as he delved deeper with his cock.

"This is amazing." Kurt was lost to his own wonder. "I can unfurl my fingers. So soft. So wet. So hot."

Becca didn't need much more encouragement. Her eyes flew open, meeting her husband's stare. And just like that, she raised their orgasm count to nine.

Kurt didn't seem very far behind. He held off long enough to extricate himself, causing Becca the least amount of discomfort possible as she continued to come in loud, erratic waves of rapture.

Her husband wrapped his saturated hand around his cock and began to stroke. He kissed Becca's belly between the restraints then allowed her to float undisturbed in subspace.

The thick shaft inside Brielle began to trigger early warning signs.

"Don't fight that on my account." Luke managed phrases and fragments as opposed to the whole sentence at once. When he began to tremble behind her, she took mercy. The instant his fingers scissored open in her ass, she relented.

Ecstasy slammed through her with every beat of her heart. She couldn't wait to see how much better sex could be when she allowed Luke to tie her up and use her. Because she knew now, without a doubt, that day was coming.

And she could hardly stand the wait, knowing how good it could be.

Nothing legal should be better than this.

Then again some of the things they attempted could very well violate state laws. She didn't give a shit.

Luke wrapped her hair around his wrist, pulled it enough that she relented and tipped her head back so he could study her face as he exploded inside her. A series of grunts accompanied his jerky, nearly violent thrusts.

Never once was she frightened.

No, she was grateful.

For him.

And his friends.

Before thinking, Brielle reached out to Kurt. He lifted his gaze to Becca, who nodded. With permission, he stepped into Brielle's grasp.

Luke's orgasm seemed to escalate instead of fade when she began to jerk his best friend. It didn't take much. She'd hardly measured Kurt's longer, thinner cock against Luke's when the shaft grew more defined and steely in her grasp.

"He's close," she groaned as Luke began to curl over her, his muscles finally relaxing after jettisoning his third load of come.

"Want some help?" Luke kissed her temple.

"Sure." She nodded, expecting pointers.

Instead, her boyfriend reached over and rolled Kurt's balls around the palm of his hand while she handled Dr. Foster's erection.

Kurt's face turned nearly purple as he coiled then sprung.

Gushes of come oozed from the tip of his erection, glazing her fingers, as well as Luke's. He clamped on to the examination table to keep upright.

"That's enough to give a man a heart attack." Kurt allowed Luke to impart one last tweak before he retreated. He tended to his wife before cleaning himself.

For quite a while, each couple concentrated on their growing bond.

After tidying them up, Luke brought her clothes over and began to dress her. Meanwhile, Kurt freed Becca, who seemed nearly incoherent.

Brielle tried to help Luke, but her utterly relaxed body wouldn't obey her silent commands. He didn't need her assistance. Soon they both were ready to go.

Kurt hugged her tight before pulling away with a wink. "You're my second favorite patient of all time."

"Damn straight." Becca grinned.

She yawned before shaking her head as if to gather herself.

"So, Tuesday is Elsa's birthday. We're having something really low key at our house. You know, dinner and some Hostess cupcakes with candles on them." She winced. "It's a crazy week with the seminar we're hosting on Dream Machine research. Anyway, I thought it might be nice if you came. If you'd like. You know, with Luke."

"Uh, I guess that's up to him." Brielle peeked up at the golden guy beside her.

"Of course I'd like you to be my date. I mean, that's what girlfriends do, you know? They attend *boring* family events." He scrunched his nose. "Don't leave me alone in Elsa's clutches. Are you crazy?"

"You tell me. You're the expert." She tried not to flinch.

"Hey, now. None of that." Luke, Kurt and Becca all keyed in to her momentary doubt.

Their intensity dared her to disagree. To doubt the experiences they'd shared over the past two days.

“Fine. I’d love to join you.” She paused. “On one condition.”

“What’s that?” Becca raised her brows.

“I’m making the cake. A real one. What’s her favorite kind?” Brielle asked.

“I vote for vanilla with pudding between the layers and lots of sprinkles in the icing. Blue frosting,” Luke answered immediately.

Brielle laughed. “I’ll keep that in mind for your birthday. Which is?”

“Not until March. Fuck.” He pouted.

“We’ll pretend one night.” She patted his butt. “But, no, seriously. What does she like?”

Becca paused to think about it. “Fruity crap. Is that too hard?”

“Nope. I can work with that.” Being useful alleviated a lot of Brielle’s concerns about attending with Luke. She didn’t plan to freeload on his friends.

“You’re a lifesaver.” Becca hugged her. “Thank you so much.”

“No, thank *you*.” Brielle swallowed the lump in her throat. “For everything.”

“Our pleasure,” Kurt answered for them both. “Literally.”

Chapter Twenty

Brielle piped whipped topping from a Ziploc baggie with the corner snipped off. She formed a decorative edge around the base of Elsa's cake. The low-cost improvisation was one of many she employed to make her treats budget-friendly. As she worked, an idea formed in her mind.

Why not start a food blog? One aimed at thrifty meals. She could cook, take pictures of her creations and share tips she'd picked up along the way. Maybe her experiments could help someone else out. And it'd be a fun side project until culinary school was a possibility. She'd heard success stories of people making a living doing things they loved like that. Being her own boss sounded like heaven. Maybe a self-published cookbook could be the way to go.

Smiling, she sliced fresh fruit to garnish the top of the cake. Pretty patterns of blueberries, strawberries, kiwi and mango emerged in a riot of color and flavor. She popped a slice of leftover mango into her mouth and hoped the bus ride over to Kurt and Becca's place wouldn't ruin her efforts.

Luke had offered to pick her up, but in addition to being out of his way on the route between his office and his friends' home, she couldn't imagine a trip on a motorcycle ending well for her present. She'd worked too hard for it to smoosh against the plastic carrying container she locked the lid on.

Still, she wondered when he'd had time to slip the note beneath her door.

See you tonight.

Butterflies winged around her stomach as she thought of just how much she'd revealed. Exposed and eager, she loved how much she could show him of herself. Everything. Trusting him had been the right decision. She was positive.

Brielle checked the oven clock. Still a few minutes to spare. So she skipped to the bathroom, touched up a couple of the gentle curves in her hair, reapplied her lip gloss and double-checked her dress in the full-length mirror on the back of the door.

The tiered lavender lace of the vintage find from a secondhand shop floated around her.

Not too shabby.

Brielle hummed to herself—one of the standards she'd danced to with Luke last week—as she collected her purse and the angel food. She took the stairs slowly in the heels she'd picked up to match the dress. Becca had it right, they made her feel powerful—sexy, confident and pretty.

At the ground floor, she emerged into the dusk. She thought she caught motion out of the corner of her eye, but when she glanced in that direction, one of the frisky squirrels twitched his tail at her as though annoyed. She'd disturbed it from absconding with the apple core he had scavenged. "I'm not going to bother you, little guy. Go ahead, take your dinner."

He scampered across the sidewalk before she continued.

At the bus stop, three college guys waited. She recognized one of them from her usual route. Before Luke, she might have thought him handsome. No one could compare to the standard her boyfriend had set. Feeling bold, she decided it was time to stop playing the meek mouse. "Good evening."

"Hi." He smiled. "I always wondered where you disappear to. Never see you out at the bars or the pool or anything. I'm Jack, by the way."

"Nice to meet you officially. Brielle. I'm not much of a partier. Usually. But I'm actually on my way to my boyfriend's friends' house tonight." The truth still startled and awed her a bit.

"Ah, damn. So there's no point in giving you my number?" He seemed genuinely disappointed.

"If you'd asked a few weeks ago, I'd probably have said yes." No reason to hurt his feelings.

"I guess that's a good life lesson, huh?" The headlights of the bus swung in their direction, casting ghastly shadows. She was glad he had been there to chat with. Being outside at night gave her the willies. "So is it a potluck?"

"Actually, it's a birthday thing." Brielle held the frosted container up so he could get a better look as the bus's air brake hissed and a couple of other people climbed on ahead of them.

"Damn, that looks great. I really messed up." He laughed, his regret the kind that would fade after his first beer and the next pretty girl he met at the bar tonight.

She sat in the seat across from him, happy to have his company as her foot tapped on the rubber floor of the bus. This was like a real date. Going to Luke's closest friends' house for a family party.

Ironing imaginary wrinkles with her palm must have been obvious.

"Don't worry, your guy is going to love that dress." Jack grinned. "And if he doesn't, just find me on the bus tomorrow."

Brielle laughed. "Will do, thanks. I think my stop is next. Good luck out there tonight."

A guy with a dark hoodie and baseball hat waited at the rear door. His face angled down, hands jammed in his pockets, making him seem miserable. Negative energy radiated off him, encouraging her to wind through the aisle to the front exit.

"Have a good night, Kevin." She smiled at the driver when she stepped onto the curb.

"You too, Ms. Norris." He warned her, "Careful out here in the dark. Aren't so many people around as at your place."

"Should only make it safer, right?" Brielle blew off his concern. She had less than two blocks to go to reach her destination. "See you tomorrow."

"'Night." He shut the doors behind her and pulled away. When the lights from the bus faded, she was surprised at how dark it was. But the moon was pretty and so were the stars, which she never could see from her place closer to the heart of the city.

Her heels clicked on the poured concrete sidewalk in the newer district. One of Kurt's neighbors was out watering plants. She smiled and said hello as she dodged the rivulets he made. The guy from the bus trailed behind her, not passing despite her careful progress in her unfamiliar footwear.

By the time she crossed the street, goose bumps rose on her arms. She could see Kurt and Becca's home just five or six houses away now. Picking up the pace, she imagined the light and love inside those walls.

"Where you going, Brielle?" The voice behind her froze her heart. It couldn't be him. "Thought I'd never get you alone."

Panic cost her precious seconds. She should have run. She should have screamed. Anything. But all that happened was a whole lot of nothing.

Until Brad grabbed her shoulder and shook her. "What the hell did you mean you were going to your *boyfriend's* house? Are you cheating on me?"

"We're through. I'm not doing anything to you." Brielle's gaze darted around, hoping for another neighbor with a green thumb, but even the first had gone inside now. Probably for the best, she didn't want to cause a scene that would look bad on the Fosters. "Now get the hell away from me."

"I don't think so." He reached for her again and she dodged.

Adrenaline kicked in big time. She surged forward, still clutching her gift. Trotting, she aimed for the sanctuary just out of range.

"I'm not going to ask nicely anymore." Holy crap, had he always been such a brute? How had she not seen it?

The street was illuminated by headlights from a car that approached slowly. Thank God. Brielle waved her free arm, trying to get the driver's attention.

"You want to say hello to Lisa?" Brad cackled. "She's tired

of doing the housework and she can't cook worth shit. So I told her I'd take it out on that brat of hers if she didn't help with this. Thought maybe you should come back and take care of your responsibilities. We won't even make you ride the bus. Have a nice spot for you in the back of the van."

"You really are fucking nuts." Antagonizing him might not have been wise, but she couldn't help herself.

"Come now and I won't have to punish you. Make me chase you and you'll stay in that closet for a year, I swear."

Instead of paralyzing fear, rage bubbled to the surface, filling her with a lifetime of anger all at once.

"You will *not* ruin this for me. Not this cake. Not my life." She protected her labor of love by cradling it close to her chest and angling away as she strode toward the lights illuminating the walkway to Kurt and Becca's house.

Screw drama. Brad had only acted like this once before—the day he'd woken her out of her seven-year daze, like some twisted sleeping beauty, forcing her to see what a fucked-up world she'd ensconced herself in.

She screamed, "Help!"

"Shut the fuck up, bitch." His forearm wrapped around her neck, choking her even as he dragged her backwards. One of her shoes fell off. She used the other to stab him in the shin.

He dropped her and she went down on her knees. Setting the cake on the sidewalk, she kicked off her other shoe and bolted, pumping her arms for as much speed as she could muster.

It didn't matter.

Brad was faster. Stronger. Crazier.

"Help!" This time she nearly rent her windpipe with the force of her wail.

"Brielle?" A young woman's voice came from the darkness. "Is that you?"

Of all people. It had to be Elsa who heard the cry. Helpless, spoiled Elsa. Couldn't Brielle catch a break just once? She supposed she had in the time she'd shared with Luke and his friends. A temporary respite before she lost it all.

"You bitch. Don't you dare answer her." Brad tried to smother her, causing a whole new set of stars to dance in her vision. The van pulled up beside him. He dragged her toward the rear of the vehicle.

If he put her in there, she'd be dead. She knew it as surely as anything before in her life.

Either he'd kill her, out of control, or she'd finish the job herself. No way would she return to how things had been before.

Brad dragged her, limping. "You fucked up my leg, bitch. You're definitely going in the closet now."

She wrenched to the side, slowing his progress though she only escaped long enough to yell for help again before Brad slammed into her back and knocked them both down.

"Brielle!" Elsa must have caught on to the scuffle. Footsteps, light yet fleet, approached.

Suddenly Brielle feared she'd only put Becca's little sister in danger instead of securing assistance.

"Call the police," she shouted. "Get inside."

Someone flung open the van door. It banged against the stop at its widest setting. The yawning black hole terrified Brielle, especially accompanied by Brad's hate-filled curses.

"No!" Elsa still closed the gap. "Take your hands off her. She doesn't want to go."

"Stay out of this," Brad snarled as he subdued Brielle. Despite her life-or-death instincts, her energy stores began to deplete. Her kicks weakened and her punches bounced off Brad's doughy arms. She'd never realized how flabby he was until she'd seen Luke...and Kurt.

"I've had enough of this bullshit," he barked then hauled back.

Fortunately, Brielle couldn't feel anything when his sucker punch knocked her out. The brilliant flash that whited out her vision was the last thing she recalled.

Luke stole another peek at his watch despite Kurt's trash talk about him being whipped. "You would know all about that, asshole."

"Generally I prefer it the other way around, but yeah... It's not such a bad thing being totally in love with a woman. Even if she flips you on your head every once in a while."

Luke wouldn't have bothered to deny his feelings anymore, even if Elsa hadn't chosen then to burst through the door, carrying on like usual.

Probably broke a nail or some shit.

"Call 911." She rushed past them toward the landline in the kitchen.

"What?" Becca emerged from where she'd been finishing her sister's birthday meal. "What's the issue now? Let's talk it through before we rush to unnecessary conclusions."

"Someone abducted Brielle. Get the cops on the damn phone." For once, she didn't become hysterical. Cold, calm and factual—she spelled things out, rapid-fire.

Luke's first instinct was to storm outside and give chase, but Kurt's hand on his arm restrained him until better sense engaged. His Cookie was long gone and they both knew it.

Phone in hand, Becca punched the three digits none of them had ever needed in their lives. They paused a split second that seemed like an eternity while the operator connected and gathered basic info needed to dispatch immediate-response personnel.

Elsa calmly recited what she'd seen. "I was outside trying to think of a way to apologize for the crap I published in the paper last week when I heard someone yelling for help. I investigated and saw a dude grab Brielle. He carted her off to his van and punched her in the head. She crumpled, totally limp, and then he stuffed her in. It happened so fast. I couldn't get there in time to stop them."

Luke only realized he'd pummeled the wall when his fist sank through the Sheetrock. "Was it Wexford?"

"I believe Brielle called the guy Brad."

"Her fucking ex!" he roared.

"I took pictures." Elsa angled the digital SLR camera hanging around her neck, lens side down. "I may have gotten something. My flash isn't that great, though."

She spun the wheel on the display.

Another tiny pause had Luke's blood pressure rocketing. He thought he might be sick. Cookie must be so scared. And there was absolutely nothing he could do to help. *I should have protected her.*

"Yes!" Elsa stood taller. "Here. It's a rusty white Ford Econoline. At least ten years old. The license plate is FPAD65. There's a woman with horrible hair driving. Think overprocessed blonde with lots of roots like in the eighties. Big poof in the front."

Luke gaped at her.

Brilliant. If Elsa'd ever had to pick a time to get her act together, she'd sure gone for the right one.

"Yes. I hear the sirens. My brother-in-law, Kurt Foster, is going outside to meet them. Thank you." She hung up the receiver, then burst into tears.

Becca surrounded her little sister with comfort. "You did terrific, Elsa."

"But I couldn't stop them. They took her. They hurt her. I'm so sorry, Luke. I tried." She sobbed. "Do you think this is my fault for showing her in the paper? It is, isn't it? Oh God. I told him right where she was hiding."

"*When* we find her, it will be because of you. Thank you." He kissed the top of her head then jogged out front, abandoning Becca to deal with the fallout.

Kurt stood next to a patrol car, explaining the situation to two officers. One looked like a living refrigerator. Luke wished he'd been around earlier.

"Officer Matt Ludwig." He extended his hand. "This is my partner, Officer Clint Griggs."

"Thanks for getting here so fast." Everything blurred around him.

"It's your girlfriend who's been taken?" The taller guy, Griggs, asked with more compassion than Luke expected.

"Yeah." He crashed onto the stone wall beside the driveway. "She's gone."

"The lady on the phone gave us great info. The lookout already broadcast to all units before we pulled in the driveway. They can't be far. We'll get your girl back." Officer Griggs paused as if considering saying more.

"Go ahead." Luke shrugged. "Can't hurt."

"The rest of my squad is tight. Several of the guys have had threats like this to their families. The best things you can do for her are stay calm, think and be ready to take good care of her when we bring her home."

"Another reason I could never be one of the men in blue." Luke groaned. "I gotta do something."

"Here. Take this flashlight. Clint and I are about to canvass the street for evidence. Scour the ground and call us over if you see anything out of place."

"I can do that." Action might keep him from going insane with worry. If Brad hurt Brielle, Luke would likely kill the fucker. Long, painful and slow. He hadn't known he had a violent side before.

"Remember, no touching. Yell to us and we'll take care of anything you find."

"Got it." He nodded. "Thanks."

Luke crossed to the side of the street the bus stop was on. He swept his beam back and forth, concentrating on every tiny pebble as though it might be a GPS device preprogrammed with Brad's address.

He'd gone about half a block when something up ahead

glinted. He directed the flashlight at it. A white plastic dome sat on the sidewalk beside a silver high-heeled shoe. The other half of the pair lay on its side in the middle of the street.

"Guys!" He turned to wave to the cops. They abandoned their searches when he yelled, "Over here!"

The officers sprinted to him, surprising him with their speed and fitness. These were no donut-eating pigs. They partnered seamlessly, not needing to talk to work as a single unit.

Luke was glad they were on the job.

They paired up and marked the position of the items, took pictures then moved on. While Luke made sure there was no oncoming traffic, they crouched over Brielle's other shoe, talking excitedly between them.

The taller guy ran back to his car, retrieved a plastic evidence bag, then returned. Pronto.

"What is it?" Kurt joined him, staying glued to his side as they approached.

"Stand back, please," Officer Ludwig ordered. "We've got blood on this one. Maybe some splatter on the ground too, if we're lucky."

Luke couldn't understand why they were grinning. He saw red that had nothing to do with the stained heel. "He cut her. That motherless motherfucker."

"No no." The big guy, Ludwig, held his hands out. "Calm down, Rambo. We think your girl stabbed her attacker with this stiletto. Check out the angle, and where it fell. She was still wearing it and kicked backward. Like this."

He grabbed his partner in a familiar bear hug that got Luke's imagination riled. Could they be…? Their sexual orientation didn't matter a damn to him as long as they were good at what they did. And they certainly seemed as if they were top of the academy.

When he didn't have an *ah-ha* moment because of their reenactment, they shook their heads. "Man, this is good. Really good. This shoe is the thing you need to lock this creep up as long as possible. Maximum sentence. Pictures *and* DNA proof it was him. Unbreakable."

"Holy fuck." Luke plopped onto the curb near Brielle's cake and her non-weapon shoe.

"You have one of the cleanest cases we've ever seen here. And almost no lead time to the perp's advantage. I'd imagine you'll be hearing from the rest of our squad pretty damn quick." Officer Griggs smiled. "This is fantastic. Best outcome given the situation. You can take the rest of her stuff inside if you want. We have what we need here."

A *chirp* from one of their belts cut the still night air. "Officer Ludwig speaking."

Luke strained to catch any hint of the other end of the conversation.

"That's great. Let us know if you need more backup." Matt smiled as he clicked the END button. "They've got the van in sight and are trailing at a safe distance. We expect they'll wait until that slimdick parks so they have a better approach. This is going to be over soon."

"Can you take me nearby so when she's out I can be there quickly? I'm the head of Elembreth University's Psychology Department. I'm an expert in trauma victims, and she already had phobias along with other issues caused by abuse from this fuckwad." He swallowed hard.

"I hope he rots in jail. We can't take you on scene. But we'll get you in the neighborhood." The bulky cop folded his arms. "You're not going to make our friends' lives miserable by interfering or interacting with the suspect in any way. Got it? You concentrate on your girl, and that's it."

"Fine. But I'm bringing my friends. Kurt is also a doctor and his wife is Brielle's official current psychologist." Luke didn't give a shit if the guy's arms were as thick as trees. He was going to be there, and he could use Kurt and Becca by his side.

If it didn't go well... No, it had to.

"Wow, cute name, bakes delicious-looking cakes, wears sexy shoes..." The taller cop winked. "I think your lady sounds great."

"You forgot gorgeous and funny and...perfect for me." Luke scrubbed a hand over his face.

"Let's go. I have a feeling this is going to go down quick." Officer Ludwig headed for the car. "You can bring one of your friends, but someone has to stay here to protect the scene until our replacements arrive."

"Elsa. The girl who made the 911 call." After tonight, Luke trusted her. Something fundamental had changed the moment she'd had to actually deal with real life and not idle in the shallow, protected bubble Becca had crafted for her.

"Yeah, she can handle it. Move out." The guys turned as one.

Brielle swallowed hard against the nausea climbing her throat. She blinked in blackness, wondering if it was that dark in the world or if she couldn't open her eyes. Why wasn't her night-light on? Where was Luke?

Her nightmare had been particularly bad tonight.

"Can't you drive this thing any faster?" Brad's derisive question shocked her awake as effectively as if she'd been plunged in a pool of ice water.

It hadn't been a dream.

Oh God.

The tiny spot in the rear of the van might as well have been her closet. And soon they would stuff her in an equally miniscule box she couldn't escape. One that would drive her mad. *No!*

Instant panic threatened to consume her. She slapped her hand over her heart.

Luke smiling up at her from the couch in her living room,

kissing her, thrilling her. His hold when he'd danced with her at the banquet. His cannonball into the enormous tub in their hotel suite. Laughing in bed with the playful man. Sex on the kitchen table. Eating dessert from his fork at the nice restaurant on a nicer day. The eye-opening session in Kurt's laboratory.

So many positive memories battled the darkness surrounding her.

He had become her anchor.

Her breathing slowed and she retained control of her logic. *Why didn't I let Luke drive me? Why didn't I run as soon as I realized someone else got off at my stop? Why...*

Anxiety rose inside her, strengthening Becca's theory. Indecision and self-doubt plagued her, damning her to paralyzing regret and fear. She had to keep calm. Had to find a way out of here so she could get back to the brilliant affection she'd only just begun to relish.

I'm okay. I made the best decisions I could. I will do the same now. Luke is waiting for me. I can do this. Survive first, details later. I'm okay.

While not completely terror-free, she managed her apprehension to a level where she could still function. A plan formed in her mind. Taking a deep breath, she invited unwelcome attention. "Brad?"

"Shit. She's awake." Some grunts and banging followed as he made his way to the back of the van. "Are you going to be a good girl now, Brielle?"

His condescending smile made her aware of how long his façade had fooled her.

"I think I'm going to be sick." It wasn't much of a stretch. She let her disgust and the roiling of her guts show on her face. Sweat beaded at her temples as she considered what she was about to attempt. She had to get out of this van before they reached wherever the hell they were going.

"Shit." He yelled at his new girlfriend, "Pull over. Right now.

I don't want that stench in here."

Brielle didn't bother to inform him that the van didn't smell much better as it was. At least not from her place with her face smashed into the dirty carpet. She swallowed hard.

They lurched to the side of the road.

She had to try twice to get her fingers to work right on the door handle. Shit. It wouldn't be easy to outrun him, given her still fucked-up state. Shaking her head didn't help much to clear the fuzziness on the edges of her consciousness.

"You can't do anything right, can you?" He opened the hatch as fast as possible.

Brielle practically tumbled from the rear of the van. She hit the pavement on her hands and knees, ignoring the shock waves that exploded from every joint. Then she took a deep breath and shoved forward like a sprinter off the block.

It seemed as if she was running in slow motion, but she put her head down and pumped her arms, tearing along the side of the road, away from the tragedy waiting to happen behind her.

"Fuck! She took off." Brad's boots pounded the road behind her. She'd never make it far. But she had to try.

About to veer off into the scrub brush on the side of the road, she was startled by the sound of an engine gunning it. At first, she assumed Brad's girlfriend had put the van in reverse. But then she realized another vehicle was coming down the road. Fast. They'd had their lights off, but flipped them on now, blinding her and Brad, who neared by the instant.

Had the world gone crazy? Were they going to run her down?

She had no choice but to keep going and pray that they might help her. Dropping her shoulders, she leaned into the light wind.

The nondescript, beige car slowed only when it drew even with her. It skidded to a screeching halt a few feet behind her. Though she heard the door open and someone jump out, she didn't pause to see what the hell they were doing, yelling at Brad. What if they couldn't stop him? At least they would delay him.

Until one word cut through her flight instinct.

"Police!"

She stumbled. "What?"

Brielle might have bit it hard, but a second car approached, drawing her up short. A man emerged. He didn't try to grab her. With his hands out in front of him, he spoke in a loud, clear voice. "Brielle Norris? I'm with the COPD. Officer Jeremy Radisson. You're safe with us. You don't need to run."

The air rushed out of her. She glanced over her shoulder to see two guys slamming Brad onto the hood of their car, facedown. They slapped a pair of handcuffs on him, even as another shorter but toned cop headed for the van.

Officer Radisson caught her before she crashed to the ground. "Are you hurt anywhere?"

"I think I'm o-okay." She tried to do a mental inventory but sorting through her chaotic thoughts was tough.

"Your boyfriend is real worried about you." He spoke low and soft to her. Something about the man reminded her of Luke and Kurt. The innate control he kept over himself allowed her to relinquish some of her own.

A tiny sob caught in her throat. "He is?"

"Hell yeah. My squad heard all about it over the radio. He's coming for you. In fact, I think that's him right there." The policeman carried her toward an approaching car. "You did great tonight. Made our job easy."

"Luke?" Only one part of his reassurance mattered.

Brakes screeched as another car stopped. The passenger door winged open and all she could see was golden hair, shining in the moonlight, mixed with the flash of red and blue lights.

"Luke!" She squirmed until the officer had to let her down or drop her.

"Brielle!" He dashed toward her, crushing her in his arms. She didn't mind one bit when he smothered her against his chest. "Are you all right, Cookie?"

"I am now." She relaxed in the security of his hold.

"Me too." He didn't seem like it—his shaking and his bloodshot eyes belied his ragged declaration.

Brielle reached up and pulled him to her for a kiss. She imparted as much reassurance and gratefulness as she could. "You might not have been in that van with me. But you never left my heart or mind. It was because of you I was able to think. Able to believe. Able to fight."

"Fuck it." His lips covered hers, seducing her mouth. "I know this is crazy, but I love you."

"I love you too, Luke." A tear tracked down her face, but this time it was born of pure joy. She kissed him again, slow and gentle, certain they had a lifetime to perfect this insanity between them.

Someone, one of the younger cops, whistled at their display.

"Razor! Behave." Officer Radisson shouted at the guy.

Luke grinned and laughed. He spun her around in his arms. "How much fucking paperwork do you think we have to fill out right now? Maybe they'll let us sneak off into those woods for a bit?"

"I'm a pretty good runner." She wiggled her brows.

"Barefoot even. You keep losing your shoes." He frowned.

"But you keep bringing them back. At least I haven't turned into a pumpkin yet." She brushed her fingers over his smooth cheek. "You make a great Prince Charming."

"Maybe I should call you Princess?" A smile spread across his lips.

The young, rowdy cop said, "Works for me. My wife likes it."

"Nah, let's stick with Cookie." Brielle rested her head on his shoulder. "Or maybe Cake. I could really use a piece of that right now."

"Don't worry, I put it in the fridge. Elsa deserves it and a million more for tonight." Luke filled her in on the girl's heroics.

"You're right, that one's all hers." They couldn't stop making out between discussions. "I'll bake something else. Something just for us. Something sweet and new and satisfying."

"That sounds delicious to me." Luke brushed his lips over her knuckles then carried her to the waiting police officers. "The sooner we start this, the sooner it will be over. Just remember that I'll be taking you home and helping you forget tonight ever happened."

"I'll talk fast."

They both laughed despite the nightmare they'd lived through.

Chapter Twenty-One

Seven months later

Brielle rode the elevator up to Luke's office, hardly thinking of anything except his birthday surprise. It was simple, but she knew he'd appreciate the significance. How far they'd come in less than a year. Brad had been sentenced last month, closing that era of her life.

It felt right that he'd be spending most of his time in a tiny cage like the one he'd tried to keep her in. And so would his accomplice. Yet far from each other.

She enjoyed the sweet smell emanating from the box of treats she bore. It perfumed the confined space of the elevator car.

The control panel tweeted cheerily as she passed each floor. And when the doors opened, she bounced out. Only because she couldn't wait to see her guy. It'd been a long time since they'd had each other for breakfast this morning.

As though he could sense her, his head turned the moment she approached.

She didn't even get to say hello to Heidi before he snagged his spring coat and met her in the waiting room. His eyes were electric as he spied her gift. "Brown sugar cookies, Cookie?"

Her eyes rolled at his silly nickname, although secretly she loved it nearly as much as she loved him. Okay, nothing could compare to that inferno. Still, it always brought a smile to her face. Even on the bad days she had so much less frequently now.

"I'll even let you keep them this time." Brielle went into his open arms, uncaring about the presence of his assistant when she accepted his mostly tame kiss.

He sighed as he wiggled the lid off the foil-wrapped cardboard. "I love you. You know that, right?"

"Never get tired of being reminded." She grinned when he popped a full cookie in his mouth. It should have taken a normal human five or six bites to demolish it.

"Want one?" His slurred offer had both her and Heidi cracking up.

The admin took two. "I've learned my lesson. Eat them while they're here."

Brielle put her face in her hands. "That was not one of my finer moments."

"I could say the same of my boss." Heidi shook her head.

"Hey now." Luke put on mock affront. "No ganging up on me on my birthday."

"Speaking of, we'd better get going. I have something for you." Brielle tugged him toward the door. She didn't have to try very hard to get him moving.

"I thought the cookies were my present." He downed a couple more while they waited for the elevator.

The doors glided open. They stepped in. Brielle wrung her hands and steeled herself for what she was about to do. She was ready. After they'd sunk a floor or two, she spun toward the control panel and slapped the STOP button.

"What are you doing, Cookie?" Luke's eyes grew wide when she unbuttoned her shirt, exposing her lacy bra.

"I'll give you a hint. It has nothing to do with being hot."

"Here? Now?" He gawked. "Aren't you scared?"

"Never with you." She hiked up her skirt, making it clear she'd opted to leave her panties at home. "So are you going to undo those pants or am I just going to keep standing here half-naked and awkward?"

He blinked.

Again.

Then laughed as he dropped the box of cookies and tore open his slacks. "This is a premeditated seduction, isn't it?"

"Been working myself up to it for weeks," she confirmed. "So let's make it good. How long do you figure we have until they send the fire department? Better hurry so we don't get caught."

He devoured her smile as he lifted her. She wrapped her legs around his waist even as he guided himself to her opening. "Damn, I see you like the idea."

"Horny and pantyless is a dangerous combo." Brielle enmeshed her fingers in his thick hair, rubbing his scalp as she kissed her way along his neck. Just as he liked best.

"Cookie, you know there's a camera in here, right?" He hesitated on the brink of entering her.

"I thought exhibitionism was your thing." Brielle relaxed her thighs, sinking onto him the barest bit. She let go of him long enough to yank the pliable cups of her bra beneath her breasts and offer herself to him.

"I'm sure as hell not a prude, and I'm not ashamed of us together. Just hoping Mrs. Allerton doesn't rat us out. Wouldn't want to get my practice evicted." He glanced down at her rosy nipples and cursed. "Fuck it. I don't give a shit. It'll be worth it."

He hunched his back, pressing into her, even as he sucked on her breast.

The thrill of doing something so naughty ramped up her arousal. The satisfaction of destroying her phobia once and for all…that was huge. Now every time she rode in an elevator she'd have this to think of and smile. Or moan.

Luke's big hands cupped her ass, tugging the cheeks apart as he hiked her up then let her ride down his entire length. They both groaned.

"I'm afraid I'm going to drop you." He walked them forward until her shoulders were sandwiched between the wall and his fine chest. "Is this okay? Me pinning you like this?"

"It's perfect." She kissed him lightly, then wild and wicked. "Stop worrying. Enjoy your birthday gift."

"You have no idea." He rested his forehead on hers, staring

deep into her eyes even as he linked them completely. His cock withdrew to the very edge of her body then burrowed deep again and again. "I'll make up for this later, Cookie."

Brielle's muscles tightened around him. His impending explosion ignited hints of an orgasm in her. All of her ecstasy was woven tight with his. When he was happy, so was she. They treated each other to a never-ending cycle of bliss.

"I'm with you. Just fuck me harder. Faster," she panted.

When he adjusted the angle of his penetration, she gasped, her eyes flying open.

"Like that?" he growled.

"Uh huh." She nodded, biting her lip to keep from screaming.

He rode her furiously, with some part of him she hadn't yet seen coming to the forefront. Untamed, rugged and a bit rough. He trusted her to take what he gave and return it tenfold.

Her hands slammed backward, splaying on the polished brass of the elevator. All around them, the sights and sounds of their lovemaking were reflected. Golden, lascivious and inspiring.

Brielle looked into Luke's eyes as she hovered on the edge of exploding. "I love you. Happy birthday."

He drove inside her once more, holding deep while grinding his pelvis against hers in a circle. Being so close to him, inseparable, did the trick.

She lifted her face and bit the base of his neck.

Orgasm crashed over her a split second later, squeezing him as tight as she could within the heat of her pussy.

Luke's attempt at silence broke when he roared her name. He jerked in her arms, shooting inside her as deep as possible. Warmth rushed into her, overflowing her with each pump from his balls. And still he came.

When finally they'd both been drained, he allowed her thighs to slide from around his waist. His cock slipped from her with a wet sound they both chuckled at. He began to rearrange their clothes and cleaned between her legs with his handkerchief, which he refolded and tucked in his pocket.

"We'd better go. Before someone really does pop in here." He looked at her with a mixture of amazement and pride and adoration. He pressed the lobby button and restarted their descent. "I can't believe you did that. Seriously. This is going to be the best birthday ever."

He'd barely finished his promise when they were delivered to the lobby.

They stepped out together and crossed the pretty marble floor. "You mean it's not already the best birthday you've ever had?"

His silence piqued her curiosity. What did he have up those devious sleeves?

Luke picked up his pace a bit as he passed Mrs. Allerton's desk, as though she'd call them out for getting it on, which they clearly had, if the state of their hair and rumpled clothes had anything to say about it.

"Have a good night." Brielle waved. Luke choked.

"So I can untape this piece of paper from my monitor now, right?" Mrs. Allerton giggled at Luke's bewildered expression.

Brielle clapped her hands as he looked back and forth between them.

"Well played, Ms. Norris. Well played." He scooped her into his arms, laughing. "You got me good."

"As long as I have you, it will always be great." She returned his lush kiss.

"In that case." He reached into his pocket. "I don't want to wait another second. I planned to give myself the best birthday present of all time tonight."

Mrs. Allerton gasped, her hands flying to her chest when Luke went down on one knee, right there where so much of their life had begun.

"Brielle Kelly Norris, my Cookie, you are absolutely the sweetest thing in my life. I will always love you and cherish you and protect you. You've already kicked Kurt out of his best-friend throne and you rule my world. Will you please, pretty please, with brown sugar on top, be my wife?" He cracked open a velvet box, revealing a gorgeous ring, complete with a honking heart-shaped diamond and pretty pink stones haloing it.

A crowd began to gather as people caught on to Luke's proposal. Brielle recognized many of them from her time in the building. They all smiled at her and Luke. Again, it struck her how he'd transformed her life. And how they might continue to build on what they'd started.

"Yes. A thousand times, yes." She nearly barreled him over before he had a chance to place his ring on her finger. They tumbled to the ground together, light flashing from where their hands were linked.

He stole another kiss before whispering in her ear, "Better be careful. I know what's not under that skirt."

Brielle laughed so hard she cried. And when he kissed away her tears and set her on her feet once more, she knew this is what all that darkness had been leading up to. All the times she could have quit, this is what she'd hoped was waiting, but what she was afraid was just a myth.

Sometimes the good dreams did come true.

The crowd erupted into applause that trailed them from the building. They hadn't made it ten feet past the revolving door, which could never scare her now, before he paused, drawing her up short.

"This is better." He nibbled her earlobe. "Now we can skip straight to your engagement present."

"I already have everything I want." She beamed.

"Oh really? Then I'll just make a quick call to tell Kurt and Becca that you've decided you don't really care for that threesome after all. No being tied down while Kurt and I ravish you and Becca watches on. No testing out the invention my best friend made to celebrate the occasion. I mean, I know...it's intense even for him." Luke hauled his smartphone from his pocket.

"Back away from the dialer!" She stared at him. Could he really be willing to fulfill her greatest fantasies and then some? "Do it and your baked-goods days are over."

"I love you too, Cookie. Let's go home."

Orange rays of sunset refracted off the glass buildings around them, casting rainbows in their path. Blinding light erupted from the rock on her finger. Brielle looked down at the spot where Luke's hand intersected hers and knew.

He had the healing touch.

About the Author

Jayne Rylon is a *New York Times* and *USA Today* bestselling author. She received the 2011 Romantic Times Reviewer Choice Award for Best Indie Erotic Romance. Her stories usually begin as a daydream in an endless business meeting. Writing acts as a creative counterpoint to her straightlaced corporate existence. She lives in Ohio with two cats and her husband, who both inspires her fantasies and supports her careers. When she can escape her office, she loves to travel the world, avoid speeding tickets in her beloved Sky and, of course, read.

When times get tough, the tough stage one scorching-hot intervention.

Hammer It Home

© 2012 Jayne Rylon

Powertools, Book 6

Morgan is happy that her best friend Kate is expecting the crew's littlest member, but helping renovate a room for a nursery is more than she can bear. Baby furniture and pastel paint are a painful reminder that she and Joe can't—and will never—conceive. There's no hiding it from the rest of the close-knit crew, either.

True to their unique brand of love, the gang rallies to find a non-traditional solution to alleviate their friends' suffering. Not with a cold, clinical visit to a sperm donation clinic, but delivering it the old-fashioned way. With a healthy dose of searing passion.

But soon after Morgan's scorching hot night with her husband's four best friends, an accident threatens the life of one of those men. The challenges that lie ahead will test the crew's powerful bond to the limit—and their long-standing promise to take care of each other through good, bad, and sexy times. Whatever it takes...

Warning: Not everything in life turns out as planned, but with love all odds are surmountable. Especially when those odds include five hot construction workers on your side. Contains m/m/f group ménage scenes.